a
beautiful
truth

COLIN
McADAM

GRANTA

Granta Publications, 12 Addison Avenue, London W11 4QR

First published in Great Britain by Granta Books 2013
This paperback edition published by Granta Books 2014
First published in Canada in 2013 by Hamish Hamilton,
an imprint of Penguin Canada, Toronto

A CIP catalogue record for this book
is available from the British Library.

1 3 5 7 9 10 8 6 4 2

ISBN 978 1 84708 847 5

Offset by M Rules
Printed and bound by CPI Group (UK) Ltd, Croydon, CR0 4YY

This book is for Joyce,
and in memory of Raymond B. Hancock,
gentleman, father and friend

one

VERMONT

Judy and Walter Walt Ribke lived on twelve up-and-down acres, open to whatever God gave them, on the eastern boundary of Addison County, four feet deep in the years of rueful contentment. Judy was younger than Walt, her dreams had an urgent truth, and five years had passed since they removed a cyst from her womb that was larger than a melon. Her uterus collapsed and for a year she awoke to formaldehyde dawns feeling sick and lonely and hopeless, no more chance of a child.

Time passed and Walt stayed near. She held his hand when she sat or when she slept. They painted the house a lighter blue.

On various nights in various ways Judy said do I feel old Walter, and he said you're too young to be old. Come here.

Walt and his partners, Larry and Mike, had built or bought more than half of the commercial space in southeast and central Vermont. They provided the roofs, walls and drains around bakeries, cheese shops, notaries public and all the unimaginable businesses sprung from the minds of people who could not conceive of working for other people. Walt believed in doing your own thing, finding your own way. The rent came monthly, businesses closed and opened. Walt made other investments, he gave thanks and shared his wealth. Paint for the church, in perpetuity. Books and shelves for the beetle-eaten library.

There were wealthy couples you read about where the man worked and the woman shopped and other people mocked or reviled them. Walt was in love, and held close the fact that there is nothing more natural or right than buying the world for the woman of your dreams. Try to name the value of that smile to Walt and his life-worn heart.

And Judy wanted little. She did not spend her days buying furniture and curtains. When dresses and shoes appeared in her wardrobe they had usually been sought for and bought by Walt. Before the operation she had wanted one thing, and after the operation she tried to get used to not wanting. They said the desire for children would naturally dissipate, but a man who loses a leg does not stop wanting to dance or kick.

In her rational moments she allowed herself to want nothing more than spending time with a child. It didn't have to be her own, it didn't have to be beautiful or smart, it just had to be near for her to care about it and give her that taste of renewal and possibility that children represent. She was calm about her desire, but every now and then, alone, she yearned like a prisoner yearns for friends beyond the wall.

I need a purpose she said.

She volunteered to visit people who were dying.

I'll keep Mr. McKendrick company on Thursday nights. They say he has three months.

That'll be good for him said Walt.

I don't know.

And good for you.

It's a purpose.

Your beautiful face every Thursday. He'll be cured, Judy. He'll live forever.

I'm young said Judy.

You're beautiful.

I just want to make you proud she said.

They bought paintings and a car and a dog named Murphy, but with every purchase and passing Sunday was a feeling that life was a collection of gestures and habits and it was hard to find surprises when most surprises were planned.

That sad light in Judy's eyes was becoming a settled part of her, and maybe, Walt thought, that's life.

His first wife had been killed in their car near Binghamton, a truck driver slept at the wheel. A lake of grief still sat in his chest and it would never properly be plumbed, but the one thing he could think of, the one fact which he could find the fortitude to contemplate, was that the trucks would never stop. He found a lesson in that. Those goods that people want or think they need, hurtling across the country. You can stand still and scream at the trucks but they'll run you down; you can hop on and go where they go; you can find all sorts of ways to avoid them. You can adjust, instead of accepting, and you can make your own world.

Walt had wanted a baby with his first wife but she was taken away so young. With Judy he had never doubted it would happen, but it hadn't and now it wouldn't. He was more than happy with the thought of looking at Judy till he died, but as for what she had to look at: Walt was getting jowly from beer and his great love of cheese. When he thought about the idea of having a child, that modern human ability to choose to have a child, and when he thought about beauty and how things can change, he could see how, maybe for a man, a child might be a way to make these moments last—some way to prolong a beauty that can't be preserved. But he simply understood it as love. He wanted what she wanted, and was sad that he couldn't provide it.

They looked into adoption for a time, but the options were limited and waiting lists long. Walt said we'll figure it out.

One of the buildings they owned in the county was a bar called Viv's. Walt met Larry and some of the others there most Thursdays, especially once the season began. Viv's was in easy driving distance from Willamette Valley where white-tailed deer would rut. The bar was a place where Walt and his friends could relax or celebrate or pay inarticulate respect to the thrill and regret of hunting for meat.

Out of season they found other things to talk about, and Viv was always good at gathering newspapers and magazines. He encouraged the exchange of facts, he said, not opinions, because opinions are like sperm: there are way too many of them, most amount to nothing, and they're more fun to deliver than to receive.

Viv usually had some newfound knowledge to announce, and in February 1972 he passed a copy of Life magazine to Walt and said now the monkeys are talking.

Walt looked at the article and it changed his life with Judy.

"Conversations with a Chimp" it was called.

He saw a photo of a chimpanzee sitting on a carpeted floor, apparently in conversation with a man. Walt read the article and learned of a group of chimps in Oklahoma who had been taught to speak in sign language. They could talk about things they saw and things they wanted to eat. They spoke spontaneously.

One of the chimpanzees, a girl, was walking with the man in the picture one day and watched a plane fly overhead. She looked up at the man and signed YOU ME RIDE PLANE.

Walt found that amazing and read that part aloud.

There was a photo of a baby chimpanzee in a diaper, sitting on a woman's lap. And on the cover of the magazine was a picture of a beautiful woman who was involved with Howard Hughes. Walt measured all beauty against that of Judy and found the woman lovely, but wanting. There is no happier feeling.

As he drove home, the thoughts of Judy, the photo of the chimpanzee in the diaper, the beer and the bleakness of February all swam in his head in a lonely and protozoan soup, till lightning struck, an idea was born, and Walt began making inquiries into how he could acquire a chimpanzee.

He had no idea where to look, what to expect, what a chimp was or whether he could in fact buy one. He thought of zoos, wondered how zoos got their animals. He thought about all the people he knew in husbandry, the friends who traded livestock, the hundreds of acquaintances involved with animals in one way or another. Judy had been at Shelburne, buying Walt some cheese. He remembered she had watched some kids getting excited about the new llamas. That was about the most exotic animal he had heard of in Vermont.

Where do you see chimps he asked Viv, and Viv said you see them at a circus sometimes, don't you.

So Walt kept his eye out for circuses.

He had spent a few years now trying not to go near things or bring up topics that would make Judy think of children. He hadn't wanted to upset her.

He went alone to a circus in Burlington and there was indeed a chimpanzee who came out a few times with a clown. The clown juggled bananas and the chimp tried to jump and reach them without joy, so he pulled the clown's pants down, revealing pink bloomers, and the clown dropped all the bananas. The chimp looked like he was laughing and so did everyone else. It was pretty funny. And at the end of the show the chimp bowed and jumped into the arms of the clown and it was also pretty cute.

Walt waited till the crowd had left and asked a guy if he could speak to the clown or the fella who played the clown or whatever you call him, and the guy said he's out in the blue trailer. Walt went through to the street out back and knocked on the pale blue door.

The fella appeared, half clown half man, and said yeah with lipstick lips.

Walt introduced himself and said he had a question, and the clown said I charge a hundred for a birthday and the kids can't touch the monkey cause he bites.

Walt explained that he was interested in the chimpanzee and wanted to know where he could find one.

Are you a clown.

No.

Wait right there for a second.

Walt heard a terrifying noise which soon became part of his daily life. He was invited in, and there in a cage on the floor in the corner was the chimpanzee from the show.

Settle down there buddy settle down.

The chimp looked simultaneously bigger and smaller somehow, and the second wave of noises was less of a shock to Walt. The chimp was in a pink dress.

The clown said she doesn't like people coming into the house. She's in a mood.

She's a girl.

Past few months or so she gets all moody.

Walt felt a strange combination of embarrassment and curiosity. He wanted to look closer, but felt he should look away.

What's her name.

I call her Buddy. They're all different. Buddy here is a good one.

Walt said hey Buddy, somewhere between the way he would talk to a horse and the way he would talk to a unicorn.

I can't rent her out or anything. But I can get you one for twelve grand.

Christ.

Sometimes as low as ten. I don't have that kind of money myself and if I did I wouldn't be a clown. You know. This is a chimpanzee. It's not a racehorse but it's not a dog. I can't tell you where I can get one, but it's not a simple thing.

Walt stared at his lipstick.

They're not born here, you see. It costs me. They travel. I travel.

The chimpanzee was looking at Walt and looking at the clown and she put her hand through a gap between the bars.

She wants to touch you.

She seemed small again. Her face wasn't as pale as others Walt had seen in photos. He looked at her fingers and something stirred in him. They seemed long and you could almost imagine them on a grandmother.

She's pretty goddamn strong. You might not want to touch her.

Walt saw no threat and softly repeated hey Buddy. He was low on his worsening knees and reached towards the cage and gently put the back of his own finger against the back of the chimp's and held it there. Buddy.

She moved her finger slightly to manipulate Walt's and the clown said be nice to the man, he's a friend, be nice, and she looked at Walt with whiteless eyes and scratched a little mole on the side of his finger.

She's cleaning you. It's a thing they do.

Walt looked at her and her eyes looked at his finger. Walt looked down at his finger and while he was smiling inside and thinking this animal's cleaning me with a woman's finger, she gathered some spit and Walt felt the splash on his face.

The clown said hey be nice now dammit.

Walt looked at her and she laughed like she laughed in the show.

I'll be.

Buddy stood up and made a gesture and the clown said okay, come out, but be nice.

She slipped the dress over her head and revealed a homemade diaper.

I keep a bat or a stick around, but I'm guessing if you're not in the trade you won't be teaching so many tricks. I put her in the cage when there's visitors or when she goes to bed and whatnot. She calls it her bedroom.

She talks.

I talk. I call it her bedroom.

I read about one who knew sign language.

Yeah, she knows signs. Tell daddy to fuck off.

She raised her finger.

Doesn't mean they're ready for high school.

Buddy walked over to the couch with her arms up like she was walking through waist-deep water. She got up on the couch and sat just like a person would sit and Walt looked at her feet. They looked like hands.

The clown went to the fridge and grabbed a can of beer which he tossed across the room to her. She made a sort of coughing noise and opened the can with her teeth.

I'd offer you one but there's only one left.

He opened it and chugged it and so did she.

When she neared the end she caught the last drops with prehensile lips, looked at Walt like she was telling him a joke and didn't care what he thought of it, got up from the couch and went to the fridge where the clown said there's no more.

She looked at him like she was making sure she understood properly. Walt watched her flip through a magazine while the clown talked business. It seemed like everything she did was either funny or impossible.

While driving home, Walt reflected on his day and acknowledged that it was always going to be slightly odd to talk to a clown about a chimpanzee. But his mind was trying to catch up to greater things—the feeling of confusion had less to do with negotiating with a clown and more to do with the simple vision of that hairy little girl sitting on the couch across from him. Was she a person or a pet. The longer Walt drove, the more he realized that what he predominantly felt was excitement. This was an opening. She had seemed so energetic, so full of stories somehow. Were they all like that. Were girls and boys different. She was eight and the clown said that was different from an eight-year-old girl, but maybe not so different except for the menses and some peculiarities, he reckoned. He didn't actually know exactly what age she was.

What would Judy think.

Walt had finalized nothing. He and the clown had agreed that Walt would get in touch in a while and the clown would make some inquiries and try to line up the right chimp. The younger the more expensive he said.

Walt wanted to think for a while and not necessarily surprise Judy with a baby chimpanzee but maybe try to find the right way to tell her about the idea. She was waiting with a roast chicken when he returned and she was the picture of his idea of home and there was gratitude in his heart. Please don't take those eyes away from me or let them get any sadder.

A month or so later he met the clown at a diner in Burlington.

He wore no makeup and his name was Henry Morris. He could line up a chimp, probably a boy, might even need bottle-feeding.

Walt was nervous, but resolved.

He talked Henry down to six thousand dollars, not knowing that Henry would pocket three of those six. Henry himself did not know that his connection in Sierra Leone, a German named Franz Singer, paid only thirty dollars for the chimps he sold for three thousand.

In Outamba-Kilimi a mother chimpanzee had been walking with her baby clinging to her chest and a shotgun blast sent bone through the back of her eyes. She was several meals for Liberians across the border, her punctured skull was ground into a paste which a man in Hong Kong bought to heal his broken arm, and her baby was put in a sack and delivered to Franz Singer's farm outside Freetown.

Nights of hunger and bony moons, steel and the rubber teat.

Singer's chimpanzees were renowned for being free of shotgun pellets, less work when they arrived. They flew in crates, Pan Am cargo, neither colonists nor slaves.

Henry met the crate.

Walt told Judy he had bought a baby chimp, and Judy looked at the painting above the mantel, oil of the lake in summer. It was night but she felt the warm breath of the sun through her dress and thought life isn't what you see it's what you think.

They slept with their bodies close that night, their minds going miles down separate roads which they never dreamt were separate.

Judy had seen enough hours and days to know that when things are truly strange their strangeness doesn't appear until after the strangeness has passed. She thought of this when she was sitting on the living room floor looking into the eyes of Looee, who was holding her fingers on the bottle with hands that had grown so much in just a few months.

The deal between Walt and Henry had been that Henry would find an appropriate place to present the chimp to him and Judy. That seemed the hardest part to Henry. He had done this a few times now. He knew to buy a small cage, rent a pickup, drive to Newark, slip cash to the right people. The laws about exotics didn't exist in those days and quarantine was a matter of money. He knew exactly what he would do with the chimp but he couldn't think of how to present it back in Vermont. He got his shoes shined at the airport in Newark by a really nice guy named Louis. He told Louis with the right sort of wink that he was staying at the Radisson and Louis recommended a girl who gave Henry a ten-dollar handjob that he would have paid double for. He wanted to kiss her but when he leaned forward she recoiled. He drove back to Vermont and thought there's that jungle gym in the park for the kids, I'll arrange that we all meet there.

two

FLORIDA

The World needs fruit. The World needs sleep. The World needs touch and the quick pink heat.

Podo rules the World. Podo chooses his moments.

He limps and others limp to be like him. He eats his breakfast with loaded hands, and alms drop and scatter like seeds from a shaken tree. He greets his friends and assesses the day and the day bows down to black Podo. He takes Fifi by the hips while she sucks on an orange.

He will play with children and pin their mothers.

Podo runs to the greybald tree and swings around it once and twice and does something else without thinking what it was, and it is always something to behold, fast Podo.

Outside are grass and dirt and swollen birds, high summer, there is concrete and society. Armpit heat and guilty meat, and friends who come and go.

Look to Podo if the food is taken from your mouths.

Look to him if you think all food can be yours.

He wants Fanta.

He will pound the eyes of detractors.

Show him your rosé.

A bird flies over the World.

Fifi watches Mr. Ghoul.

Mama likes Fifi.

Fifi likes Mama.

Magda slaps Bootie.

Bootie likes Burke and hitting Magda, his mother.

Podo is pinning Magda and neither really wants it.

Bootie and the new one are jumping all over Magda and Podo.

Bootie slaps Podo on the leg.

Podo is busy, sharp Podo.

Bootie and the new one want to understand.

They want it to stop, continue.

The new one is looking at Magda's rosé getting pin, pin, pinned by Podo, and Bootie is thinking about slapping or biting the swinging balls of Podo.

Podo thinks a thought that he can taste and the World swells hot and dark.

He has finished.

Magda walks away without looking over her shoulder.

Bootie and the new one are bewildered.

Podo feels the oa, grateful Podo. Magda feels safe.

He is huge, black Podo, and he walks with black hair raised, and daylight blue and slick on his body, and his shoulders are widening, legs surprising, he coils and uncoils with prowess and venerable grace.

There is oa in the ground and oa in the wind and everyone knuckles and bows, how-do.

Mr. Ghoul spends the morning eating onions.

three

Looee reached for Judy before conversation began. The little guy in the diaper and red shirt. As soon as she was near he reached out with both hands, apparently not caring if he fell from Henry's neck. Henry introduced his burden by name as he was losing it. L-o-o-e-e he added, spelling it thus because he reckoned the woman would find that cute.

All the way to Burlington her anxiety had grown.

What will he eat she said.

I don't know. I don't know all that much Walt said.

She tried to calm herself by not thinking deeply. Walt had said they seemed so human. She sang and ignored the cramps in her belly.

At that moment of meeting, Looee lunged and nuzzled and squirmed and settled. He and Judy made unwritten noises and he looked at her with eyes of eagerness and purity, and she understood his hunger.

Walter she said.

Henry looked around the park, at the jungle gym and concrete.

Looee was not a conventionally cute little baby, but there was something about the fact that he had hands that made Walt and Judy feel right away that he was more than a hairy beast. And the way he moved in Judy's arms made Walt say that's a cute little guy right there.

Henry said just give him plain old milk and you'll find soon enough that they'll eat just about anything, too much if you let em. He looks good and healthy to me.

Judy carried him away like she was determined to take him somewhere better.

It was April and snow sat on the mountains.

Judy held Looee in the backseat while Walt drove to various stores after Judy said there's all kinds of stuff we need. Looee stayed still in her arms like a newborn baby, alternately dimming and shining his eyes.

At Kmart a woman said how cute, when he was wrapped up, and screamed when she saw his face.

When they all arrived home Looee seemed awfully hot. Judy got a thermometer under his tongue and his temperature was 103.

That might be normal said Walt.

They gave him milk and bananas but through the night he grew weaker and hotter and Judy could swear he stopped breathing sometimes. She was sure he had a fever.

At dawn when things seemed worst Walt said do we take him to a doctor or a vet.

Judy said doctor without hesitation.

What on earth have you got there said Dr. Worsley, and Walt said that's a baby chimpanzee.

The situation was inadequately explained, and Dr. Worsley said I'm just not sure you shouldn't take him to a vet but I'd be lying if I said I wasn't curious, Walter.

He had a look at weary Looee and thought his private thoughts about bodies and death and how he and his medical brethren found thrills in life and love despite their knowledge of flesh and its banal truths.

He took his temperature but frankly wasn't sure what was normal for chimpanzees.

His lungs sound congested, so as far as I can tell it's a respiratory illness. I'll do some reading about it.

Looee coughed a lot at home like a baby and Walt and Judy ran the shower in the bathroom and hugged him in a way his body remembered. The steam did him good and drenched them all in sweat. When Judy dried him with a towel in the bedroom on the bed, it seemed for a moment that he might be ticklish under his arms.

I think he's smiling, Walter.

That second night felt longer than the first. When Looee slept and his chest stopped moving Judy would panic and wake him up and think what on earth have we done, who is this. He developed diarrhea and made a terrible mess of the bed.

He truly seemed pale under his hair and Walt thought that maybe they should have taken him to the vet but Walt was in a jungle of sleeplessness and confusion.

They waited, like they waited with each other when they were sick, ultimately relying on the instinct of the body to live and find its own solutions. Eventually his fever broke and his limbs regathered their twitches and kicks. The three of them slept.

four

Mr. Ghoul was there from the beginning, before Podo, before anyone but Mama. No one remembers as well as Mr. Ghoul that the World was once white and square.

He pulled the lever marked GO and the World grew piece by piece.

He remembers Mama who was not much bigger than her cat.

Everything that Mr. Ghoul wanted and learned began with the lever and the machine.

David was his friend.

? Machine make Dave tickle Ghoul

They used to smoke together.

Some of the people used sticks in those days and there were rules and customs which he can't find anymore.

When he got things right, the machine gave him pieces of apple.

One of the pokol-people who smelled like vodka would come in the morning and rattle Ghoul's bedroom with a stick, gangalang. And Ghoul would not want to go so the man would hit him with the stick. Sometimes the people were good and he would walk with them down the hall and hold their hand.

Dave would pick him up and put him on the desk and show him how the pictures on the machine lit up. Dave took his finger and they pressed each picture together and different things would happen.

The machine made milk. A small white room and a machine with lights and colours. None of it remains.

He spent his days in that small space, the Hardest of the Hard. Sometimes they put Mama in there with him. Also, for a while, they put the gentle idiot Orang in there with him. Ghoul had little interest in the machine when Orang was there for company.

Mr. Ghoul used to think of Orang.

The machine was the means by which the people taught them words. There were no words on the machine, but there were pictures which were pictures of words but not pictures of the things that the words were meant to picture.

This is an apple: Ж.

At first if he wanted an apple he learned to press that picture and the machine would give him a piece of apple. It soon became more complex. The picture for apple was in a different place on the machine one day, and the next was in yet another. Ghoul had to find the picture. And later he had to make sentences, which are the longest routes to getting what you want.

Dave would say put it in a sentence.

Please machine give apple.

Dave was in another room with a window and would communicate in the big Dave voice and then through the machine. He made Ghoul's machine light up from the other side of the wall and Ghoul could see the pictures inside Dave.

Dave was full of questions.

? What does Ghoul want.

? What is name-of this which-is black.

And Ghoul had to answer in a certain way or Dave would not understand.

Banana give Ghoul which-is black.

That is not right.

Please machine give Ghoul banana which-is black.

He grew very tired. He tried to stay out of ¡harag! but it was sometimes much too hard. The machine was very strong and Ghoul could never smash it. He banged his goon on the wall sometimes and for a while his favourite thing was to throw Coke at the machine and listen to the fizz.

The machine was turned on by the lever marked GO. Ghoul pulled the lever and conversed with Dave and sometimes other people. They would punish him if he made a mess or if he played when they didn't want him to play. They locked the lever so he couldn't move it, and without the machine he could neither eat nor drink nor get tall Dave to come into the room for a tickle or a swing.

Mr. Ghoul jumped around the room, wanting chomp and not understanding a sentence. Mama wasn't good at the machine but she knew everything Mr. Ghoul wanted. She tried to pull the machine off the wall, and nothing ever happened unless they made a dirty sentence.

Please machine put dirty cabbage outside.

Mama was a friend he wanted in those days, but they took her out of the room like Orang because he didn't use the machine as much when she was there.

He liked Dave very much.

? What does Ghoul want.

Make Dave into room.

? Ghoul wants Dave in room.

Dave tickle Ghoul.

They would do what each other wanted, as long as Ghoul found the sentence.

The World is not the World.

He ate well. Each time he made a sentence he got a raisin or an M&M, a Coke, a coffee, a thing he can't remember the name for. Lettuce.

He learned to love Twizzlers and vodka and smokes.

The machine did more and more.

Please machine make music.

Please Dave dance with Ghoul.

He wanted the machine to make music while he and Dave made sentences but in the earliest days the dirty machine could not. There were simple things that the words, the machine and Dave could never understand. Things in Ghoul that were part of the World.

A sentence is not a sentence without a period

Please machine make vodka sentence.

? What does Ghoul want.

Make vodka. Dave. Make sentence.

? Ghoul wants sentence or Ghoul wants vodka.

Vodka sentence

That is not right.

Please Dave vodka sentence Dave.

Dave does not understand.

?

? Ghoul wants vodka.

No.

? Ghoul not make sentence.

No. No No No No No

? Mr. Ghoul wants a raisin.

The machine learned more and more and Dave and Mr. Ghoul understood many things and the machine got bigger.

Sometimes he could see Dave through Dave's window and sometimes he could not.

A man would wake him up with his stick and walk down the hall and he wouldn't let Ghoul take his hand. Ghoul learned the sounds of pokol-people, the filthy dogsmell cunt, and on those mornings when he was led into the Hardest and could not see Dave in the window it was lonely. He pulled the lever marked GO, the machine lit up, and even though he knew that someone was behind the machine he was alone.

Please machine put dirty radish behind-the-room.

He liked saying that because Dave would have to come into the room and open the drawer on the machine with the radish in it and take it out, and when Dave came in they would laugh because they both hated radish and Dave would touch him and hug. He could only do that once a day, and then Dave stopped putting radish in the machine because he no longer enjoyed the game.

When he walked by Mama's bedroom at night they touched fingers through the plekter, if the people let them. Their bedrooms were smaller then. There weren't many soft things, except the yellow duck, the small grey boy.

But there was music.

Smoke on the water.

And movies.

Ghoul would get tired from all the questions and so full of raisins and coffee that he filled the room with urulek and the Fool would hit him with the stick. And sometimes as he grew tired and full there was nothing he liked more than a movie.

Please machine make movie.

Movies were like being swung very gently by hands you cannot feel. When he learned what a movie was, and that it was called a movie, he wanted to share it. Every now and then he got up and typed on the machine:

Movie name-of this.

He wanted to remark how special it was.

He liked the movie about fish.

And the machine made things called slides as well, which were a feast of apples.

? Ghoul what is name-of this.

Horse name-of this.

Out came a piece of apple.

When Dave was in the room in the morning, Ghoul was very happy. Dave taught him to wave hello and goodbye, how to give him five, play peek-a-boo, which he never tired of. Ghoul liked Dave's smile, and learned to make one. He smiled with people whenever he could.

And the World was not the World.

Sleep after sleep and some of it grew less frightening. They put a new window in the Hardest, which looked into another room, behind-the-room, and another window behind-the-room looked out into the open, and Ghoul kept learning that the World was not the World.

They put a new phrase in a picture, ₪, which meant open-the-window. The blind over the window rolled up when he put that picture in a sentence, and Ghoul could see into the other room and outside.

He and Dave developed a beautiful game together. Ghoul would say

Please Dave go behind-the-room.

And Dave would say

? Ghoul wants Dave behind-the-room.

And Ghoul would say

Yes.

So Dave would stare through Dave's window and smile and he would disappear. But he would knock on the other side of the walls, and Ghoul would follow the sounds around the room feeling heegly, and then Dave would knock on the new closed window.

So Ghoul would then go back to the machine and say

Please machine make open-the-window.

And the blind would roll up and there was Dave and he was always doing something funny. Once he tied his long thick hair back on his goon so it looked like the ass of a horse. And once he wasn't there and then he sprang up from below and poured Fanta over himself. And the one Ghoul liked the most was when Dave was there on the other side of the window with a smoke, and with his yalamak and lips he made shapes with the smoke that came out. Beautiful shapes like circles.

He can taste that game.

Mr. Ghoul can make smoke rings.

five

What do you see when you look at me.

The Girdish Institute had its origins in the 1920s, when William Girdish made a trip to Buenos Aires. He had heard of a large private zoo owned by a wealthy woman in that city, and it was there that he saw his first chimpanzees. He was beguiled by them and endeavoured to learn as much as he could about their nature and habitat. He heard stories from the staff and zookeeper and witnessed their obvious empathy and charming curiosity, and he bonded with one in particular.

At dinners in the US he would tell stories from this place, like the one about the chimp who developed an attraction to one of the pretty cooks of the household. This chimp would watch her in the kitchen from his cage with obvious desire, and over time she grew unsettled by his attention. She asked one of the staff to erect a barrier to his view, and boards were nailed to the outside of his cage. The man with the boards who took away the sight of his beloved was attacked a year later. The chimpanzee had harboured a grudge all that time, and found an opportunity when the man was doing repairs to the door of his cage.

Girdish set about gathering his own collection of chimps and other primates, bringing them over to one of his properties in Florida, near Jacksonville. He was a gentleman amateur, the only son of a land-owning family, and he had property throughout the South.

He believed that much could be learned from primates, chimps in particular, that they were a link to our past and could explain much of our behaviour. In this respect he was ahead of his time, and there were few in the world who knew as much about apes as he did. He travelled and sent envoys to Africa and housed a growing collection of apes and monkeys in and around the greenhouse, observatory and staff buildings of that property.

He established the institute and started a breeding program. He developed a philosophy of what the ideal research subject would be in terms of health, size and character. He and his colleagues steadily developed tests, both mental and physical, which slowly confirmed, in demonstrable scientific terms, how closely we were linked to these creatures.

When he died in the 1940s he left a large endowment and his work was carried on. Through the development of breakthrough drugs the institute attracted funding from the federal government and from companies around the world.

The old observatory and staff buildings were kept and it was here that behavioural studies remained and the field station developed. The new main building expanded and the biomedical studies became the lucrative focus of the institute. But the beating heart for many was the field station.

The original buildings had an Art Deco quality, soon hidden by various additions. There were the sleeping quarters, which had expanded over time, a winter playroom and a large safe area where cognitive tests took place. There were kitchens, offices, bedrooms, a garden which supplied some of the produce for the chimps, and numerous old rooms whose purposes changed over time.

David Kennedy eventually became director of the field station, and oversaw its expansion. Since the late 1970s you could say that this part of the institute mimicked the life of a man. Its early days were of directionless and unlimited enthusiasm and were shaped over time by conflict, financial reality and the needs of others. When David realized his personality, where his true interests lay, the field station took its present shape. But while curiosity sometimes dies and old enthusiasms seem foolish, the nature of the field station prevented it from ever being static, and passion never diminished.

Even when the population settled, nothing was ever settled.

In vivid memory, his family were Podo, Jonathan, Burke and Mr. Ghoul. Bootie, Magda, Mama and Beanie. Fifi and her open heart. All the names he didn't want to give them and the sadness that he didn't want to see.

David tells his assistants, when they first arrive, that they can never choose favourites. Observe, but never judge. He knows that it is an ideal—as if any ape can look without assessment: fruit is never fruit, it is either ripe or rotten. People are never people.

He had an assistant once whose logs were always coloured by her distaste for promiscuity. It was never simply *Jonathan mounts Fifi*; there was always a hint of morality, a suggestion of wantonness or assault. He sat her down and said do you have a boyfriend. She was twenty-nine and had been married for seven years.

He said when you go home tonight and you find whatever way you find to encourage your husband to hold you, make sure that you forgive him.

His staff have come and gone in numbers. He has grown, he hopes, more compassionate with age.

It's a guideline, a piece of advice that David repeats, despite himself. Try not to choose favourites, try not to dislike some of them.

He brings prospective assistants out to one of the towers and tests how quickly they can distinguish between the chimps. If they have that rudimentary skill, he gives them twenty minutes to observe a group. If the group seems peaceful and pensive and the kids have fun, a bad observer will say they were peaceful and pensive and the kids had fun. A good observer will say the alpha slept, as did two of the females. Male chimp C sat near the moat as if on guard, and the juveniles alternately rested and played. Male chimp B, before he lay down, bowed to male chimp A (though asleep). The females stayed closer to male chimp B as they rested. Female chimp C would look towards sleeping male chimp B whenever the juveniles made noise, instead of reprimanding them directly or looking to the alpha, suggesting a possible shift in power.

Small things are big, every movement matters, morals blind us to seeing the bigger picture, and if you don't have the empathy to watch for these things, get out of here.

But, at some level, it really was impossible not to judge. Their talk over lunch was always about personalities. Who was mean and what was wonderful.

Do you have a favourite, David.

He could rarely think of Podo without imagining some beloved, long-reigning king.

Something about Fifi, who weighed two hundred pounds, made him think of Farrah Fawcett.

And he had never met a chimpanzee as gentle as Mr. Ghoul.

six

Looee was quiet and still for over a month, waking only to feed or if he felt Judy moving away. His lips quivered whenever she put him down, though he was neither feverish nor cold. She knew he needed the feel of her body and she felt his panic when she saw him shiver. She rested him on her shoulder when she cooked. Applesauce, candied carrots, everything warmed by stove, mouth or hand till it held the heat of a body surprised by love. She crushed bananas, scooped the purée with the tip of her little finger, felt the tickle of his pink boy's tongue as he sucked, the pull inside at her feet, groin and heart.

Walt got sick and said I think I caught whatever it was he caught, and Judy looked after them both. Walt was ever brave before the wailing train of life's horrific surprises, but he wasn't good with the flu. Judy he said, and nnn he said, and I feel sicker than, and he rarely finished a sentence. He wondered whether it was right to be sharing a bed with a chimpanzee and he dreamt of eating prunes on a wavy sea.

New life was in the house. Two arms, two legs, grasping fingers, inquisitive hunger, a shock from a dream that freezes the limbs, subsidence into adorable sleep, and mouth on skin, he needs me I need him to need me I need him. I'm tired. She slept.

She kept the fire burning into May and the house acquired a sweeter, nuttier smell that was unpleasant to visitors. The bedroom grew layers of terry cloth and tissue and she kept the bathroom hot in case Looee needed warmth and wet for his lungs. Walt was hot, Walt was cold, Walt was grateful and uneasy and finally hungry and better. He explored the changing house and watched her cook with their new friend over her shoulder.

He'll hold your finger like a baby.

I know.

This house is hotter than inside a moose he said. Maybe it's time to crack a window.

The cloud of rheum, the film of incomprehensible memories, was lifting from Looee's eyes, and looking down was Judy. The more his eyes cleared, the more curious and intimate Judy got.

Walt bought some toys like a ball and a doll and a bone. He wondered what the hairy little guy could do.

These were the days that Judy, months later, remembered when she sat on the living room floor and pondered the strangeness of her life, how none of it seemed strange till now, and now there was nothing strange, this was her little Looee. She fed him formula, not plain old milk as Henry Morris had suggested. He was fifty percent bigger in four months and Dr. Worsley was correct in figuring he was smaller than normal when he had come to them. He figured he was possibly a year, year and a half, who knows.

The loss of a mother and the travel from Africa typically killed most chimps his age, but Judy's presence saved him. Questions naturally occurred to them about where he came from, what ground, what air, but Henry and the circus had moved on. When you plant a sapling, sometimes you don't care where the seed was from. They decided that as far as Looee was concerned, this was where he came from, right here.

He slept in their bed for the first several months. Walt would sometimes be awakened by Looee running his fingers through his hair or playing with his lips and trying to pry his mouth open with those little fingers of his, I'll be darned. They always woke up with him in the middle of the bed—he never liked anyone coming between him and Judy.

The difference between Looee and a less hairy baby was that he could move a lot better. He could support his weight, hang on to things and climb. He never left Judy, but she could usually rest her arms.

And he did enjoy a tickle.

Walt thought back to the laughing chimp in the circus and figured Looee's laugh was different. Looee's laugh was real. You'd get him on the bed and when you'd wedge your fingers into his little armpits he smiled with his lower lip more than with his upper and then he started this little chuckle like the uck in chuckle or the ick in tickle but softer and Christ it was funny and cute. And he'd stand up and squeeze your nose then throw himself down again and away you'd go with more of a tickle on his belly and thighs, Walt and Judy's four hands on their little hairy piano.

He had pale hands, black fingernails, a pale face and feet, and a little white tuft of hair on his rump that Judy liked to pat before she put his diaper on. The hair on his body was a little wiry, though Judy found ways to soften it up. There was a little boy's body under there.

He was squirmy in their bed and they didn't sleep well for a long time. Walt set things up for the future. It was a large old house, with a couple of spare bedrooms that Judy had long ago decorated with insincere finality. Solid desks for future business, beds that only existed to display her latest linens. Walt took a big oak wardrobe, laid it on its back and made a sort of crib.

They were happy to see that room change. Walt took a chainsaw to the mattress and resized it so it would fit in the flat-lying wardrobe, and why they thought the walls of a crib would contain a chimpanzee was part of a daily chorus of I didn't think of that.

He caused quite a fuss later when he had to sleep in his own bed. He jumped on the dresser and kicked Judy's makeup, jumped down and halfway up Walt to hit his chest, and sometimes he removed his diaper, smeared his mattress and returned with a look that said you can't expect me to sleep there it's disgusting. He would walk to Judy with his palm up and whimpering, and she was quite susceptible to that. But Walt prevailed and Looee later loved his bedroom and bed.

He hung around Judy's neck or back throughout the day watching everything she did. He slept a lot, but wouldn't sleep unless she lay near, and Judy cursed the noisy floorboards whenever she snuck away. His screams when he awoke had a visceral effect on her—she had no choice but to drop whatever she was doing because it felt like either the world was ending or his noises would make it end.

Sometimes he played on his own, but never beyond the bounds of whatever room Judy was in and not for very long. He was a toddler with the agility of an acrobat, so his play was usually spectacular.

She had to think of him constantly—that's what occurred to her over the years as she looked back; that's what soon made him more than a pet. He wasn't self-sufficient, he always needed company—not just the presence of bodies, but society; he needed the emotional engagement of others. There was no denying him. You could step over Murphy on your way to doing other things or tell him to shush if he was barking. With Looee you simply couldn't ignore him, and if he was complaining about something it would have to be addressed with just as much care as with a child. When Judy first used the vacuum cleaner, Looee screamed and leapt onto her face. She had to turn it off, show him how the power button worked and how the hose sucked up dirt. He was in a heightened emotional state whenever it came out of the closet, but he was soon able to turn it on, pull it around the house and vacuum in his own way.

The truth was that Walt and Judy woke up most mornings with the happy suspicion that something today would be new.

Despite her tiredness there was a new sense of vitality in Judy, and as much as she sometimes yearned for peace she couldn't imagine returning to their old routines or waking up to days without these fresh concerns.

You look rosier in the cheek said Walt. Let me kiss that.

There was a loss of spontaneity in their lives but it was more of a shift than a loss. They couldn't decide out of the blue to drive to Stowe for dinner or make love on the couch with that surprise of skin and heart. Looee had an especially uncanny knack for knowing when they were getting close to each other, sensing the change of energy between their bodies like a blind man knows that a flower is red. He added a different range of surprises to their life.

Looee wasn't keen on going outside at first, but he ventured onto the verandah. He was so attached to Judy that she was never worried about him going far. When it was really warm the following year she let him roam without clothes. She held his hands above his head and stood behind him, trying to teach him to walk upright— assuming that he would one day walk on twos despite his arms seeming longer than his legs. They walked hand in hand to the old apple tree which had just lost its bloom. He sat down and picked up some dry blossoms, smelled them, scattered them, made a soft noise and handed some blossoms to Judy.

Thank you Looee.

She didn't know that he had ridden his mother's back when she had climbed trees and he didn't remember himself, but one day he looked up the apple tree and climbed it.

He went to the top and she told him to come down. She tapped on a branch that was just above her head. He came down and hung from the branch and she couldn't believe how strong and dexterous his limbs had become.

There was a long period of keeping to themselves, making adjustments, enjoying the fact that sometimes family is society enough.

He understood a lot of what they said, and they were regularly surprised. They sensed how he learned, and taught him the names of body parts. The three would sit on the couch, and Judy would say where's daddy's nose. Looee would point to Walt's nose. Where's daddy's eyes. Where's Looee's belly.

Sometimes he stared off in space and sometimes he pointed to his own eyes when Judy asked him to point to hers. He was either getting it wrong or showing there was no difference.

He was always watching, and aware of anything new. A wallet in the hand, a hairpin, rubber boots on a rainy day—anything unusual attracted his inspection. And he had unusual preferences which might otherwise be called taste. He screamed at a La-Z-Boy that Walt bought and was terrified when it reclined.

The house was mapped in his mind, and he didn't like change unless it came from himself. Judy had a rubber plant which she was very proud of, that she would move around the house at different times of the year to find the right light and humidity. She moved it to the landing and found it later in the living room where it had been for its first few months. She moved it again, and again found it back in the living room. She asked Walt why he kept putting her rubber plant back in the living room and he said why do you keep stealing my toggle bolts. Looee rested on Judy's hip and stared at a pendant piece of amber as though it was a caramel Shangri-La.

Judy stared at Walt. I don't think I know what a toggle bolt is she said.

The work required was staggering. For the first year or so Looee stayed close to Judy, and even though his curiosity meant spills and surprises, it was kept within a limited range. His constant presence would have been a trial for any mother, and Judy was the tiniest bit relieved when he got bored with her for a moment. But when his range expanded, they had to be prepared.

A padlock on the fridge was an obvious measure. The old high doorknobs on most of the doors in the house were a boon to Walt and Judy because he wasn't tall enough for a while. But he had quietly observed them in all their daily tasks and soon knew how to deal with every handle, knob, lever, door, switch, clasp, plug, button, tie or unlocked lock in the house. And because he was so good at climbing there was little they could put beyond his reach.

Walt remembered the cage which Henry Morris used for Buddy. He proposed it, and Judy said absolutely not.

Judy made checklists all around the house and tried to keep loose objects secured unless they were willing to sacrifice them as missiles or toys. Walt put padlocks on most of the cupboards. He tried to make the electrical outlets safer and always kept an eye over his shoulder when he was manning the grill; but he also figured a burn here and there was the surest way to learn.

Looee had an insatiable appetite for playing. And because of the weather in Vermont it often meant that diversions were required indoors. He loved hide-and-seek, but sometimes played it when others didn't know he was playing. He climbed onto the mantel one afternoon and watched as Judy walked around the house calling his name. Looee it's time to clean up the dining room, come on my little man, my Looee where are you. When she came around the corner he leapt from the mantel onto her shoulders and she lost control of her bladder. He then walked to the bathroom, took toilet paper and ran around the house, unravelling it and laughing.

Judy's concern was not her own emotional state so much as how he reacted to it. When he saw her fear or anger he got frightened himself and he would run around screaming, trying to find comfort where he could until he felt he could touch her or get a hug. It magnified the impact of simple frights and required massive mental energy from Judy to feel calm almost before her fear.

They usually found such delight in seeing how much he could do, though, and, when they were in the right mood, they loved to watch him play. He learned by observation, by staring and remembering. He learned to crack eggs. You sit up on the counter there. He held the electric beater. He could spread butter on his toast with a knife. It was rarely done with grace or without a mess, but they imagined he would one day be more careful.

He loved to wear Walt's ski-doo helmet, which was half the size of his body. He wore it backwards and walked into furniture. He laughed every time he hit something, and it was impossible not to laugh when he laughed. Larry saw him do this, and Walt said do other animals laugh.

Sometimes he could sit still. He liked magazines, especially ones that focused on home decoration and women. He loved pictures of women sitting in family rooms and he would make his I like this noise, that creamy repetition of ooo through his soft lip-trumpet, and he would look at Judy and tap the page with the back of his fingers. There were lovely minutes where she could settle him down with a magazine and read one of her own or do some work in the kitchen with the sound of I like this in the house.

When he misbehaved they tried to be patient with him, but they had their own ways of making him obey when patience was exhausted. With Judy, the most effective was to make him feel guilty. You're going to make mummy sad if you do that. Do you want mummy to cry.

His natural way of apologizing was to come to you with his hand held out, shrugging and bowing as if to acknowledge that, while he had had no choice, what he had done was wrong.

Walt found that shouts and threats were the best way to bring him in line. He was never physical—he never had to be. Looee instinctively understood that shouts were a prelude to something worse. Shout at him, and be done with it. They always got on well immediately after an outburst.

At some level these negotiations and struggles for power meant that Walt couldn't help but see him as an equal—a child perhaps, but certainly not an animal. There was never any sense of ownership or mastery.

Walt shouted and took Looee in his arms and they went out for a drive, and Walt slapped his hands away whenever he reached for the wheel.

When it came to the artificial niceties of human life, he had his own approach. He ate with cutlery. They never taught him or said that he should; he just saw them doing it and wanted to do everything they did. If they presented him with a bowl of food, he never dug in without a fork or spoon. He only drank from a cup or glass.

He wore diapers for the first couple of years and they tried to train him to use the toilet. Looee had always been fascinated by it; he would let neither of them go into the bathroom alone and would flush for hours if he had his druthers—but getting him to use it himself had been a struggle. Walt had placed a step up to the toilet to encourage Looee to pee standing up, but he wouldn't. Walt demonstrated how it was done but Looee either tapped on Walt's penis or drank from Walt's stream, and the two would emerge from the bathroom confused for different reasons about the significance of urine. Looee now went into the bathroom on his own sometimes and otherwise used a portable potty. There were accidents, of course, as with any other child, and sometimes he was deliberately dirty.

They learned that the ability to lie comes naturally to everyone. They never taught him to toy with the truth but they saw him do it early and it was often potty-related.

Judy had annoyed him by refusing to tickle or play with him, having done so for two hours. He went into the living room and shat on her sheepskin rug.

She was very upset when she discovered it and said why did you do that. He shook his head as though it hadn't been him and he gestured towards the garage where Walt was tinkering.

It was daddy who did that, was it.

He nodded.

Walt put up a swing set in the front yard. Looee helped him fetch pieces to put it together, and as soon as it was upright he couldn't get enough of it. He ripped the seats off and swung from the chains. Walt built a wonderland for Looee out front. Tires from tractors and cars which he flipped, hid in, gnawed on and rolled. Looee spent hours out there, not yet eager to explore beyond the property.

He and Walt would come in sweaty and hoot when Judy said we're eating Italian rice balls tonight.

Judy bathed Looee and relaxed him with body lotion. She put him to bed while Walt envisioned his next day's work downstairs. Conversations foreseen and successes planned, if this goes that way and that goes that way.

On the weekend Walt and Looee worked in the garage.

Walt said get me the ballpeen hammer. The one with the black handle.

seven

Podo's back hurts, and when he holds up a leaf to look at the ants on it, the ants grow invisible when he brings it near his face. He wonders where they are.

Fifi walks over and touches his balls and they both feel better for it.

Burke doesn't want to play with Bootie. He pushes him, and Bootie thinks he is playing and won't go away. Burke bites him.

Magda hits Burke and sticks her finger in his eye. She too finds Bootie annoying, but he is her son. Magda complains to Podo, who bluffs at Burke and nudges Bootie.

The rebuke stings Burke all the more because he wants to impress no one more than Podo.

Magda shows Podo her rosé, which looks to him as pale and unwilling as the winter sun.

He chooses to eat an apple. Fifi comes over and takes the apple from his hand, which he allows because she touched his balls.

eight

Not all the guys were keen on Looee when Walt first brought him to Viv's. One of them in the corner said is that a dog and Mike said that's a monkey in a suit. Mike's wife Cindy had been through a bout of cancer and was saved by the Blood of Christ. Mike would not want Cindy to know that he had been at Viv's with a monkey, they're full of disease. He watched Looee from the corner of his eye and thought of how guilty he had felt when he had tried certain things with Cindy after marriage and how the sin of the world caused good people to hurt each other, monkeys jeering at our earnest efforts to live in this quiet valley.

Susan was friends with Cindy, and while Susan was not, in Cindy's mind, assured of escaping damnation, she believed in an eternity blanched and rich as cream where understanding would land like feather on skin and her faith was so strong she was breathless some nights. Susan just wasn't sure that her friend Judy was spending her days as she should, and was really, frankly, afraid of seeing her with that chimpanzee.

So tell me what he's like she said to Judy.

Judy wondered if Susan really wanted to know, and she was sometimes unsure if her words had any value when Walt was not around.

He's just so special she said, already knowing she could never say how. He's just so special.

Tell me about your days, do you still read on that couch by the window or is he always … Is he clean.

She tried to tell Susan what it was like to be surprised all the time and to feel a spread of warmth after each surprise. She tried to tell her that what he looked like didn't matter but there was no certainty in her mind about what Looee was, and of course she looked down sometimes and saw this little hairy creature and thought is he my baby or a beast. He handed her blossoms and smiled. She could tell him to fetch his toys from the upstairs landing and he would. But he walked on all fours, always grunted before he ate, and idly put his finger in his anus and smelled his finger, sometimes licked it, although he heeded Judy on occasion when she said dirty Looee don't do that. There was so much inhibiting Judy's mind from following certain thoughts to their logical conclusions, and so much inhibiting her tongue from telling Susan about the contradictions and complexities of her days, that she simply tried her best to mention cute things like you know, Susan, he's eating with a knife and fork like a real little gentleman.

Susan's scone was dry in her mouth and the image of a chimpanzee with cutlery made her think of hair and tongues. She wondered how big Looee was and she was aware of the pain in her cheeks as she smiled.

Judy said we're animal people, Walt and I. You know that. I grew up with horses.

She wanted to say something that would keep the conversation within the mountains of Vermont. She thought of her horses and how no two horses she ever knew were the same, that animals have what you might call personalities. And Looee had such a personality that you might not even call him an animal. And what's an animal. And none of the thoughts that rushed in would she dare or be able to say.

He kisses me goodnight she said. He climbs up and kisses me and I put him in bed with his toy gorilla.

That evening when she was washing dishes she said to Walt I was thinking about some things today and feeling really … There were things I wanted to sort of explain to Susan but I couldn't get them out and I don't know if it was Susan or me or what it was. Maybe I should read more.

Walt said those chimps I read about with the sign language. I've been wondering if we shouldn't teach him to speak like that. Sign language.

She was pensive and kept washing the dishes. Walt looked at her and thought she's gaining weight and she's prettier.

There's plenty I don't know how to say he said.

When he next went to Viv's he asked where Viv kept all his old magazines, there was one he wanted to look at. Viv said I used to keep all my magazines in bags in my basement. Then last year every time I went down there I caught my son Jack jerking off. I said I'm gonna throw those magazines out and you're gonna get a job.

Walt couldn't remember the name of the man in the article, he just had the photos in his mind. The library didn't have space to keep old issues of all its magazines and Walt walked out before they asked him for another donation.

Where do you find out how to teach a chimpanzee sign language. Walt felt his old feeling that there are people with words and people without words, and the ones with words think they run the world and the ones without words will get the job done.

He thought about how he did well in life despite his failures in all those institutions that are meant to define what is smart. There are those who build and those who live off what is built—professors, councilmen, tax collectors and all those swarms of managers and middlemen making words we never needed, and all those terms of art are how they keep their sting in.

He nonetheless wanted to teach Looee so Looee could tell him what was wrong sometimes, so Walt could tell him more clearly what to do because it was occasionally more difficult to get Looee in line.

When Walt and Judy both had colds, Looee made them open the pantry. He got down from Judy's arms and found a bag of onions and took it to the garbage can. He obviously assumed the onions were making them both sniffle. They made connections every day without words, but there could be so many more. Walt really didn't know where else to look to teach him how to speak. There were those with words and those without.

Their first couple of winters had passed in the fog of exhaustion which envelops all young families, but time was somehow more regular this winter and they were more awake to its challenges. Despite all his hair, Looee really didn't like the cold and was often sneezy and sick—and every illness he suffered, Walt and Judy caught as well.

He would go outside in his snowsuit for little more than a minute, and whenever he went back in he sat right by the fire. Sometimes Judy would be peevish because she needed her fresh air and she would say you know I don't like it when you sit so close to the fire, and Looee would know it bothered her so he moved a little closer to it to punish her for taking him outside.

He was very sensitive to the emotions of others, and knew how to manipulate them. When Judy was sad he could tell as soon as he saw her. He would hug her and bring her something, and if she had any cuts on her hands from the kitchen or bruises on her legs from the furniture, he would kiss them. He was very protective of Judy, and if anyone, even Walt, made a movement towards her that seemed remotely threatening, his hair would go on end and he would scream and stand in the way.

He was also reliably mischievous. They tried to have parties with old friends, and Looee charmed many of them, but there was an uneasiness with some which Looee usually exacerbated. He had a keen eye for insecurity. Chimps will naturally extend a hand in greeting, but Walt encouraged this to mimic handshaking. Guests would be at the door and Looee would amble towards them and stretch out his hand. Not everyone would take it, and things went down the wrong path from there. He went through ladies' handbags and looked at himself in their compact mirrors. He took their lipstick and smeared it wide of his lips, or took men's cigarettes and pipes and put them down his pants. Often the owners would feel he was mocking them. If he knew that they weren't enjoying the joke, he pushed it even further. There was nothing so power-fully unsettling as his stare. Walt and Judy would scold him, and he might be good for a while, but if he sensed already that someone didn't like him, their scolding only encouraged his own dislike.

He could learn to trust people over time, but it was obviously something immediate as well. He either liked someone or he didn't, and sometimes he slithered out of someone's arms no matter how much that person liked him.

He was on better behaviour when he was away from home, when he felt less secure. But at home he had an amazing ability to dictate the mood of any gathering.

Judy had two sisters who came at Christmas, and one of them had a husband. Looee was immediately suspicious of the way they all behaved. He didn't like the way the sisters hugged Judy and he tried to get in the way. He particularly didn't like the way Carole, the unmarried one, always touched Walt on the shoulder and laughed at whatever he said. He emptied her handbag on the floor and threw the bag in the garbage. She said that's all right. He heavily powdered his face with her makeup and she said that's all right, it's funny. He looked in her mirror at himself and laughed.

He disappeared and played with Murphy, and when he came back he saw Carole laughing and talking and no one else looking at her. He bit her toes under the dinner table, not hard enough to draw blood, but hard enough to be sent to the garage.

Time passed and friends came and went, often hastened by their distaste or discomfort at the thought of a chimp being raised as a child.

When Looee was older, Susan came over and Looee was very excited. He didn't go to shake her hand, he crawled right up her and Susan said oh.

He liked her big stiff boobs.

Judy told him to get down and pour them all some tea.

I was telling him stories she said. I tell him stories about a boy with a hairy face. He loves it.

Looee was walking and showing that he loves it.

Pour some tea for mummy's friend Susan, okay Looee. It's so good to see you, Susan, I've been craving some grown-up company.

It's mummy's friend Susan. Looee. Remember. See how happy he is.

He's getting big said Susan.

Looee made his food grunts as he carried the tea to the table.

He's getting bigger all right. He's hard to keep a handle on.

Looee poured tea for himself and blew on it to cool it off but he wasn't good at blowing.

He drank it.

Pour some tea for Susan, Looee.

No that's all right.

You don't want tea.

No, I.

Looee poured tea.

He really likes you. It's easy to tell when he really likes someone.
Well.

I was telling him stories I make up. Give Susan milk, please
Looee.

Susan watched Looee pour milk into her cup and it overflowed
extravagantly.

Good boy. Now come here. Mummy tell story. There, see.

Looee was sitting on mummy's lap.

The boy with the hairy face was running through the summer
flowers and sneezing and laughing, and sneezing and laughing and
laughing.

Looee laughed.

That's his laugh.

Looee looked at Susan and Susan wasn't laughing. Looee
wanted to make Susan laugh.

And he was laughing and laughing until he met his friend
Murphy. Why so sad, Murphy. Don't cry, friend.

Looee walked to Susan and got up on her lap.

Oh oh oh said Susan.

It's okay.

He won't be comfortable on me.

Sure he will.

Boobs.

He's happy. You don't mind. He loves you. Do you mind. Sit
still, Looee. That's mummy's friend. There.

Looee put his arm around Susan's waist.

Nice boy. That's my nice boy with Susan.

Looee looked at Susan's boobs.

Is that a new blouse, Susan.

I got it in Boston.

Wow.

I was visiting James at Harvard. His graduation.

Oh my god, already.

Yes. It's gone by so fast.

Susan, you must be so proud.

Mummy was excited.

I'm relieved. I am very proud. But I am relieved. It was so expensive. And I feel like I can move on. To a new phase of my own. A different time of life.

Judy looked sad but she was smiling.

You must be so proud.

Looee dug his overalls into Susan to try to feel her warmth.

Susan went stiffer.

I'm very proud, yes. He is a hard-working man. I can't believe he's a man. But we all move on.

Looee looked at Susan's pretty face.

She wouldn't look at him.

Looee looked at Susan's cheek. There was toffeecream-pancake-sauce smeared all over her pretty face, and lipstick.

Susan looked at him for a second, his face so close to hers.

What does he. What else do you do these days, Judy.

Looee touched her face and looked at his finger.

Gentle, Looee.

My leg is cramping a little, actually.

Okay, get down now, Looee. Come on down. Some people aren't comfortable, remember.

Oh no, it's not that.

No, no, I know.

Susan looked sick.

Looee squeezed her boob and she jumped.

Looee.

Mummy was shouting.

Looee!

No!

Looee hugged himself.

I'm sorry, Susan. He's sorry.

It's nothing.

You remember what it was like. It's just his age.

Well, yes, but he's not.

Go play upstairs Looee. Go on.

Looee walked to the stairs.

It's a relief these days when he plays on his own. He's clinging to me less, you know.

Looee walked up the stairs.

Tell me about James, now. What's next.

Looee walked up the stairs thinking this one's mine, and this one, I know this one makes noise.

He looked for a surprise in his room.

The following year, summer settled early. Cottonwood seeds had blown from the banks of the stream at the end of the Ribkes' land. Maple, beech, white oak and elm, everything was rooting deep and surging beyond this world of English and taxonomy.

Walt sat on the porch, late afternoon, Looee sat way up high in the oak just there. The feeling of warmth and promise on Looee's face, kind needles on lips and cheeks, was identical to that on Walt's. And while Walt was saying nothing, Looee was saying it all in a medley of heart-deep hoots and ultramontane trumpets, sounds never heard in the forests of Vermont. Millennia ago they had never seen a naked ape nor centuries ago a Frenchman.

Looee's shouts of victory made Walt think of summer, peaches in the mouth and almost-kisses, howling with his friends in the forest. He felt his arm outside the window of the car, pleasure in the moments when he knew he was stronger and smarter than some. He and Looee felt all of it the same, and none of it by name. Judy came out on the porch with a Coke for Walt and said sounds like someone's enjoying the weather.

Mm.

I should water those fuchsias she said.

I should kiss your lips.

If I sit on your lap do you promise to be good.

No.

Good.

Smack smack.

I'm getting heavy she said.

The more you push on me the closer you are to my heart.

Walt said all the right things.

Judy looked down at her thickening ankles and silently blamed the heat. Did you read about the mayor in Burlington she said.

No.

Had an affair with a young woman.

Did he.

It was in the paper she said.

Well Walt said.

Looee saw Judy from up in his distant tree and hooted.

Judy said I guess just because he wears a sash and necklace doesn't mean he's not a man.

Walt was in the middle of summer. He reached up and took

her by the chin and turned her face so she could watch him say I don't know how you keep surprising me, but I'll tell you this: you keep surprising me.

It was Looee's first summer that he could take to the next summer—his first real season of memory. He could look down at Judy from his tree and choose not to run to her, knowing now that he could do so later. And later he could sit on the porch and clean Walt, suck the salt out of his jean cuffs and think back to being in the tree. Memories were blue and yellow sheets hanging from the line (don't pull those down please Looee): fixed but restless colours blowing soft across his face. Memories made him pound on the porch, wanting to make more. He wanted to roll through all those flowers.

Looee found Walt's spare key to the front door one night that summer and ran away.

He was afraid of the stream so he ran through the woods to the Wileys', the neighbours on that side. It was dark in the woods and he wanted to see another house. He ran through the woods in his pyjamas.

No lights were on in the house, and the front door was open because the only people who locked their doors in that valley were the ones who housed chimpanzees. The hall smelled like bread and Looee was scared and excited. He found their kitchen in the dark.

There were no locks on the fridge like at home.

Looee's food grunts alone would have been enough to waken the Wileys upstairs but they had been stupefied by chicken and brandy and were lost in nonsense dreams of things less likely than a chimpanzee at their fridge.

Looee sniffed the leftover chicken, licked it and put it back. He dropped a jar of Mrs. Wiley's pickles and liked the way they spilled.

He put one in his mouth and it tasted like the bitter insides of Walt and Judy's ears. He screamed and spat it out.

He ate carrots, a jar of jam, half a bottle of cream, some raw eggs that he mopped off the floor with Mrs. Wiley's raisin loaf. He opened a can of beer with his teeth and almost liked it, opened another and liked it more.

He heard a noise upstairs and remembered he wasn't at home. He had seen the Wileys a few times and they were very tall and grey and he had never been close enough to touch them. He thought about going upstairs to see if they wanted to play.

He heard the howling of a dog outside and got frightened. He wanted to go to bed and thought maybe the Wileys have a bed for Looee.

He knew exactly how to get home.

He held a can of beer and an egg in his lips, held another can of beer in his hand, and walked on threes through the front door, closing it gently, Looee, gently.

He wanted to walk farther that night but his cargo of eggs and beer prevented him. Murphy barked once when he saw Looee come through the door at home and Looee dropped the egg from his lips and it broke on the floor by the stairs. Murphy lapped it up and Looee was sad, angry and jealous. He made noises he wasn't aware of, but Walt and Judy heard nothing. He forgot to lock the door behind him.

In his room he hid the beers under the bed so Judy couldn't have them.

The next morning, Judy was perplexed by the eggshells at the foot of the stairs. Murphy held his head low when she was sweeping them up, so he must have been somehow responsible. Looee was sleeping in, which was nice. She noticed they had forgotten to lock the door last night, but she knew that Looee was in his room.

When she checked on him later there were food stains on his pyjamas. Where'd you get those from she said. Looee gave her lots of kisses on her neck, which he didn't always do first thing in the morning. She loved it.

That night Judy made sure she locked the door, and Looee used Walt's key again and went out into the warm darkness.

Tonight he knew clearly that he was going to the Wileys' fridge, and the now known goal made the journey more fraught and rich. He noticed sounds he hadn't heard the night before.

In the woods at night he could see no farther than a boy could. Two white-tailed deer had seen his blue pyjamas coming long before he might have seen them run. Looee's nose wasn't sensitive enough to smell their timid spoor, his hands and feet were dull and dumb compared to those of the raccoons that mapped those woods with constant touching and probes. He heard sounds in the dark, and throughout the state and country was a generation of people either supporting or reviling the superstitions of others. The sounds in the dark made Looee think of the drain in the upstairs bathroom, the drain that made him scream for reasons Walt and Judy could never understand. Looee feared that if he didn't move quickly he would be swallowed by a drain.

There are leopards in the memory of every ape, leopards we've never seen. Some look like dragons and some look like drains.

Mr. Wiley was sitting on his porch in the dark with his shotgun across his lap. Last night his kitchen was taken apart by a bear or some hippie desperate for beer.

Looee came to the outer edge of the woods with the mind of a four-year-old boy, the coordination and strength of an eighteen-year-old, a throat, tongue and teeth that could never form consonants, and even if he was able to speak he could never tell those deer how deep those woods can look in daylight. And the deer could never tell Judy that the soft blue pyjamas she bought her boy were actually fierce and electric and the world was a long horizon of threats.

Mr. Wiley will kill that bear or hippie.

He's not too old to get angry.

He was staring at the distant road thinking if it's a man he'll come from there. He figured if it had been a bear that came into the kitchen, why would it have taken the beer and not the chicken. And what kind of a bear opens and closes the front door without leaving a scratchmark or two. What kind of a man would come into the home he bought for his retirement and not respect the fact that he would offer food to anyone in need.

He didn't want to kill someone, but he'll shoot. He will stand tall and fire.

Looee came out of the woods unfrightened, thinking there are no locks on that fridge. He walked across the lawn.

Mr. Wiley saw a bear coming out of the woods wearing a grey garment. He had enough time to think that he might be getting cataracts again and of course the bear isn't clothed; enough time to think that's a smallish bear and mother won't be far behind.

A bear, he could shoot without regret.

He stood taller and Looee saw him.

Jesus Christ what is that.

Mr. Wiley thought he was looking at a nightmare, a perverted little outcast, half-bear, half-man, and he was hot with pity and terror.

He aimed squarely at Looee.

Peace is a result of curiosity, when one ape wonders about another.

Mr. Wiley got down on his knees and said Christ it's the neighbour's little gorilla.

He wished his wife were awake.

Looee kissed his hand and put his arm around his waist and tried to get him moving towards the fridge. And Mr. Wiley had no idea what to do.

So how do I … You're wearing some pyjamas on yourself.

Looee was making his I like you I'm excited noises and stayed still for a moment while he pissed in his pyjamas, calmed by what we would call the kind and curious shyness about the eyes of Mr. Wiley.

And now he would get what he wanted.

He urged Mr. Wiley towards the door with his hand on his lower back.

Okay okay.

Mr. Wiley felt as though an excited friend was saying I want to show you something. He opened the door and Looee took his hand and pulled him towards the fridge. Mr. Wiley couldn't help but smile and think that really is a hand.

Looee was grunting and making excited noises.

I guess you know the place pretty well.

He watched Looee look for things in the fridge. Whenever he wanted something he looked up at Mr. Wiley as though he were asking.

You want the sour cream. Go ahead. I like it on baked potatoes, but you'll. Yeah. You'd need a baked potato with that to like it.

Looee grabbed a beer and Mr. Wiley said how old are you and reached for one himself.

Looee pulled on Mr. Wiley's belt and persuaded him to sit on the floor.

That creature is neither wild nor owned, he said to his wife the next day.

That beer is for sipping now, sip it. Sip it.

He had driven past Walt and Judy often and seen their little pet, but now that he was sitting across from him he was thinking that right there is not a pet. He was feeling just the right mixture of fear, curiosity and confusion required to make meeting a stranger memorable. I want to get to know that little fella more than I ever wanted to know a cat or even my brother-in-law James.

He watched Looee get restless, and when he settled again Mr. Wiley touched himself on the chest and said Joseph.

Joseph.

Looee stared.

Looee and the Wileys became good friends. Their fridge was a memory that stayed with him.

When Walt and Judy were awakened in the middle of the night and found Mr. Wiley on the porch with Looee they were angry and embarrassed. Looee was very affectionate with Judy.

They found the spare key in his diaper.

He can come over any time said Mr. Wiley. Just maybe not alone and not in the middle of the night.

Only Looee and Mr. Wiley knew what it was like to walk through those woods hand in hand.

He's a nice … it's an … he's an unusual situation, was all Mr. Wiley could offer.

Judy felt the urge to close the door on the outside world.

Walt was just plain mad.

Goddamnit Looee, you can't walk out like that.

To Judy, in bed, he said we've got to make him understand.

They both felt surprisingly betrayed—that he would want to run away, that he would be curious about another home, that he always hid things from them.

He's always wanting what other people have said Walt.

He's only little said Judy.

He's gotta learn.

I agree.

Daylight offered some clarity.

I'm gonna think about what to do said Walt.

He went out that day to buy the same tractor Larry had bought last month. It was better on gas and was blue, kind of handsome and unusual.

nine

Please be my friend Podo.

 Please come down Dr. David.

 Please machine make movie.

 Money name-of that.

 Dog name-of that.

 You have that. Ghoul has this.

 Money buys dogs.

 Money buys friends.

 Yellow colour-of dog.

 Money is bowing without bowing.

Podo watches Jonathan stand and sees his pink needle. Mouths are wet and chests are aching. Podo is alert to the wants of others today. Fifi feels good on his lap. A wind creamed with birds and clouds blows over the belly of Fifi and she is heavily fond of everyone.

 Fifi is pink, and men delay their breakfast.

 Burke is confused and needs to be alone.

 They left their bedrooms this morning and Fifi was the last to leave and when they were out in the World they saw why: rosé behind her as large as a goon, splendid as a picnic of plums and cherries and soft as a person's neck. Podo was the first to run to her but she did not fall forward right away. He touched her rosé with his finger, put his eyes close to her heat, and when she sat he felt the breathless give-and-take of being protector and abuser together.

They rested in the shade while the others grew to realize that this would be a day of permissions, of careful walking and making up tasks that kept them away from Podo.

Fifi lay on her side and Podo sat with his hip to her back and they contemplated the sky (pink), the flowers (pink), the sun soaking trees, and the heat from skin to ground to skin, limpening hair and engorging everything else.

Podo made a noise. Fifi looked at him. Podo opened his legs and flicked his wakening cock. Here. Fifi made a noise that was appealing. She rolled and leaned forward, pushed her rosé up to the sky and felt the counter-push that balanced the world and the quick hard dance of very serious laughter.

Magda's back was turned and she sat in different shade.

Mr. Ghoul sat close to Mama, thinking thoughts that were like the movies of fish, so quick and incomprehensible.

And if the growth of every seed and leaf, every pump of hungry wing, could be amplified to sound the unremembering surge of life, it would find its equal orchestra in the core of Jonathan's body as he squeezed his erection between his legs and wondered what to do. He had seen her rosé as she painted a line from her bedroom. He could taste her smell and could eat no fruit and he rested his chin on the ground.

No good would come from whimpering or complaining but the whimpering came nonetheless. He put his hand across his mouth to hide his smile of fear. He walks away and sits. He lies down and tries to rest but all he can think of is Podo's broad back

between him and what he wants. He thinks about ways to please
Podo, things to offer his great black protector to secure his benedic-
tion and pin fat Fifi with impunity.

He barks without thinking, hoots before he thinks of why
he barked, and is suddenly aware that he is making a great noise.
Podo turns, Magda gets up to join Jonathan, movement is created.
Nothing comes of it, except a small good feeling.

He thinks again of Fifi. He thinks of her bent over, her plump
and muscled flower.

He lies down again.

Jonathan will never get what he wants unless Podo wants to let
him.

He stands and looks at Magda.

Jonathan is looming, stubborn black cloud, bedoulerek radish
pointing hot and urgent from under his belly.

Magda runs away and Podo watches.

Mr. Ghoul walks to Podo, a supplicant. He holds out his hand,
which Podo touches. Mr. Ghoul grooms Podo and they are both
now aware that Mr. Ghoul, at some point, might stick it to Fifi but
probably not today.

Mr. Ghoul knows that the new one has a mother. Mama.

Mother.

When Mama came out from the Hard she had an eety little
new one and she fed her from her chest. So did Magda, and Fifi fed
Burke from the bottle.

When Mr. Ghoul looked at the new one he felt new confusions.

Mama feeds the new one.

She rides Mama's back through the World.

Mr. Ghoul had a mother named Dave.

*

Mr. Ghoul and Mama learned the people's culture for longer than some of the others.

Be nice.

Don't bite.

What's the name of this. Look at me. What's the name of this.

You can't always have what is yours.

There were sticks and electric sticks and the short woman Mary with thunder in her mouth. Mary taught them signs with their hands and when Mr. Ghoul or Mama wasn't interested she would slap you in the snut or grab you hard under the mouth to make you look at what she was saying. Always moving her sharp bald hands.

They wanted Mama and Mr. Ghoul to talk to each other with their hands. They only did it sometimes when Mary was around so she wouldn't hit them.

Then Mary disappeared, like Orang and the others.

Dave liked the dirty machine, and Ghoul liked Dave.

They made the Hardest bigger and brought new toys and paints and Mama made paintings and Ghoul liked watching her make them.

Dave taught them colours, and colours were the way you could describe the pictures that can't be pictured.

Mama liked red.

Dave would talk through the machine and hold up the fire truck.

? Mama what colour-of fire truck.

Red colour-of that.

? Mama what colour-of lipstick.

Red.

And then Dave held up one of their favourite things, the whistle. Dave could put the whistle to his mouth and fling a twirl into the air that made your ears and hair and back stand up and look for what no one could see. And Ghoul knew the whistle was black.

? Mama what colour-of whistle.

Red.

? Mama what colour-of whistle.

Red colour-of that.

No.

Dave held up a black pen.

? Mama what colour-of pen.

Black colour-of that.

And he held up the whistle again.

Red.

Red red red.

And she was happy.

She called magazines red, her blue hairbrush red, the blind uncovering the window red, and Dave grew excited. He gathered the other people to his window and he and some of them smiled because they knew that anything Mama really liked was red. When the Hardest grew softer and they saw the trees, Mama went to the machine and said

That red.

Dave liked it best when they shared like that, the pictures beyond the pictures. His face changed.

? Ghoul what colour Dave's eyes.

Dave was at the window pointing to his eyes and neither smiling nor crying nor frowning. Dave's soft face.

Please Dave swing Ghoul.

? Ghoul what colour Dave's eyes.

? Tickle.

Later. ? Ghoul what colour Dave's eyes.

Red Green Green Blue Black Green Blue.

ten

We wanted to know what friends were, says David to a conference.

Girdish was a warren of different interests in those days and when he thinks of it he remembers a time of great excitement. From room to room there were studies of intelligence, memory, communication, breeding, all distinct and diverse but united by a sense that we were always on the verge of something. Staff would smoke pipes and pot and sit with the younger apes, and ideas were openly traded. Few people shaved, and some of the male and female researchers kissed and thought we might as well be honest.

David was young then, as was his profession. And when you're young it sometimes seems like the world, no matter how old, is being shaped anew. It seemed like everyone was talking about primates. Journalists often visited, and some of the research was published in the popular press around the world. The Naked Ape was a bestseller. Konrad Lorenz had explained our warmongering and violence by looking at us as animals. It seemed like humans were at least talking about kinship, if not actually acknowledging that they were apes.

There were reports from field studies in Africa, from Gombe and the Japanese groups. Much of it was anecdotal in the early days. Chimpanzees have culture. In Gombe the chimps were wiping ants off sticks with their hands and bringing the wad of ants to their mouths, but in the Taï Forest they were bringing the sticks directly to their mouths. This was behaviour that they had learned and passed down through observation and imitation. Strangers would be recognized by how they ate. At the time, most Americans were eating with their forks in their right hands, and being mocked by Europeans for doing so.

David used to envy the people doing the field studies. There was a growing rivalry between those who worked with apes in labs and those who observed them in the wild. Do we know them better when they interact with humans or do we only understand the traits we have in common. Isn't it best to see them behave as chimps in the wild, or is every ape, humans included, always adapting to some sort of culture imposed by others.

From the field came reports of chimps doing dances or displaying whenever it rained. They were seen to marvel at water-falls and to act unusually when they saw some wonder of nature. There were chimps in Kibale who used small sticks to clear their noses, and there were others who laid floors of branches across thorny ground to protect their feet.

David wanted to see these things in the wild, but he also had plenty of his own stories, his own examples of culture and of inventiveness. Much was made of the fact that the Ugandan chimps used a unique hand clasp when grooming—something that no other colonies were seen to do. At Girdish, when the field station grew and the population was stable, Podo clapped his hands whenever he wanted to be groomed, a ritual Podo would not have seen anywhere else. All the others in the colony copied him. As new apes were introduced they either learned to clap or were shunned. Wherever they are, apes invent culture, and their culture is strengthened through the exclusion of others.

So while David heard field reports and felt excited by the broader world, he felt as though he had his own small country here. There were experiments that made him feel he was part of a family, and his memories of the early days are not just of youthful enthusiasm but of iconoclasm. Like all his younger colleagues, he wanted to demolish beliefs about what it meant to be human.

They wanted to see whether chimps were capable of doing favours for others without reward. Was the celebrated altruism of humans unique.

We devised trials with several of the chimps he says to the conference. We put them individually in their cells, and outside the cages I and another researcher would pretend to fight over a stick. The other researcher would win the fight and walk away, dropping the stick within reach of the chimp but beyond my reach.

At that point I would make noises and stretch for the stick beyond my reach, and would plead with the chimp, gesturally, non-verbally, to reach outside the cage to get it for me. There was no incentive for the chimp to help me, no food or praise, yet every chimp retrieved the stick and gave it to me.

We refined the experiment and made it more difficult for the chimps to get the stick. The other person who won the play fight would put the stick high up beyond everyone's reach, but the chimp could get it by climbing up and opening a door. And again, even in the face of effort and obstacles, they always got the stick and gave it to me.

I love remembering those trials. We often did similar tests with humans, to compare. We created a similar scenario with toddlers, twenty-month-old babies who couldn't speak. Two women would pretend to fight over a crayon, and the winner would drop it beyond the reach of the loser and leave the room. The losing woman would reach out but be restricted by a desk, and the toddler could see that the woman really wanted the crayon. The toddler would watch the woman reaching and pleading, non-verbally, and the toddler would walk over and pick up the crayon and bring it to the woman. We made obstacles again, like we did with the chimps, and the kids still picked up the crayon and handed it over. None of them kept the object for themselves.

It was moving to see these little creatures helping each other. That's what I remember.

This was decades ago.

It's hard to find anyone outside my profession who talks about these things anymore.

David pauses and remembers that in all the human trials, the toddlers had their mothers in the room. They sat in the corner and were instructed to be neutral, and the kids usually looked towards their mothers before they did anything.

We never had the choice of chimps that I wanted. When I was younger I had an ideal subject in mind, but as I aged and got to know the chimps I realized ideals were nonsense. Our chimps came from everywhere, and it soon appealed to me as a city in microcosm. Of course backgrounds and personal histories mattered, but, just like in a city, those personal histories would have to come up against the reality of this new society.

We had a chimp named Billie for a while. He had been part of NASA's space program, so I expected him to have difficulty with some of the others—too humanized—but he quickly behaved like a typical male chimpanzee and had alpha status briefly.

When I think of friendships I remember Rosie having her baby, Burke. It was never clear who the fathers of any of the children were because when the females were in estrus they had multiple partners. But it was pretty clear that Billie did not consider Burke to be his own. Rosie never took to motherhood, but on the first day when we reintroduced her to the colony with her baby, Billie moved aggressively towards her. His hair was on end, as scary as an alpha could be, and he was clearly intent on harming the baby.

Podo and Ghoul, as if they had been planning it, stepped directly in Billie's way. They actually had their arms around each other and stood between Billie and Rosie. We have photos of it.

One thing we noticed whenever we introduced new chimps was that the older ones, those who had been reliable, compliant subjects in the past, were suddenly less consistent in their performance of various skills. The more we got them working together, the more difficult it was to gather data. It was as if they had suddenly forgotten all they had learned, or that their prior learning had been an illusion. Sometimes it seemed to put all earlier findings in doubt.

The cooperation tests were telling. There was a famous old video of a study by Nissen and Crawford. Two juveniles sit side by side against a cage and each pulls on a rope attached to a heavy tray, upon which is piled food. If the chimps pulled the ropes cooperatively they were able to pull the food towards them. The video shows the chimps cajoling each other when one or the other is unwilling to work, putting an arm around a shoulder or giving encouraging shoves. It seemed proof that chimpanzees were willing to work together for a common task, until it emerged that the chimps had been trained to work together and that some of the test subjects would simply refuse to do the task. There was no real proof that chimpanzees would cooperate.

At Girdish we devised a series of tests which showed the importance of prior relationships. If the test subjects had got on well with each other, in advance of the cooperation study, they performed quite predictably in the advancement of a common goal.

The real test was whether or not they had succeeded together in the past. Our trials, and several others around the world, have shown that personality differences, tolerance among individuals, can be the deciding factors in these cooperation studies. Dominant chimps in a pair would dictate the progress of a trial, as would the question of whether the other in the pair would truly accept that dominance.

We eventually came up with a test where a chimpanzee could choose which partner he or she would work with. They were given a key which could open any cage, and they were free to release the chimp of their choice for the trial. What we found was that if the chimp with the key had been successful with a partner in earlier food trials, he or she would always open that other chimp's cage and they would perform a new task. If the new task was a success they would work together again, but as soon as there was a failure the chimp with the key would make a different choice of partner in the future. The other chimps in the trial would observe the successes and failures beyond their cages, and there was evidence that they would all shun the chimps who failed in tests which they witnessed.

There was clearly memory involved. On one occasion there was a gap of a week between tests. The chimps with the keys exclusively chose whatever skilful partners they had worked with the previous week. Over time it amounted to the development of what we would call reputation.

We know from other tests that chimpanzees will help each other, and humans, when there is no obvious reward. But when there is a third party and motivational reward involved from the beginning—in these trials, food—the matter of altruism is muddied.

The bottom line seems to be that if a chimpanzee does not need another to acquire food, he will not bother trying to get along with anyone.

And if he wants the help of someone, he will regularly choose the one he has found success with in the past, and consequently shun all others.

How many of you have lost friends.

eleven

They had parties.

M&M's.

Dave lit vodka on fire and Mama went to the machine and said That red.

Dave played a guitar that made Ghoul want to leave the room.

Some nights he slept and some nights his arms and legs ached and his bedroom was too small.

Ghoul thought more on his own sometimes and squirted white on his belly and leg.

New pictures were put on the machine.

Cassette

Microwave

Cockroach

Visitor

The greatest changes came with Visitor.

Some of the people then were Dr. Duane, Dave, Mary, Mama, Ghoul, the Fool, Orang and Sue. These along with others came and went. Anyone new or yekel was called Visitor.

And usually a Visitor meant Ghoul would have to work and not relax with Dave. The Visitor watched while Ghoul named pictures, looked at slides, worked for raisins and coffee till the ache bloomed in his goon. Sometimes there was more than one Visitor and Later Later Later when the window was bigger there were ten, twelve, fifteen of them sitting and watching Ghoul work.

Visitors could become many different things—a Visitor one day was Julie the next.

Dave stayed later than everyone sometimes and walked with Ghoul to his bedroom. Sometimes Ghoul took Dave's cigarettes from his shirt.

One night in the Hardest before bed Ghoul was saying

Bedtime swing Ghoul yes yes Dave

And Dave said

Visitor.

Dave went away and came back to the window with a Visitor. She leaned on Dave and looked through the window.

Ghoul did not want to work.

Please bedtime swing Ghoul

And Dave said

Twizzler.

Bedtime.

Later.

No.

Dave was talking to the Visitor who was smiling in a way that Ghoul did not like. She smiled at Ghoul too and he felt tired.

No No No.

Dave said

? Ghoul what colour-of eyes Visitor.

She was standing at the window, looking to Dave and then intently at Ghoul with big white eyes and Ghoul was too tired to tell if she was a friend or a mindling liar. You need to touch and bother someone to see if they like you.

? Ghoul what colour-of eyes.

Please bedtime swing yes Please. Machine make Visitor off.

The Fool came into the room and took Ghoul by the hand and Ghoul looked over his shoulder at the Visitor and Dave, and they both looked shiny and lucky and stupid.

She came back another night and Dave made a new picture which meant and sounded like this when he said it:

Julie.

And Ghoul was not nice at first.

One day Dave said

? Ghoul what in corner low-down.

Julie.

No. ? What in corner.

Julie in corner.

No. ? What dirty thing in corner low-down.

Ghoul went to the window to look at Dave's face to see if he was laughing but he wasn't.

? Ghoul what in corner.

Cockroach in corner.

Ghoul did not get a raisin and was sorry. When Julie came that night Ghoul said

Please Julie chase Ghoul.

She looked at Dave and Dave said

Ghoul be good. Julie chase Ghoul.

Visitors were not allowed in the room, so chasing meant Julie had to run from Dave's window to the new window and all the way around outside to the window where Dave blew smoke rings.

Julie ran around outside and Ghoul followed her inside and

sometimes she would appear at that window and sometimes not and she was happy and good at the game.

Ghoul said

Again.

And they did it again.

And Ghoul said

Again.

And Dave said

No.

? Julie tickle Ghoul.

No.

? Ghoul tickle Julie.

Later.

Ghoul felt very happy and now liked Julie, and really liked the picture of tickling Julie, and he squirted white on his leg.

He squirted white on Julie. Dave came into the room with Julie one night and Ghoul could finally touch her and she smelled like apples.

He took off her shoes and liked her feet and liked the look of her small teeth.

He lay on his back with his legs spread to let her tickle his klopsiks but she didn't.

The three sat on the floor and Ghoul walked over to her and sat on her lap. Her leg felt warm underneath him. She talked to Dave, and Ghoul stared at her, and she turned and looked at Ghoul for a long time. Then she talked to Dave and had her arm on Ghoul's lap where she held him and it was warm on his leg and he stared at her teeth and squirted white on her arm.

They tried to put his cock into Mama later but it was bent and he didn't want to, and the days were sad and cold.

Mama wasn't good at the machine.

*

Ghoul had a birthday party. 1, 2, 3, 4, 5, 6, 7. There were hats and candles that burned the lips and Mama put lipstick on her face. That night Julie came to the room and gave Ghoul a present: a comb. Ghoul gave Julie kisses on the neck and lips and nuzzled and shnuttled and put his yalamak in her mouth to touch hers. He squirted white on her pink shirt and Dave said dirty, and Julie was red and happy. She sang happy birthday in the hard square room, with the lights of the machine and Dave's face. She sang it quietly, like they hadn't with Mama, and Ghoul missed sleeping Mama in a happy way, and he swung from the bar above the machine and hooled because tonight was rich as butter.

Dave and Julie put Ghoul to bed and it's a night he still thinks of and tastes.

Please machine make party.

Julie kept coming at night and sang quiet songs.

When Julie stayed behind-the-room she gave Dave lots of kisses and Ghoul threw an apple at the window and screamed.

But Julie always came into the room, even when Dave hung on to her and said no. She didn't talk through the machine, she came in and said where's my Ghoul, my big Mr. Ghoul, and sometimes if they were sitting still for a moment he would go to the machine.

Dave looked different around Julie, like he was keeping a secret he really wanted to show. Sometimes Ghoul wanted to be alone with Dave and sometimes alone with Julie but he never wanted them together without him.

Mr. Ghoul stopped using the machine at night and Dave didn't like that.

Julie said how's big Mr. Ghoul, I missed you I brought you a present. He liked her so much he backed into her all the time, and she would scratch him. Whose little butt. Is that Mr. Ghoul's. He felt excited and calm at the same time like when he drank coffee. He didn't know what he wanted to do with Julie but he could taste it in his hips.

He pulled Dave's hands off her whenever he could.

When she touched, it didn't tickle.

I missed you Mr. Ghoul.

During the day, Ghoul would say

? Where Julie.

And Dave would say

Julie later.

And those were the days when Ghoul didn't need to eat M&M's when he made sentences.

Dave taught her to talk on the machine sometimes.

? Ghoul want nature.

Nature was a movie about trees.

? Ghoul want tickle.

Julie walked in calm and warm.

Then Dr. Duane came back one night and found Dave and Julie and Mr. Ghoul in the middle of games and talking on the floor with smokes. Dave and Dr. Duane shouted at each other and the Fool came in and took Mr. Ghoul to his bedroom.

He never saw Julie again, and then there was no picture of Julie on the machine.

Ghoul could only say

? Where.

? Why Ghoul make dirty. ? Why Ghoul make dirty machine.

The picture for Why was this: ↔.

He knows the answer for When is Then and Where is There and What is That, and What is that, it's a coin. But there is no answer for Why, neither in the World nor in the Hard nor in the dreams of young Ghoul or old. He never understood it.

Whenever Ghoul was asked Why, Ghoul did not know what to do, so Why, like Julie, disappeared.

The walls and floors and ceilings of the Hardest were white and he jumped up the walls sometimes in ¡harag! and Dave stopped saying Why.

twelve

The Wonder of Growing by Esther P. Edwards was a book which accompanied a range of toys, all designed for a child's first few years of life. Judy had ordered the book and toys from the Sears catalogue when Looee was a baby. When she was a girl her parents did the same thing. She tried to enrich his childhood as much as she could.

Most of the toys came from the Christmas Wish Book or the general Sears catalogue when Judy ordered things for the house. The Big Toy Box, Twisting Turning Teddies.

When he was a toddler he bit everything in sight. When he grew up he could bite off a finger in minor irritation, bite off someone's face or the scrotum of his tormentor. But Judy said no, Looee, we all have teeth but we don't approve of biting.

Naturally she did not expect as much from his encounters with books as she would from another child, but he liked the talking books whose pictures made noises. What he loved from an early age was drawing or painting or colouring. He marvelled at a line emerging from a pen.

She bought a Little Learners two-sided wood easel, and she would stand and paint on one side while he sat up on a stool and painted on the other. He regularly came around to her side and made his noise for I like this. Sometimes she imagined she could see real shapes in his paintings. Maybe that was possible. When she looked at pictures or puzzles with him and said where's the tree, where's the cat, which one's the front-end loader, he always got it right. He recognized representations, he just couldn't create them. His hands were strong and capable, but not dexterous.

She bought him a flip-top desk because she realized he could never go to school. She watched him sit and draw. He banged on the desk in the way he did to say that this is mine.

He beat his hands on the living room floor, on the porch, on the lawn, to say that this is mine.

He sat more still now when they drew, groomed her with more love when they looked at pictures and she explained the dimensions of her world.

Looee was learning how to wash dishes in the sink when he was smaller and he slipped on the edge and fell in. Judy said sorry sorry sorry, hug hug hug, hugging herself before picking him up. And when she told Walt about it later, Looee overheard and hugged himself. It was one of those miracles of comprehension in tiny children that make all parents proud. He gets everything we say.

Sorry, hug became the gesture of regret, the one that was made whenever someone did something wrong. When Looee got too rough with Murphy and heard Murphy whine or Walt shout ENOUGH, Looee hugged himself before hugging Murphy's head. Or when he tore the stuffing out of the cushions in the living room and Judy turned her back and walked away saying I'm not talking to you today, Looee walked after her upright, hugging himself repeatedly until she knew he was truly sorry.

It became a giveaway or sometimes a pre-emptive gesture. If Judy walked into the room and Looee was saying sorry, hug, she knew he had been up to something, that she would find a mess or something broken. Sometimes he would say sorry, hug before he did something wrong, knowing he would get in trouble but doing it anyway. On those occasions she was less convinced by his contrition.

The day after Mr. Wiley brought him home and Walt and Judy were mad at him, Looee sat in his room waiting for Judy to come and see him.

He stared at the wall across from his bed. He didn't want to be in trouble; he wanted to play chase with Murphy and go to the Wileys' fridge. He wanted to be nice to Judy so she would be nice to him. When he heard footsteps near the door he hooted and hugged himself several times to say sorry, sorry, sorry, but no one opened the door. A long time passed and he played with things in his room. He drank the two beers he had hidden under his bed and felt relaxed.

When Judy finally came in, feeling she had punished him enough, Looee was asleep next to the empty cans of beer.

I'm not sure what he's growing into she said to Walt later.

thirteen

Visitors came to the window and Ghoul put urulek in his hand and threw it at the window, and the Fool came in. The Visitors were never Julie and now whenever he heard that sound

Visitor.

whenever he saw that picture light up

☺

he tried to hold the urulek-heat inside in case the Fool came in with his stick. He refused to work till he burned and burned.

And one day he heard Visitor, and no one was at the window.

He looked at Dave, and Dave looked nice today.

Visitor.

Ghoul got up on his chair and said

? Where

And looked for the picture of Julie on the machine.

Dave said

Visitor behind-the-room.

It was the day that Ghoul met Podo.

Sitting on a chair behind-the-room with a long black string

hanging from his neck was young Podo, not yet known to Ghoul as Podo and not much bigger than Ghoul himself when he ate too much popcorn. He was sitting behind Dave with his back to the wall and the Fool was there also with his stick.

Podo was staring at Ghoul and Ghoul could not look him in the eyes. He was wondering what the Visitor was doing, why he was behind-the-room with Dave, when Ghoul was not allowed to be.

Ghoul looked around at the machine and the desk in front of him and picked up his orange ball. He got down from his chair, threw the ball at the wall for a while, and got back up on his chair. He looked at the machine and said

? Who that.

Mr. Ghoul has a handful of pebbles. He is sitting on the branch above Fifi while she eats her peach. He makes sure Podo isn't looking, and he drops a pebble on Fifi's back.

When Ghoul looked again at the Visitor he was eating an apple. Ghoul wondered how the Visitor got the apple.

Dave give apple Ghoul.

The drawer under the machine slid open and delivered a piece of apple.

When Ghoul worked with Dave he only got pieces of apple: one good sentence meant a piece of apple. But the Visitor was eating a whole apple.

Dave give apple Ghoul.

Another piece came out.

Please Dave give apple Ghoul.

Dave said

Apple in hand.

Ghoul pressed the picture for more-than.

Nothing happened.

Please Dave give more-than apple.

The Visitor got down from his chair, walked towards Dave, got something that Ghoul couldn't see and returned to his chair. He had a whole can of Coke.

Please Dave give more-than Coke.

It took Dave a while to understand that more-than meant everything.

Dave said

? Ghoul go behind-the-room.

And Ghoul wanted to go behind-the-room to see Dave and get whole apples and Cokes, but the Visitor was there. Again Ghoul said

? Who that.

Dave walked over to Podo and was saying things that Ghoul couldn't hear. Dave took the string off Podo's neck. Podo looked at Dave and looked at the window where Dave pointed, at poogly Ghoul who would not look him in the eyes.

Dave came back to the window and said again

? Ghoul go behind-the-room.

Ghoul looked at the Visitor and said

No.

Dave walked over to Podo and started tickling him under his arms.

Ghoul watched and felt the heat he felt when Dave and Julie kissed.

Dirty.

Then he said

Dave tickle Ghoul.

Dave looked at the machine and the window and was smiling.

Podo was making gestures with his hands for more tickling.

Ghoul started screaming.

Dave came into Ghoul's room and the Fool stayed behind-the-room with Podo.

Ghoul ran to the corner away from Dave because he would never let Dave tickle him again, unless Dave tickled him.

Dave came closer and Ghoul complained but Dave came close anyway, and Ghoul knew that Dave still liked him so he tackled Dave and they rumbled.

Podo watched from the other room. The Fool was close.

Dave went back behind-the-room without closing the door and Ghoul watched him give the Visitor a whole banana, for doing nothing but being a Visitor.

Ghoul went back to the machine and thought. He summoned the pictures of what might happen, but there were no pictures.

Please give Ghoul more-than banana.

Dave came to the door and said come, and withdrew behind-the-room.

Ghoul got down from his chair and walked carefully. He looked through the open doorway and the Visitor was eating and making noises. Dave was sitting on his chair and Ghoul looked at all the chomp that went into the machine and wondered whether to eat or run or jump on Dave or hide in his bedroom with a doll. Dave said Ghoul be good in his normal Dave voice and he got down on the floor and they sat. Podo got off his chair and Ghoul was scared and wanted to go back to the machine to ask what the Visitor was doing.

But the Fool had shut the door.

Podo came near and his hair was raised.

Ghoul turned his back to Podo and looked at Dave.

Dave was smiling and saying with his hands and mouth

That Podo.

Ghoul felt a wind that wasn't there on his back and his cock stood up with fearjoy. Podo might do anything.

Dave was still smiling and Ghoul wished he could ask questions. He couldn't remember what dirty Mary had taught him to do with his hands to ask questions.

The wind that wasn't there grew stronger on his back.

Dave was smiling and looking at the Fool over their shoulders.

Dave and the Fool saw Podo and Ghoul sitting on the floor with their backs both turned to each other.

Ghoul heard Podo make noises and Podo heard Ghoul do the same. Podo made one noise and Ghoul made that same noise and Podo wriggled backwards a little. Ghoul looked at Dave.

Dave got up and walked behind Ghoul, and as Ghoul started to turn to see where Dave was going, his back touched Podo's and they both jumped up and screamed.

Podo jumped on the goon of Ghoul and Ghoul found it funny to bury his face in Podo's belly and he flipped Podo over and Podo put his foot in Ghoul's mouth and Ghoul nibbled. Podo laughed from the tickle and Ghoul laughed for the laughing and they rolled and rolled in black animalalia while Dave and the Fool were pinned against the wall.

Ghoul had a friend named Podo.

Yesterday Jonathan tried to push into Mama and Podo bit his arm and drove him to the ground, with fists more than fists like hail is more than water.

Jonathan was chased to the edge of society and lurched like liquid meat. No one would go to him and Podo went to Fifi, and they shared the question and answer of race, if that was everything there will be more.

There is a great blue wall around the World. Sometimes they think of it and sometimes they don't.

And Fifi is still pink today, but it is different. A new flower is red one day and red the next but the next it isn't new.

She is the first to step out after eating cheese and two fists of bananas, and her lips and feet carry peaches out to the morning heat. Mr. Ghoul is last to the food.

It hurts when Podo breathes this morning and he needs to be alone but doesn't. He needs some hands on his back, and chomp in his mouth, and will not abide demands. He claps and a skrupulus forms. Fifi and Mama and the new one gather around him. Podo reaches over his shoulder and taps on his back, and Mama goes to him. She tries to see pictures of Podo and the secrets in his chest and she touches his back while her mouth makes sounds of loyalty and care. He coughs his complaints and she hears his breath, and she thinks of rain and the loss of her cat and wants to keep the new one close.

Fifi rests on Podo's lap but it irks him. He flicks her off and she arphles and fleps and goes elsewhere to eat her peaches.

Mr. Ghoul sees his opportunity.

Fifi feels the pebble on her back, looks up and sees Mr. Ghoul in the tree. He drops another pebble which lands on her shoulder. She understands.

Fifi feels the twitch behind her legs like her hips want to eat their own peach. She puts the peach on the ground and makes soft noises to Mr. Ghoul who feels rich involutions from his throat down to his tightening balls of all that is unknown and good. He almost jumps down, but remembers the need for discretion.

He tosses another pebble at Fifi.

She wonders why.

He looks towards Podo who is lying on his side with his back against Mama. Mr. Ghoul climbs down to the ground and touches Fifi on the neck and leads her into the first grove of trees. It is cool in the grove and they move fast and shaky. Fifi bends forward and manoeuvres in the way she must for bent Mr. Ghoul. She looks over her shoulder and his hair and nails catch fire.

In the grove of trees are a million sugared hummingbirds screaming more is never enough, and before Fifi can blink there is a burst from the needles on the trees and ground that says, in fact, that's enough.

Mr. Ghoul feels the oa.

Podo is asleep.

Fifi leaves the grove.

Mr. Ghoul stays behind.

There is no beginning and end to the trees, the ground, Mr. Ghoul and the wall.

He feels the oa.

He stays behind and thinks nothing.

He smells something and thinks of Fifi.

He would like to do that again.

fourteen

Daily, monthly, the force of Looee's moods increased, and whether he was happy, depressed, mischievous or malignant, he was growing and making more noise. Almost everything he did had an accompanying noise, and some grew so loud that when Judy was tired or uneasy she would shush him and say the neighbours are going to think we're running a zoo.

Their house was indeed becoming infamous. They had no idea how many acquaintances and strangers drove by and said that blue one there's the monkey house. People would knock on a Saturday afternoon with children wondering if they could see the circus. Looee was friendly at first, just as curious as they were, and Walt didn't mind showing him off sometimes.

Looee was very excited around kids. He took the hands of those who were his size, or smaller, and showed them his toys and the kitchen. Their parents were worried and amazed. Judy didn't so much like the look on some people's faces—she saw judgment or arrogance or hints of dark questions she had not yet found the answers to.

Walt was not exposed to Looee's moods as much as Judy was, but he sure knew it when Looee wasn't happy.

Can't you just tell us what the trouble is, you're not a baby anymore.

Looee woke them up one night with screams that came from the hollows of everything manmade. They ran to his room and found him sitting up with his bedside light on, shrieking at something on the wall that none of them could see. He wouldn't stop.

What is it Looee said Judy.

When they settled him and went back to bed they were less awake than they thought they were.

I'm wondering if you stop feeling blue just because you can say I'm feeling blue said Walt.

I feel better when I say it said Judy.

Their bodies were united by Looee's screams and Judy thought there are no words for what you do not know.

Are you blue, Walter.

I think it's just winter he said.

Looee reached his sixth or seventh year. He was more or less the size of an eight-year-old boy. He was big for his age because of Judy's good food. Sometimes he looked small because he walked on his knuckles, and he still liked to be carried when he was tired.

They couldn't take him out in public as much anymore. Walt took him to his office sometimes and had shown Looee how to use the phone. He would call Judy (Walt would dial) and she would tell him stories about the boy with the hairy face. He kissed the mouthpiece and heard very little.

He ate forty cobs of corn with Larry one summer and was proud. Judy dyed her hair more blond and Walt said I didn't think you could look any younger. Looee was scared at first because he thought she was Barbie. Earlier that summer, Barbie had given him strange feelings and he sat on her, naked, on and off, for a few afternoons.

He stayed up at night in his room thinking of ways to get out and visit Mr. Wiley and his fridge. For a few nights he heard small scratching noises coming from somewhere in his bedroom. He walked from his bed to the wall and put his ear to the wainscot. He tore the wood off the wall and discovered the tickles of feeding termites.

If he had grown up in Sierra Leone he might have developed a taste for termites, but he was full of chicken Kiev and wanted to play or make friends. He tore the rest of the wainscot off the wall and covered it with pillows and cushions to keep it quiet.

Judy discovered the torn-up wall in the morning. She told Walt who said goddamnit when he saw it. The wall would have to be replastered.

Later that week Looee threw the radio through the living room window because something in the song American Pie made him think that Judy was going to be attacked. He hugged himself but was heavily scolded.

Walt said when will enough be enough.

They built him his own house. Walt hired some contractors to make a reinforced concrete building adjacent to theirs, nicely hidden by the maples. It was attached to the main house by an inward-opening, self-bolting door and a short concrete corridor with high windows. The building was one large room, twenty-five by thirty feet, twenty feet tall with climbing bars and a raised pedestal bedroom that had a large reinforced window looking out to the front through the maples. Looee climbed a steel ladder to reach the bedroom, or he could jump to it from the climbing bars. There was a drain in the middle of the floor and a squat toilet in the corner.

It was concrete because of practicality, and it was only ever thought of as his own place, his suite, his domain. Walt had proposed it and Judy hadn't objected in the least.

He would now have his own space to do whatever mischief he could, and would have to behave all the more when he was invited into the main house. There was a doorbell placed low beside his door and he learned to ring that whenever he wanted someone to get him.

Judy had sensed that Looee wanted to be alone more anyway. By the age of nine he was well into adolescence. Looee would sit with Judy reading magazines and she would wonder sometimes why he would suddenly start to display.

Not inside, honey. Not in the big house.

He had trouble stopping.

If Walt said not here goddamnit he would stop, but when Walt wasn't around Looee might flip the coffee table over or run around the living room as fast as he could.

It took her a while to realize that things in the magazines were triggering his displays. Men holding up large fish in Walt's Game and Fish magazines sometimes set him off: he wanted to be one of the men.

Bras in the Sears catalogue.

Pretty pretty pretty pretty pretty pretty pretty.

Judy saw him with his hand down the front of his pants as he lay right back on the couch. She wanted to give him privacy.

He didn't seem to have much shame, but sometimes she would see him get up and leave the room, watching with the wisdom of a mother, sad about the things in his future that she might not be a part of.

He loved his house. He rang the doorbell constantly, often at night when he had a bad dream or to make sure that Walt and Judy weren't asleep. But when he was in his own house he never heard no, Looee, no.

He swung on the bars and wanted Walt to see, and imagined Walt was watching.

Looee's house was the grocery store.

Looee was jumping from shelf to shelf and no one said no, Looee, no.

Walt was watching Looee jump from shelf to shelf, can Walt do this, it was fast. But Walt wasn't there.

Popcorn.

One more swing.

Two more swing.

Popcorn.

Looee wasn't in the grocery store, Looee was swinging over the creek. Look how far. Looee's not touching the water. Swing. Don't touch the water.

Popcorn.

Looee wanted popcorn.

Looee rang the bell.

Walt unlocked the door between houses and said mummy's asleep, it's Sunday.

Looee rang the bell again, and Walt said Mummy's asleep I said.

Looee was hugging Walt's waist and he took Walt's hand and took him inside Looee's house. Looee screamed louder than Walt could scream, and swung from bar to bar.

Wow said Walt. That's great. Fast.

Looee wanted popcorn.

Looee swung and Walt said that's amazing. Don't hurt yourself.

Looee took Walt's hand and pulled him down the corridor and Walt said I told you buddy, mummy's sleeping.

Looee tasted popcorn butter and Walt knew his noises.

You're hungry. I gotcha.

They made popcorn and watched the game.

When the fall came there was the usual feeling of melancholy and fragile possibilities. It was Walt's favourite season and he told Judy he wanted to take Looee hunting.

She said I think he's still too little.

You think.

I think so darling.

Walt rarely made the connection directly, but the richness that filled his nose and eyes when he stood in the middle of the woods made him think of his first wife and the fact that these colours will be taken by winter and today he can pluck meat from this waning abundance, and there's permanence in that.

One day I want to take him.

They took him for a picnic instead. He watched them from his window as they loaded the pickup and he was screaming and jumping up and down. Walt put two gallons of gas and a chainsaw in the back so he could make a fire in the woods while Judy and Looee played. They packed baloney sandwiches, a Thermos of coffee, light beer and a bag of dried fruit. Judy went through the house to open Looee's door and he ran out ahead of her, grabbing a work shirt and a plastic gun from the kitchen.

He sat between them and no longer grabbed the wheel when they drove, and the only time he was tense was when they went over the long Scott Bridge. When he was afraid or in pain he pulled his lips back over his teeth—it was the same smile you see on liars or half-brave men in pain, civil servants walking calmly through rough neighbourhoods. He made low mocking noises at cows and horses and dead raccoons by the road.

*

Freedom is eating and not having to give thanks, not sharing, not working for the food, wondering about its source, caring about when and how you eat or when it will run out.

Nobody is free said Larry. Looee's got his own little place here, but nobody is free.

Looee let no one cross his threshold unless he really liked them. Larry came over a lot and they drank beer, and Larry and Walt talked about work while Looee swung and groomed and told jokes with his face like a grandpa to a baby.

Walt and Larry's partner, Mike, was the planning commissioner for Addison County that year and was drifting away from their business. As owners of commercial property Walt and Larry had long ago realized the need for political connections, and both of them had served as selectmen in their towns. Mike was someone Walt brought on board for his political interests, and he was always the most eager to have his voice heard.

When there were efforts to rezone or raise taxes Mike would work in their mutual interests, but he wasn't working so well lately, not always making decisions in their favour. Larry said he's got his own life. Nobody is free. He looked at Looee and said Looee's got his own little place here.

Pretty pretty pretty pretty pretty pretty pretty.

Looee woke up and climbed down to the squat toilet in the corner. He liked to leave a small mess around the edges on the floor for mummy to clean.

Summer heat was sweet as Tang. He rang the bell for breakfast.

Susan was going to come over in the evening to take Judy to her book-of-the-month club.

Looee was excited when he heard that Susan was coming over.

You really love Susan don't you.

He felt nervous and happy and gagged on the egg in his throat.

The morning drifted invisibly and Looee watched Walt do this and that. Looee went back to his place and swung around. He thought about spaghetti and pretty ladies. He looked through a Better Homes and Gardens and rubbed the lips of a pretty woman on his balls.

He wanted a friend and no longer fully understood that Susan was coming over.

He grabbed his overalls and walked pantless to his door and rang the bell for mummy.

You want me to wash those.

He shooed her away and wedged the door with a rubber eraser—something he regularly got away with when mummy paid a visit. He looked for his pants with suspenders.

Walt wore suspenders on the days when he did little more than eat—holidays, mostly—and Looee learned to associate them with special occasions.

He felt like dressing up.

He collected some favourite things.

He felt a growing importance.

He had his own comb, which he put in his pants.

There was no mirror in his house but the clothes felt good. He smiled and made proud noises like when mummy says how handsome! and he grew more restless.

He heard a truck on the driveway and screamed.

Walt had arranged for some landscaping to be done, and the workmen arrived at noon. The men didn't know what those noises were from the house, and knew even less when Walt simply said that's Looee.

They unloaded their gear from their truck and Looee watched

them from his bedroom. One was skinny and one was hairy. He wondered if these men were staying for dinner, and he wanted to show Walt and Judy how handsome he looked.

Judy had felt fulfilled that day, rooted happily in her life and enjoying the summer, eager to reach out and be accepted by Susan and her friends. They were supposed to talk about a novel called Trinity by Leon Uris. She was slightly nervous about discussing books because she hadn't been to university, but she was curious about what the other women thought. Susan wasn't much older than Judy, but had reached life's milestones early. She had married and lost her husband. She raised a son to maturity on her own, and instead of coming to terms with the imperfection and unpredictability of life, she celebrated and embraced the opposite. She knew that things would be perfect, that they ought to be, and there was a positivity to that which Judy admired. Judy unconsciously adopted Susan's elegance as she moved around the house and thought about her friend.

She heard the landscapers at work outside and thought she would bring some lemonade to them.

Looee had watched them from his window unloading machines he had never seen. A Bobcat and a gas-powered weed trimmer. He was impressed by their violence. He wanted to meet the men.

They were addressing a slope on the front lawn and the wiry one said there'll be too much slip. Walt had asked them to add a low stone wall and steps to make the place look like it had been there longer, like it had grown from the earth.

They looked around at Walt's property with their hands on their hips. Like all with a knowledge of craft, they imagined how they would have built and shaped things differently.

It was a short drive from the road to Walt's house so there was no real mystery about the nature of the place. Big blue house stretching through a few new additions. There were tires all over the front lawn and in one corner was a swing set with the seats missing. There was some sense of a thwarted childhood or an incomplete past which the wiry landscaper found familiar and discomforting. Dirty wet shed where his mother sent him. He felt pity for Judy's children, however old they were.

I've got to do some work for my lady's dad this weekend he said.

The hairy one was looking at Walt's old pickup sitting on blocks. He was wondering whether Walt was rich or not.

Looee watched as Judy walked across the lawn with a tray and glasses of lemonade. Looee loved lemonade. The men heard a loud whoo from inside the house that sounded like a teenager admiring a hot rod.

Judy had tied up her hair to look smart and taller for the book ladies, and to the men it looked gigantic.

They heard another whoo from the house.

How old's your son.

He's around nine or ten said Judy. Which I think is more like fourteen.

She smiled as she said so.

The men were confused.

Looee assumed that these two were special—the way they shifted dirt and got lemonade from Judy.

His hair was erect and bursting out of his collar.

After Judy had taken his overalls, Looee's eraser left him free to go through the door.

He walked down the corridor to the front of the house and stepped out into the sun.

Looee was usually best at disarming workmen or macho types; the coldest and toughest personalities often relaxed like they did for no one else. Walt and Judy had been careful to control most meetings, though, because there was always some opportunity for surprise.

When Judy saw Looee walking proudly towards them, her accustomed caution was pushed to the back of her mind. She wasn't surprised by his being outside so much as she was by his outfit. He was wearing something special and he looked so proud, and instead of thinking about the situation and encouraging him to go back in, she smiled and said oh my Looee, you look so handsome. She knew that was the reaction he wanted.

The landscapers saw a chimpanzee walking towards them. He was wearing a plaid jacket backwards with suspenders pulled over it, and a long pearl necklace which Judy had been missing for months.

He was smiling his genuine smile and bobbing his head to Judy's lovely words.

The wiry one said what is that, and started laughing. Then his partner laughed and soon it was hands on chest and thighs and that is the weirdest fuckin thing I've ever seen.

It took Looee a moment to get over his excitement and realize they were laughing at him.

Judy watched his expression change and there was nothing she could do. Don't make fun of him she said.

When Looee screamed, his lips pulled right back over his teeth. The men thought this was even funnier. When he pounded the ground and screamed and cried they had visions of everything ridiculous, of old women dressed as tarts, of children thinking they were strong and wise.

Looee ran at them and they pivoted out of the way and spilled their drinks. He kept running and picked up the weed trimmer and threw it at a tree. They registered his strength.

He ran back in their direction and his nails tore the grass as he sprinted.

He ran directly at Judy at first. She thought he was going to attack her.

The hairy one felt the ground hit the back of his head. He was winded and thought he had slept. He tasted blood when he was driving down the highway and asked his partner what the fuck just happened.

Walt had heard all the noise and ran out to tackle Looee, who was pounding and stomping on the man's body. By chance he got his arm across Looee's mouth before he could bite him between the legs.

When they couldn't sleep that night, Walt said we're just lucky they were workers. Rough-and-tumble. Anyone else and Looee wouldn't be here.

Looee had bitten Walt's arm, and Walt had hit him across the back, held his face down in the grass till Looee struggled out and ran up the tree.

Walt wrote a cheque for the landscapers, for two thousand dollars, for forgiveness, and none of the work was finished.

What kept Judy awake was the thought of Looee running towards her. Those men made fun of him, but he ran at her as well. She didn't stand up for him.

There was no one she could explain that to except Walt.

I want to do the best for him she said.

She felt aware of other realities: that what she saw was not the whole truth, or what other people saw was simply not her truth. It was a lonely feeling.

fifteen

Burke has taken to bothering the women.

He used to make them proud. He used to do their bidding.

Some days they don't see him. He sits in the grove and licks his teeth.

Whenever watermelon is thrown down from the roof of the Hard, he runs over everyone to get to it first. He knows Mama loves it and he taunts her with it. He knows she likes to eat it in the shady grove so he walks there first with the watermelon between his arm and belly.

Mama can't believe it at first. She brings her fists down on Burke's back and he drops the fruit and runs. He doesn't scream or show much fear, but he runs.

He used to play with Bootie and show Bootie how much better he was at everything. Bootie followed him and mimicked all he did. They wandered away and Bootie felt nervous being out of sight of the others, but Burke never seemed nervous. They made fun of poogly Mr. Ghoul. They copied Podo's gait. They wandered the edge of the World like the men did before bed.

No one else was welcome here, no one could break this unity.

But now Burke stays apart.

The next time he steals Mama's watermelon she shouts. Through her feet she borrows the authority of the ground and she shouts inarguable justice in his ear. He feels as if he has been bitten and this time he screams in fear.

The next time he holds the great green fruit in his hands and runs around Mama and Fifi and Magda. He smashes the fruit on a rock and kicks pieces through the filth. They scream and pound the dirt and make a cloud. Burke walks and sits on his own and frowns like Podo at nothing on the ground.

He has been strong.

Fifi doesn't know what to do. Burke is the burst and fruit of her chest, like Bootie is Magda's and the new one is Mama's. Everyone is Fifi's. She hugs Mama to console her. She gathers pieces of the broken fruit.

She walks to Burke and grooms his long bluffing hair and he is calmed. He doesn't know where to go so he lies on the ground in front of her and sighs, and her hand is on his shoulder.

Burke tries to join a skrupulus of Podo, Jonathan and Mr. Ghoul, but his bows are short and perfunctory as if he were an equal. None of the men will look him in the eyes and he knows he is not welcome. He sits apart and does not appear to care as much as he cares.

Bootie walks to Burke and Burke pushes him away.

Later Burke changes, puts his fingers in Bootie's armpits, and colours arc kind again. Bootie wants to look for squirrels, but they sit and smell the day.

Jonathan is watching Burke these days. He feels that if Burke is ever attacked he will defend him, depending on who attacks him.

Podo sleeps, awakes, and feels old.

*

The Hard closed down when Podo arrived. They tried to teach the machine to Podo but he couldn't use it, couldn't use the pictures like Dave couldn't use the guitar and Mama couldn't use the lighter.

They were bored until new games arrived.

¡Pong!

¡Pac-Man!

They tried to keep Mr. Ghoul using the machine but he attacked the Fool. They made a keyboard, a piece of hard paper with all the pictures on it, and now they could leave the Hardest and wander and Dave and Mr. Ghoul would talk. In each new room Mr. Ghoul thought he might see Julie saying where's my Mr. Ghoul.

Mr. Ghoul was taken on trips to the woods with Dave. They roasted marshmallows and Mr. Ghoul got sick in the van.

He learned to get used to the rinjy feeling of grass between his toes and that trees could be useful and fun. Those trips stopped long ago, but he was one of the few who had these early visions.

He did not see Dave at night anymore and there were no longer vodka and smokes.

Fences of plekter arose in the Hard after Podo attacked the Fool.

But the Hard also finally opened to grass and monkey bars.

They were no longer led from their bedrooms to the Hardest or the playroom. They walked on their own through tunnels and emerged in various places. Their bedrooms grew.

New Visitors arrived. One was a black-brown yek who looked like he could reach across the length of any room.

Dave, from the other side of the plekter, said

That Jonathan.

Mama liked him and wanted to look after him like her doll that had one ear.

He had tremendous balls.

He sat and pressed his balls against the plekter and Mama felt a strange flush of oa when she touched them through the grid.

Podo and Jonathan screamed at each other from either side of the plekter and Podo tried to hit him. They were all kept apart from him until one day Dave put Mama in the room with Jonathan while Mr. Ghoul and Podo watched from the other side.

Mama's rosé was pink as a mouth and she let Jonathan clean her neck and pin her

¡Hoo!

And Podo and Mr. Ghoul were hanging from the plekter and screaming and mounting each other for comfort.

Dr. David watched through windows.

When Jonathan hung from his side of the plekter he looked like a wall of thorns and threats. Mostly he sat in the corner.

They soon emerged in the playroom together.

Jonathan and Podo groomed each other after bloning and bluffing, and it was grooming like a conversation between men is a test, not a connection; it was touching like you touch a suspect tree—not to sit in it but to see what it will take to push it down.

Jonathan was bigger than Podo.

He learned nothing in the Hard. Instead of learning how to dip the skinny stick into the honey, he begged for the honeyed stick. If the honeyed stick wasn't passed to him he would pleen and pleep and make annoying faces, and Mama would always pity him.

This was not admirable.

But Mama seemed to want to please him no matter what he did. And Mr. Ghoul and Podo wanted to please Mama.

Mr. Ghoul would feel drawn as much as obligated to groom Jonathan because awful people are strangely compelling.

Strange smells are sniffed at not once, but thrice.

Podo was good at getting food.

Whenever they worked in the Hard, Mr. Ghoul would wait for Podo, defer to Podo, just as he did for Dave sometimes. Dave wanted Podo and Mr. Ghoul to identify faces on a screen, match a man in a hat with another man in a hat. Dave would try to get Mr. Ghoul to go first, but Mr. Ghoul wouldn't go unless Podo went first. Podo sometimes wouldn't go unless Mama went first, especially when she was pink.

Dave played Pac-Man and sometimes looked swollen and sadder.

Mama had a birthday.

Dave gave her a cat.

Mama loved the cat and said on the keyboard

That red.

Cats are quiet and soft and can twist around the room like a lie.

She learned how to hold it without the cat getting sharp, and soon it rode her back like a little one. She shared food with it.

Jonathan and Podo never learned the keyboard or the machine. Mama and Mr. Ghoul were the only ones who knew the pictures with Dave, and Mama only wanted to play with her cat.

Everything was changing.

sixteen

Looee ate more often than he thought about eating, and played more often than he thought about playing. He swung more often than he thought about swinging and the swinging was more than swinging, it was training and claiming and delighting and boasting, and was more than he really knew.

The man who knows his mind is not a man who knows his mind, he's a man who acts and feels good for it.

He liked the smell of his house whenever he walked through the door. He looked at magazines and tried to sing like Judy, and there could be no telling that singing was what he attempted.

He masturbated in ten-second bursts, a puff of flavour in the middle of his eyes as he looked at pretty pictures.

Sometimes he waited without knowing he was waiting. And when he was lonely he rang the bell without dwelling on the fact that he was lonely.

He loved jackets these days, and he really wanted to meet certain people. He loved anything to do with Mr. Wiley—his house, his wife—and he was curious about any car he saw slowing down near the Wiley house.

And he loved tall dirty-blondes, like Susan.

He loved his walls and yearned to get out of them. He hated strangers and needed people to visit him. He was bored and spent agreeable hours looking out the window and dreaming.

Judy had bought him a snare drum which he loved so much he tore the skin. He tried to make it loud again by putting his trumpet inside it. He banged the trumpet-filled drum against the wall, and Larry walked in with a six-pack of Michelob.

We've got to get you a girlfriend said Larry.

They clasped hands by the thumb and Looee panted with passion and care, you're my brother, you're here, let's begin.

They sat on the hairy plaid couch at the end of the room and drank beer. Larry had just had a rye with Walt, who had been with Looee earlier.

Looee listened to Larry talk and picked up on a few words like girls, beer and movies.

Larry stared up at Looee's high platform bed and remembered younger days.

Looee got up often and occasionally swung from his bars.

I'm not saying that romance is everything. You get used to other things, find other things to put in its place. Between you and me, Elizabeth and I haven't really said more than goodnight for over a year.

Looee wanted to watch a movie with Larry in Walt's house, but Larry didn't seem to want to go anywhere. Looee pushed the trumpet-filled drum along the floor and wished he could drum it for Larry.

A hobby can work for a while, sure. You've got your music, your magazines, but you're young. It's not enough.

Looee got back up on the couch and made grooming noises without knowing he was making them. Larry chatted while Looee groomed, and there was no difference in kind.

Looee's days seemed sad to Larry, sometimes, and he would feel angry with Walt for taking him from wherever it was he belonged. He looked around the high concrete room.

There was a scab on Larry's bald head from banging it on the doorframe of the car the other day. It made Looee sad for Larry. He picked at it and it bled. He hugged himself in apology.

Would you call yourself happy, Looee. You seem like a happy guy.

Looee made his happy smile because he thought Larry was telling him to be happy.

It takes a while to get over how you look, buddy, you know, thinking you're not old or some rotten son of a bitch. That funny face of yours. You've got an old-looking, mean-looking face. Don't get me wrong. You don't see anybody smiling much. We're supposed to be happy all the time. You make a guy talk more than he wants to.

Looee opened another can with his teeth.

It got dark outside and Larry thought about going home.

What do you think you'll do tonight, young man. You need a new drum. Are you going to be all right.

Looee nodded and Larry thought I think that he just nodded.

They clasped hands by the thumb, their palms made the sound of a pact, and Looee had a shallower sense of the future.

Larry started his car and looked up at Looee in his lighted window. Larry waved at him, knowing that Looee wouldn't wave back.

Looee watched the car reverse.

He wanted to watch a movie in the dark.

Larry drove and looked at his hands on the steering wheel.

Looee felt itchy in a place he couldn't scratch.

Larry didn't feel like going home.

Looee rang the bell and Walt came and got him.

Larry drove around Mount Wilson and illuminated the eyes of deer. He took the long way home and wondered what would have happened if he had married someone other than Elizabeth.

Looee, Walt and Judy sat on the couch with the lights off. They watched 60 Minutes and Dallas, and Judy and Looee ate pie.

Summer waned and Looee sat on his high bed, looking out the window at the driveway and the black-and-yellow trees. Walt had asked Looee if he wanted to watch the game but he turned his back.

He watched the rain slap leaves near the window and some of them fell off the tree.

There was a ball on his bed but no one to throw it at.

Walt took Looee on a hunt the next day. He bought him some small man's camouflage and thought he would enjoy sitting in a tree stand or a blind with him and Larry. Looee loved being out in the woods and was lousy at sitting still. Whenever a deer came near he screamed and ruined every shot.

His relationship with bigger animals was of fear and fascination—the fear was diminished if the animal was penned in. He was terrified of cows if he was in the field with them, but if he was outside the fence he would taunt them, throw Walt's hat at them, let them know he was their master.

Deer and gunshots made him lose his bowels.

Mike shot a twelve-point buck. Looee saw it lying on the roof of Mike's Volvo in the parking lot at Viv's. Looee was scared of it at first and then its tongue hanging out of its mouth made him laugh, and then he wanted to be at home with Judy and hot chocolate and felt afraid of cars and the sky.

Mike couldn't stand the sight of Looee in camouflage, it was like a chihuahua in a tuxedo or a nasty comic telling jokes at Mike's expense. Mike had said earlier I don't know why Walt doesn't let that poor animal go back to where it belongs.

When Walt and Looee were sitting at the bar, Mike came over smiling and said hey Walt, hey Looee.

Nice buck said Walt.

I got lucky.

Looee here wasn't the best spotter for us said Walt.

Well he looks good.

Mike was smiling when he said so.

Looee stared at Mike.

How're you doing Looee.

Mike just asked a question of a chimpanzee.

Looee kept staring at Mike.

How's he doing Walt.

He's good. I'm just not sure I'll take him hunting again.

Mike slid a bowl of peanuts towards himself and Looee watched him.

Looee was still feeling uneasy from the deer he saw on the roof of the car outside. He was sensitive to how everyone was acting, how Mike was smiling.

Mike reached for the peanuts again but they weren't there.

Looee held the bowl and ate and stared at Mike.

Mike smiled at him.

There's something I'd like to talk to you about this week said Mike.

You bet said Walt.

Larry came into the bar and grabbed a handful of peanuts from Looee's bowl. You're the worst hunter I ever knew said Larry.

Looee felt good having Larry around. He put his arm around him and made him sit on the stool on his other side.

Mummy taught him sharing.

Looee pushed the bowl of peanuts along the bar with the back of his fingers, towards Walt and Mike as he had often seen others do.

Mike found it offensive.

Mike was forty-one years old.

He thought vaguely of Vermont.

He had felt proud of his kill and proud of his state when he drove to Viv's, proud that there were no billboards, that wildlife and trees abounded, and he said to Viv we have the best syrup, the best game and the best local government in the United States.

He looked at Walt and said how does Tuesday sound.

There was something about the simplicity of Looee, his forthright behaviour, that Walt unconsciously bonded with from the earliest days. You knew where you stood with Looee, and people said the same about Walt.

It wasn't a calculated or carefully expressed philosophy, but Walt was drawn to people who made mistakes. There was something honest about it.

He always had a good eye for buildings and he had a talent for knowing whom to fill them with. He had an equal knack for acquiring land—for spotting future access roads and lots that were ripe for development. But every now and then he chose to fill a space with a person or business with little chance of success: a physician nowhere near any conceivable patient. His partners had often complained, but Walt could appease them with the profits of other endeavours.

Sometimes Walt carried the rent for them or helped them out directly. He liked driving the roads and seeing tiny signs of hopeful businesses—Bath and Radio Repairs, Boyz Toyz for Girlz; places where people were being themselves but reaching out at the same time in whatever way they knew.

He couldn't stand people who instructed but didn't create. Legislators, bureaucrats, journalists. He couldn't read newspapers or listen to talk shows—people always explaining after the fact or predicting what will happen. Fifteen years ago he came home expecting stew for dinner and met a state trooper who said his wife was killed. Even this day right now could not have been predicted, you prognosticators, it's your own entrails you're blind to. People will go on expecting, but making money from telling them what to expect seemed like a cheat.

Make something. Make a mistake.

Mitch Randall was one of Walt's long-time beneficiaries, a man with brown teeth who had suffered the pursuit of some of the stupidest ideas that had ever taken bloom. Walt had loaned him more than ten thousand dollars over the years and housed him for free, and he was just such an innocent and honest man that Walt saw him as neither a caution nor a nuisance but an animate speculation on the accident of days. He was a brother. We could all be Mitch.

We could all be Looee. What upset Walt about the incident with the landscapers last year was not the violence but the mockery that had set Looee off. You don't make fun of a sensitive little fella, even if he looks like a child-sized grandpa and dresses like a moron.

He fixed the pickup with Looee on a cold day in the fall, Looee tightening some of the lugs. They both caught a terrible cold.

Looee and Walt sat on the couch and Judy made them both better.

She and Walt made love that winter with an unexpected sense of novelty and thrill that made them both quietly think that after all these years, who would have thought.

And Walt felt himself growing ever closer to Looee.

He named himself father and Looee son, and we can ponder the novels, cities and excuses based on the carriage of those words. We can say that paternal or filial pride comes naturally or sometimes must be willed, or that without the bond of blood there can be no father and son. And when it comes to connection, the attraction of one body to another, friend, lover, guardian or admirer, the names and certainties can accrue all the more, and we can spin in bewilderment when a friend marries the wrong man, a man leaves the perfect woman, a daughter refuses to call her own mother and a dotard wills his fortune to a boy he barely knows. The names and bewilderment won't stop, and the connections will equally gather. A woman will walk into a room and others will believe that she literally brought light in with her, that they had known her all their lives, the friend they always wanted, the endless golden fuck they never had.

All who drew the warmth of Walter Arnold Ribke; all who opened his eyes to lover, friend and son—the hundreds over the decades who drew fantasies and smiles, and made what we call connections; all were members of the scattered tribe of Walt.

There were Walts long before him and Walts long after, they were bald and gorgeous and brown and pink, and some were tyrants and some so tender, and they liked each other equally, knew each other well and never met at all. And no matter where their yearnings took them or what their mistakes were called, they were never able to do other than they did, and, because they were Walts, they did it for each other, did it for themselves, and felt no real need in the surge of the present to explain their peculiar joys.

So look through the window at the man and the chimpanzee, sitting on the floor together doing a puzzle. The man instructing, the chimp in a T-shirt that says MY DADDY DRIVES A FORD. Look at the chimp years later handing the last of his milk teeth to the man who says I am not going to give you a treat for that, there is nothing more useless than a tooth outside a mouth.

Call him father.

Call him son.

Walt's heart was warm, his house was his, he was happy with the questions of his days.

seventeen

Burke grabs a squirrel.

It is hissing in his hand and is weightless. Its tail is twitching and Burke squeezes to calm it down. A surprising flower of meat, grey and purple, comes out of the squirrel's mouth. Burke puts it down and thinks he wants to see that again.

Burke picks up the squirrel and takes it to the foot of the electric tree. The squirrel doesn't move so Burke tries to scare it. He sways back and forth on his thick black legs, but the squirrel lies still on its side. Burke touches it with a finger. He picks it up and ponders its limpness more deeply. He begins to walk with the squirrel between his knuckles. He walks towards Podo to show him what he has done, for explanation, for admiration.

He stops and feels he does not need the admiration of Podo. He feels alone, and wants to be alone.

Bootie watches Burke walking back and forth. He watches Burke wave the squirrel at him. The squirrel's little goon flies off and Bootie walks near it and sniffs.

eighteen

Word had got around last year about Looee and the landscapers. They talked about it at Viv's and at church. Mike heard about it.

He had paid Walt a few visits when Looee was much younger, before his house was built. Looee brought Walt and Mike a couple of cans of Coke—one in his mouth—and Mike said it's really amazing what you've trained him to do.

Walt said it's not training. I haven't trained him at all. He just watches and learns.

Mike remembered Looee sitting on an armchair looking like an abomination. He thought there was a cruelty in Walt, a wickedness.

They did the dairy barn deal together. The dairy industry was suffering, and Mike had been one of those who found new modes of production. He managed to triple the milk per cow, and was able to cut his herd by half, but still produced more than he had started with.

Walt had sensed that something could be done with all the barns that were vacating. He bought one of Mike's and kept his eye out for others.

Mike suggested to Walt that he donate the barns to the state as part of its local heritage program. Walt would get a tax break and the barns would be preserved. Walt bought up a few more with Mike's help, and a society emerged to protect them.

It was a happy moment—Walt and Mike in a private deal, their interests coinciding. Mike liked visiting Walt's home instead of meeting at the office.

Mike wasn't ashamed of his own house, but Cindy was still recovering from her illness and Mike didn't like to force company on her—not while she was neither feeling nor looking her best.

Mike had to admit, as well, that Walt had found a lovely woman in Judy. Very soft, very charming. He sensed that she was not as happy as she could be, and he tried to cheer her up whenever he saw her, with his smile or clear-minded vigour.

They sat in Walt's living room and Judy wore a white dress, white as the lilies. She asked if there was anything they needed and Walt said no, honey, you go get some rest. Looee will get us a couple of Cokes, won't you Looee. Mike watched Judy leave and the chimpanzee grunting its way to a fridge that Judy unlocked.

When they had started the barn deal together, Mike had thought it was an opportunity for him and Walt to get to know each other better. They hadn't had many conversations about matters beyond work.

Was the chimpanzee more suitable company for Mike than Judy was?

The only polite thing he could remark was how well Walt had trained it.

Mike tried to talk about his growing interest in the community, but he wished that Judy was near because somehow it sounded flat or insincere when it was shared with just one man. He felt tested by

Walt, even though Walt was mostly silent. He noticed that Looee wouldn't look at him when he talked, but Mike caught him staring surreptitiously. It was unsettling.

Looee abruptly climbed the arm of Walt's chair and kissed Walt's cheek, and Walt said don't go misbehaving. Looee left the room and chewed a hole in Mike's winter boot.

It was a devilish scene, as far as Mike could tell, and, as much as he had thought he wanted to get to know Walt better, this congress with a man-animal was repulsive. Circus stuff. Worse than those who keep a hundred cats or kiss their dogs with their tongues.

He's something else he said to Walt with a smile.

You should look closely at his mouth said Walt. Next time you see him. His lips are big but when he's looking normal they're exactly like ours. His lips remind me of my father's. And his tongue.

He's something else. He truly is. What else can he do.

You know, Mike, it's funny. People never ask me what my dog can do.

Well. I didn't mean anything.

Next time you're at a town meeting, look around the room and look at people's mouths. Don't listen to what they say, just look at the way they sit. The way they argue.

Ha.

I'm serious. You know his feet, when you don't wash his feet they smell cheesy just like ours.

Goodness.

Mike felt that he was being challenged by Walt or that Walt had taken offence, or that he was expected to know how to talk about a creature that did not belong in a living room save as an imaginary caution. There are monkeys in old paintings, in papal processions, risible in their garments.

He can do all kinds of things said Walt. I've stopped counting.

You could probably get him to milk your herd. He wouldn't even need a reason.

Pretty pretty pretty.
　　Rain.
　　Blankets.
　　Looee wanted to put his cock in Susan's face.

The time will come to judge and to rebuke. Mike was open to the interests of all others. There is nothing easy in the affairs of men, and Mike held this wisdom with a light in his eyes. Judge not according to the appearance, but judge righteous judgment.

Mike had mellowed and grown over the years. Strengthened. He truly enjoyed meeting all kinds of people. He believed that we could all, in time, move together.

He joined the Rotary Club for fellowship, and when it came time to publish his resumé for the Senate he could claim membership in over sixty-four associations, unions, cooperatives and clubs.

The Addison County Independent published profiles of all candidates for the State House, and their political columnist, who was professor emeritus of political science at Middlebury College, forecast a competitive race for the county's Senate seats. Mike was singled out as one who would give the Democrats a run for their money.

That same columnist characterized Mike, years later, as a determined supporter of agriculture and local industry, a thoughtful legislator who had been quite successful promoting and passing bills (eight of ten in the past session alone).

So while Looee was looking at lingerie and had a concept of tomorrow as a thing that happens later than right now, Mike was carefully plotting his journey to the Vermont state Senate.

Over fifteen years, Mike had sat on planning commissions, conservation commissions, select boards and development review boards. He knew local politics as well as anyone in the state.

He had had a hand in forwarding the Land Use and Development Act, which was the first of its kind in America. The act was created with the idea that the state was essentially a garden to be enjoyed by everyone. It put strict rules on any development that might impact the state's environment or small communities. Mike had been one of the private citizens appointed by the governor to approve or reject development applications.

He had tried to be practical about the concept of a garden. It was a place for people to relax and recreate, but it was also a space that provided food. It had uses.

He was long into his partnership with Walt and Larry, and the more they succeeded with their properties, the more complicated his concept of a garden became. His power on boards and committees over time was useful to the three of them.

The heart of politics in Vermont was the town meeting, and Mike hadn't missed one in eighteen years. He had learned early on that a confident side of himself emerged whenever he joined these gatherings, and he felt he had an ability to direct the mood of the room. He wanted to test this ability in a bigger forum, and he was encouraged by his wife to seek election to the State House in Montpelier.

She told him to dare to take power.

When he sold his share of the business back to Walt and Larry, he didn't get as much money as he deserved.

You know I've done a lot for this company Mike said. I shouldn't need to point it out.

You know the books better than I do said Walt. We can't afford to pay you that price. You're betting on the future. That's not current value and we'd be doing you a favour. I like doing you a favour and I appreciate everything you've done, but we couldn't afford more than seventy-five percent of that—not without selling those same properties. They're worth nothing now.

Well if Vermont doesn't go in the right direction, you never know. That's my point, Walter. I feel that I can get things done for your cause, for the common cause, that will make your properties an important piece of an important state. But you never know.

Walt went to eighty percent having talked to Larry, thinking they were buying future favours from Mike; but eighty percent only bought a lingering grudge. Mike knew he had saved them hundreds of thousands through his bookkeeping alone, never mind all the passages he had smoothed through being on boards and councils.

It was Walt's company initially, but when he brought the partners in he never quite let go of a sense of entitlement. Mike had often felt unrecognized.

Where he did feel recognition, however, was in town meetings and his exchanges of ideas about the state and its environment. He gained a reputation as a champion of local produce and local industry. When companies from out of state or out of country wanted to build plants in Addison County, he not only helped to thwart them as planning commissioner but he was also a Jeremiah at monthly meetings. This will be a disaster for our communities. Let them be California's problem. Vermonters make what Vermonters want.

This was the idea that took root and eventually led him to Montpelier. There is nothing this state needs that this state cannot produce. Like all Vermonters he loved the woods: their trails, their lumber, their syrup.

Mike's other business was dairy farming. His family were in

dairy, back generations. He loved ice cream, cheese, this morning's curds.

He loved hiking, hunting, orienteering and fishing, cross-country skiing from dawn till dark.

Where Larry would look at Looee's burgeoning manhood and say I was your age once, Mike would never admit that that age had ever passed—not except in the briefest or loneliest moments, when shopgirls would only give him perfunctory smiles or when he closed the doors of hotel rooms after company had left.

He even loved beer. Vermont was brewing the best beer in the Union. Small, careful, artisanal products, that's what Vermont excelled at; things created modestly, low to the ground, things that were other people's business only when they were made well, made here, and people chose to come to them.

He was a proud Vermonter, and only those who were from here could truly know what that meant.

And over the years, as his political ideas matured, the thought of a chimpanzee in his midst made him angry. It disgusted him.

A creature should be in its rightful place. Let the land produce living creatures according to their kind.

Mike respected all animals, but he knew that ultimately all must be measured for their utility each to each. There is a chain of being, and where there is killing there is also thriving. A lion despises a lamb no more than Mike despised a deer—there is gratitude and communion throughout the chain, and ultimately mankind must show the highest gratitude and bear the burden of being a guardian. Mike read an immense responsibility into the passage of Genesis, where the fear and dread of mankind will fall on all the beasts of the earth. They were given into our hands. He did not see this as a licence to kill indiscriminately; he saw it as a duty for us to manage our dominion.

He understood that some of this language did not have a place in political discourse, and when he spoke at town meetings he put his thoughts in terms that everyone could appreciate.

Do we want to eat the chemically fed and foreign cattle of Canada? The blind and featherless chickens of Kentucky? I have never tasted corn as sweet as the corn from here or St. Albans. I don't know about you, but I don't need to eat corn all year or save a dollar on a chicken. Let's eat what our gardens give us.

It was no great adjustment to apply these ideas to industry. He spoke of his preference for local knowledge and local experience. These big-box stores that were starting to sprout across the country. I would rather get the advice of my local hardware store owner, Bill over there—Hi Bill—who has known me for years, knows my land, my house, my machines—I would rather get his advice than have to deal with strangers just to save a nickel on a box of screws.

He opposed all developments that would bring more of what the state already had. Let others do what they do, and we'll get on with our business.

Good fences make good neighbours.

And now that he no longer had business with Larry and Walt, and didn't have to be troubled by the imperiousness of Walt, he could focus, once again, more clearly, on the concept of a garden. The greenest state.

He joined the Vermont Natural Resources Council and broadened associations throughout the state. There were elections every two years for seats in the Senate, and his county had two seats. It was all within reach.

As he made his speeches and refined his thoughts, he sometimes pictured Looee.

What on earth was the purpose of that animal.

nineteen

David's belly pushes against his belt and he thinks he might skip lunch today. He says how are you to Pete at the gate and parks in the space labelled KENNEDY. It is a ten-minute walk from his car to the field station, longer if he takes the hallway near the cafeteria. He used to be able to walk outside, but the front of the institute was sealed years ago to keep it secure from protestors.

When he leaves the main building there is just enough distance to the old observatory to make it annoying when it rains. When it is dry he walks slowly and pensively, forcing a brief meditation, trying to forget the noise of his own life. He deliberately smells their air, feels their sun and breeze. He can hear them on the other side of the wall.

His office is upstairs now. He walks through the security doors and through the once open area that is now walled in as winter and sleeping quarters. This used to be where he had all his interaction with Mr. Ghoul and Mama. Concrete cannot bury memories but it makes them harder to envision. It is only when he wills his recollections that he can picture what these spaces once were.

He greets his colleagues and assistants and every day a miniature history of the species plays out. Jokes, testiness, grievance, ease, illness and maternity leave. His days are filled with administrative duties, staff meetings, board meetings, negotiating the movements of those above and those below. A life like no other, identical to billions.

His office is small but has a floor-to-ceiling window, which he insisted on, that looks out over the enclosure. From here he gets a good enough sense of what goes on that he rarely walks out to the roof or the towers. He thinks about looking out, spending the day watching and speculating. He wishes he could smoke.

He will turn his back on the window and work at his desk. Letters. I. They. Tiny flagpoles staking claims on pages and screens.

The day shines behind him.

He hears a chorus of hoots and turns away from his desk. He looks down at them. If he missed something important he will hear about it.

They see him watching from the window sometimes, and of course when he is out on the towers. He sees Mr. Ghoul looking up. Most of the time they are all in the mire of their own moments, and he is sure that the buildings and the eyes of humans are incidental and faded decorations to the action of their days. He must be as remote to them sometimes as they are to him, those days when he lacks empathy and sees nothing but dirt and hair and clouds of animal scurf.

Here he is, high above. He used to like taking his daughter here on the weekends when she was little. She always said can't we go down. I want to talk to them.

twenty

Magda and Fifi arrived a long time ago and the World began changing entirely. The World became the World. For a time there was also Billie, Rosie and Bongo, but they all left the World.

Doors opened and they went outside. At first there was a small space outside with a hard ground and wall, which wasn't really outside, it was inside with no roof.

They were not afraid.

Then there was another space, with grass and monkey bars. Mama recognized this space from seeing it through the window and wanted the keyboard to say: that red. She hugged Mr. Ghoul and waited for him before they went out. Mr. Ghoul was the wisest and strongest for a moment.

He had been to the woods with Dave and knew the feel of grass. He knew how to climb outside. For the rest there were memories and ideas of what to do and some were more excited than others. Mr. Ghoul went out in this new World and sat atop the monkey bars and hooled. He smelled fresh smells.

Mama had never stepped on grass before and was frightened.

She made sure her cat was on her back so it wouldn't feel the grass.

Jonathan and Podo watched Mr. Ghoul and touched each other and arphle-coughed noises of wonder and lost certainty. Podo walked to the monkey bars and looked up at Mr. Ghoul. He held the bars and got a feel for them.

Jonathan wandered over to the fence, never having known electricity before. He smelled the faint hum, put his hand around a wire, jumped without knowing he was jumping and saw all colours more clearly. He sat and now realized he was terrified of the fence.

Magda and Fifi were friends already, having learned how to skate for

¡Holiday on Ice!

They never knew sex before but spent a long time getting pinned by yeks in hollow rooms in the Hard with bars for walls and people wearing masks and watching.

Fifi liked it.

They were moved to the World and no one liked Magda. She still did tricks from when she performed on skates, but she no longer wore skates and seemed poogly. She did lipflips and grins, pulling her lips back over her snut like she was taught or stretching them hard across her teeth to make everyone laugh, but here in the World it looked weak, like she could not control her fear or disapproval.

She had trouble making friends and sat in the corner of her bedroom for a long time pulling out her hair.

Not liking anyone comes from not being liked, but not being liked comes from not liking anyone: there is no beginning or end.

Fifi made friends with Podo, Jonathan, Mr. Ghoul and Mama, and Magda tolerated Fifi's arm around her shoulder, and needed it.

The women sat apart sometimes and there was something about Mama that made them look up to her as if she were always tall. She let them play with her cat.

Magda took Mama's cat and ran to the edge of the World and Mama chased her while Fifi screamed and Mama pounded on her back until she dropped it.

Later Jonathan felt like someone was pouring hot Coca-Cola through his cock. It swelled and burst greenyellow like a squeezed caterpillar, and Jonathan showed it to Dr. David through the plekter like he did with all his booboos.

Jonathan was put in the cold white room.

So was Magda, who felt the burn when she pissed.

They got needles. Magda liked needles. Pain made sense to sadness like food makes sense to hunger.

Magda and Jonathan were welcomed back to the World and hugged.

New doors opened and the World grew even more. The great blue wall appeared and its base was flooded with pokol-fear and many things felt less urgent when the limits were expanded and cries did not resound from walls and ceilings.

A huge new space and days outside, an electric tree and birds. They were amazed to see such open space, and afraid. There were needle trees and the greybald tree, and groves and corners to hide in.

Mama's cat got bigger and climbed the electric tree. It went electric and fell over the other side of the wall, and Mama still looks up there some days.

There are parts of the World where some are still afraid to go. Slowly, though, they explored.

They got used to grass and dirt and most climbed trees if they had the inclination and Podo could do so like a thought cannot be stopped. Black Podo.

The more the World grew, the less they went into the Hard except for dinner and sleep.

Billie and Rosie arrived and they were kept apart from the others for a while because they were yekel. Then Billie made friends with Jonathan through the plekter.

Rosie came out, Rosie long and dulchy.

Podo liked Rosie.

Podo grew bigger.

Bongo came, fat grey Bongo, old as a stone and slower. He didn't wake up one day.

Mama missed her cat.

Podo and Jonathan and Billie fought. Jonathan rarely bloned before he attacked, he would bite without warning like Magda.

Billie and Jonathan tried to keep Rosie to themselves. They beat her face and gave her treats, and interfered when she tried to sit with Fifi. She couldn't leave their side sometimes. Billie pulled her by a foot and his heavy slaps made her fly and roll through the dirt.

Podo sat close to Rosie, and Jonathan attacked him. Podo lost a piece of a finger and hurt his wrist and he walked with a limp for the rest of his days.

Podo sat with the others.

A great fire arose in the world beyond the World, a constant heat, breath of a thousand mouths, and ash on the wind like black feathers. Podo and Rosie sat far apart from each other, but Podo knew that there was something wrong, a small hot thorn in her sight. She called and he knew she was calling for him and he walked to her. He removed an ashen splinter from an eye and she saw again. She gave his fingers a kiss and rubbed him and she looked at him, searching and seeing.

They smelled smoke and wood, and the sky was orange at night and grey in the day, and everyone sat and moved together forgetting complaints and dislikes and uniting in their worry. When others slept, Rosie lay on Podo's chest, hot black feathers floating down.

Rosie looked at Podo, longer looks than any before or since, and she knew when he needed a friend and was the maker and cure of the ache.

They groomed close and snuck to corners of the World on their own and Rosie stood on her goon. She opened her rosé to the sky, to Podo, and gave the World her pinksalt. Podo invited her to him and she came and turned and arose before he felt her heat and she sat ahead, just ahead. She came back and did the same, again and again, and Podo leapt and showed her his worth. Rosie stretched up and stood and scratched her long body slowly and did this again, a dance for no one but Podo, and she turned to him so often those days, his cock so tired he had to use his finger. To Podo, she couldn't stop coming.

Billie and Jonathan pinned her, over and over, and Podo watched, and her pink made the ground a bed of bleeding nerves.

Rosie got fat.

She had a new one in the cold white room and people helped her and pushed her and wrapped her, and her dreams might not have been dreams.

She was scared of her new one and didn't know what to do. He hurt her and she didn't know these people and felt sad.

Rosie walked like no other.

She was long and Podo's friend: sad Rosie, dulchy-fruit lips and long stares.

Rosie's new one scratched and sucked and screamed. She didn't know him and he hurt her legs, sucked out her light, made her weak, and when she looked at Podo she had nothing to give, far away no matter where she was.

She left her new one on the ground.

*

People took Rosie's new one and gave him to Fifi and taught her the bottle and called him Burke.

Fifi liked milk and drank the bottle herself, but people got angry and shouted whenever she drank it. Dr. David sat and showed her how to put the bottle in the tiny lips of Burke, and she pretended not to look in case Dr. David saw how much she wanted to kiss the new one and hold him and mimble yamyum, he was so chewy-eety she could feel him in her gums when she stared.

¡Baby!

She held him and gave him the bottle and cream came from her bones and one day dripped from her nipples.

Mama was sad, like fruit wasn't in her hands even when it was, and when it was it didn't taste like fruit. She sat in a corner of the World watching trees blow back and forth. They blew back and forth while Rosie wasted; and while everyone worried and arphled and wept, Mama sat still and heard nothing.

Rosie's sadness was younger and more vicious than Mama's. It ate her.

Billie pushed into weak Rosie, and Podo saw from afar Rosie being hurt. Billie pinned her and beat her and she couldn't stand up.

People took Rosie back to the cold white room.

Podo waited and watched, dark Podo.

He sat with sad Mama and patted her goon. He groomed the tangled hair of Magda and tried to envision her unhale visions.

He waited for Rosie.

It got cooler outside then warm again, and no one saw Rosie, ever again.

Podo watched and scratched and frowned, and when Billie slapped Mama for not giving him watermelon Podo took him by the foot and bit between his legs. No one had heard such sounds.

Billie tried to fight but Podo pounded his face and jumped on his cracking and weakening body until no more noise came from Billie. Podo dragged Billie through the dirt. He dragged him and waited and pounded the ground and jumped, and dragged him farther and pushed him into the chill of the pokol-fear, no matter how the others screamed.

Fifi walked with Burke beneath her belly.

Mr. Ghoul saw dark Billie face down beneath the cold surface. Red was rising from between his legs like smoke from a blown-out match.

The death of Billie stayed with them. Podo dragging his body.

They needed protection from the things you cannot see. They were afraid of those things; they were not afraid of Podo.

Podo threw urulek at uninvited Visitors.

He helped all who lost—the losers of fights, the losers of food, the losers of new ones and oa.

He knew how to choose his grudges.

He never forgot that Jonathan made him limp and took a piece of his finger.

As Mama watched Fifi feed Burke and protect him, she wanted a new one all the more. She waited for Fifi to put Burke down so she could take him. Days passed and she got used to change. People had shown Fifi what to do with Burke and now Mama understood.

Burke watched what everyone did, learned how to eat and climb and his little eyes were open to everything, he never turned his face. Mama helped Fifi and kept Burke away from harm.

Jonathan thought Burke was in the way of Fifi. Burke would climb all over her whenever she was pinned, and Jonathan could not tolerate being screamed at when he tried to enjoy the heat.

He slapped Burke off the back of Fifi and this put everyone in ¡harag!

The young ones must be tolerated.

Fifi and Mama chased Jonathan into a needle tree and everyone circled and screamed.

It was then that Podo sensed how weak Jonathan was in the group.

When treats were thrown down from the roof of the Hard, Podo took what he wanted, but he also made sure that Fifi got extra, and that he got in the way of Jonathan.

He watched as Jonathan screamed and turned to others for help, hand held out, embraces neglected.

At first he and Jonathan fought, but Jonathan no longer won. And as this all continued and Jonathan's begging was ignored, Podo found the solution.

Podo gave Jonathan food.

Jonathan began to beg from Podo, to turn to Podo for help and rely on no one else.

As Burke moved from Fifi's belly to Fifi's back, from Fifi to Mama and up his first tree, Jonathan began to believe he was beholden to Podo, indebted to his wisdom and generous hands.

Magda slapped Jonathan for sitting in her shade. Podo shouted at Magda on Jonathan's behalf.

So convinced was Jonathan of Podo's strength and beneficence, he greeted Podo more often than anyone, and eventually more loudly. Mr. Ghoul could hear Jonathan's salaams from the other side of the World. Whenever Podo approached directly, Jonathan bobbed and slithered backwards.

Jonathan made himself small.

Podo did favours for everyone, and they naturally turned to him whenever they wanted something that they couldn't get on their own. They turned to him or feared him whenever there was a dispute.

Fights broke out involving everyone sometimes. It was impossible to know how they had started unless it was a watermelon being thrown down to them by someone on the roof. Podo chose no sides. He fought until fighting stopped, smacking goons and pounding backs in the middle of the rolling krieg. Podo helped the ones on the bottom, the ones whom no one helped, and everyone needed help sometimes. And when he bit and tried to hurt, he hurt everyone. And the feeling that lasted for not very long was that fighting shouldn't happen. Another short-lived feeling was that no one was to blame. The feeling that lasted longest was that Podo hurt everyone and thus hurt no one, because the pain that is truly longest is the one that comes from knowing that someone else was preferred and protected before you.

Tired Podo.

Fifi and Magda had new ones of their own in the cold white room and never saw them again. Days and dreams are light and colours and some of them disappear.

Then Magda had one which people called Bootie: that Bootie.

Mama felt slow and the World seemed slightly tilted. She got fat and felt like her belly would touch the ground when she walked.

There were new high stones to climb in the World, and Mama climbed them. She wanted help but wanted to be on her own. She felt a need to be away from others and wished she was in her bedroom.

She climbed to the highest stone and felt sick, and the melon, nuts and scallions which she ate that morning burst up from within and spilled out on her arm and the stones.

She descended one level and held on to the highest stone with one hand, leaning for support.

She felt pressure in her rosé. She closed her eyes and hid the World and the movements inside started hurting so much she kept silent instead of screaming and could not be alone enough.

She stayed standing on two legs and put her long fingers inside her rosé to relieve the pressure. It was warm and wet and she withdrew her fingers and licked them. She reached back and put her hand inside herself again and felt a tickle of warmth between her fingers.

She sat.

She thought.

She stood up again.

She put her hand inside again, deeper, and she moved around, got down on threes, stood up again with her fingers inside and felt something tighten and release.

Something poured out and soaked her arm.

She got down on all fours and felt nothing.

The pain returned and she sat with her back against the stone and rested. She felt as though she was dropping to the arms of untrustworthy yeks. She put a hand across her belly and liked the weight of it, watched her arm rise and fall through a contraction.

She held a hand outside her rosé. She squeezed around the outside, then held her hand beneath it, expecting something.

She felt tight inside and made a noise that unsettled the World. Fifi had been watching her for a while and walked towards the stones when she heard the yekel noise. Fifi climbed up some of the stones and watched Mama, who turned on her side and looked at Fifi and some of the pressure receded for a moment when she could see the face of her friend.

Then it came back. Mama moved around in silent agony and Fifi felt sad but had no pictures and watched like the innocent watch a thing they cannot expect. Fifi's new ones came out in the cold white room and she was always made to sleep.

Mama put her hand under her rosé and Fifi watched it open. It closed and opened and closed and opened and dirty fruit was emerging.

Then the fruit was a tiny goon with a face and in a hot wet rush a body came out and Mama caught it in her hand.

Mama hauled the body onto her belly and hugged it. A yellow string was attached and was wrapped around her tiny chest. Mama unravelled some of it.

Fifi looked at the lek all over the stones and the new one on Mama's belly.

Mama felt a memory in her rosé and something else came out, which she caught in her hand and brought directly to her mouth. She ate some of it while the new one lay on her belly.

Fifi looked at the placenta and held out her hand for a piece but Mama kept it and ate.

She licked the red from her hands.

The new one was still on her belly.

Mama bit the yellow string, ate some of it, and the cincture was undone from the new one's chest. Mama removed it and put her lips to her tiny lips and snut and sucked out the salt and the new one became more lively. Mama hugged her and she pleeped tiny grief and Mama made noises quiet and soft and rarely made. She kept sucking and licking the salt and red spit from this vivid apparition and felt stunned and short of breath.

Fifi walked back to the others and sat with Magda near the monkey bars.

Mr. Ghoul saw a small brown bird.

Mama slept and when she awoke she gave the new one some kisses and hugs and kept her on her belly. She remembered Fifi and

Magda, how Burke and Bootie ate, but the new one wouldn't wake up on her belly. Mama got up and carried her like her cat, and climbed down the stones with no strength in her legs. She took her across the grass and sat on her own and wanted no one near her. People stared that night through her plekter bedroom.

Everyone wanted to see.

She touched her with the back of her fingers in the night and she sucked.

Mama stayed in her bedroom for days and people brought her food. No one could come in and she lay her new one on the floor. She lay next to her and stared.

Mama smeared red on the floor. The yellow string dried up.

She lay on her back with the new one on her belly and wriggled and wanted to squeeze. She ground her back and legs into the concrete, looked to the ceiling, tried to wriggle deeper into that memory, this floor, don't squeeze, those fingers, are true. Softbone body, chest on Mama's belly.

Nothing ever slept so small and still on an earth so heaving with want and satisfaction.

twenty-one

Montpelier's golden dome.

Smooth wool against the leg or khaki or cavalry twill. Dry-handed handshakes and echoes of Mike, get it to Mike if you want to get it done. The Senate Chamber was intimate, elegant but modest, and the vessel of his happiest days.

He had won the most votes in every town but two. All the shoe leather and meetings paid off. While Walt and Larry searched for ease in their days, seeking distraction and toying with nature, Mike had come to be known in different towns—a new barn near Goshen; Rotary in Middlebury; in Ripton, years back, he had gained popularity by preventing an eighty-thousand-square-foot box store from arising and choking the land—and everyone came to support him.

He was humbled.

For the land and the people's wishes he had learned to take down giants. On councils he had stalled applications, using wetlands as obstacles, demanding elaborate and unaffordable sewerage, using utility poles, traffic lights, sidewalks, winter maintenance in such a powerful combination that most developers went running. Early on, this was sometimes in the common interest of his partnership with Walt and Larry, but that interest never did anything but enrich the state of Vermont.

He had done his work for the towns, and now that he was in the Senate he could focus on higher things.

Every year he attended the Addison County Fair and Field Days, and now that he was senator he had the privilege of serving food in the fairground's main dining area. He made a point of serving Motts Vermont chicken from the Motts farm eight miles away, with mashed potatoes.

It was such an opportunity to get to know his constituents and their concerns, to touch each other with words, to showcase Vermont's products and to celebrate the fact that food is more than food, it is communion. When it comes from the right place and is touched by hands that care, it is goodness. It is health, not mere survival. When harvested locally, sustainably, it is giving back to the earth. A chicken with no beak, pumped full of steroids and preservatives, suffering an unholy immolation and travelling by jet and truck to packing plants in the dirty corners of fallen cities—that is not food. That chicken knows no more of what it came from than those who make a living in the theatre.

I know the people who raised this chicken: Robert and Jennifer Motts. They live just up the road.

To know our food is to know ourselves, to know our place on this earth.

On the night before each Fair and Field Day he had a waking dream of himself, a benefactor at the centre of a long table, grateful for his responsibilities and for the gratitude he receives. He saw the smiles and the beautiful little mouths.

Judy came one year while Mike was attending. She said it's

nice of you to take the time to do this and he said to serve is the highest thing I could do. He smiled and laughed because a laugh commands another's smile.

She was a very charming woman, a little older now. She had never had the chance to congratulate Mike on his appointment, but he could tell from her behaviour that she was pleased for him.

Mike was wearing an apron and he dared to look long at her.

The centre of the eye is a tunnel through the past to the future.

I think about our ancestors when I do this said Mike.

He offered Judy some chicken.

No thanks.

Somewhere way back a man was doing this for his family. For his tribe. Sharing the meat that he earned. Not that I earned this, he laughed, although it was an ordeal getting the Motts to sell these chickens at the price I offered.

Salt on the lips, grease on the fingers. What dim light did they work with in cuttings and in caves.

Please at least try these potatoes. Please.

Judy explained that she had to run. She had an hour to herself and wanted to get some cheese for Walt and something sweet for Looee. He loves maple candy in decorative shapes—like a moose or a maple leaf. He sort of talks to it like he's saying wow you look like that and I can eat you!

A veneer came over Mike's eyes.

He wanted Judy to linger but he wanted richer talk, or no talk at all. He didn't want to mention his wife but he wanted to take Judy's hand and say my wife and I, too, are childless.

Judy bought two of every shirt for Walt—one for Looee and one for Walt. Looee was growing weekly. His arms were now so thick that extra-large Hawaiian shirts were the only ones that fit. Walt thought I'm from Vermont and a businessman, and he buried his own Hawaiian shirts in a box.

Looee still needed help getting into certain outfits. His fingers couldn't manage buttons. He was long reluctant to be helped. He strapped on his overalls by himself and spent the summer days bare-chested.

He collected quarters in a jar in his bedroom. He stole tools from the garage whenever he had a chance. Larry brought him Penthouse and Hustler instead of a girlfriend and said those are the real deal as far as fake things go.

Larry found Looee energizing and thought of the days when he ran and kept running and the earth didn't call him in like it does its rusty products. He told Looee about a plot of land he owned off Highway 7 and said I'm going to build something there someday but I'm not sure what.

And through the summer the afternoons swelled and Looee ate a lot of spaghetti.

The noise in his concrete house was truly painful. When he attacked imaginary enemies or displayed for the women in the magazines it was best not to be around.

He wanted to run like the skinny men in the Olympics. Sebastian Coe. My money's on Coe said Walt.

Judy watched his shoulders grow, his movements become more manly. An idle glance at his rolling walk brought muted memories of dances and yearning, whispers and surprises, a distant history of romance that passed behind her eyes like a storm drifting miles behind a traveller.

She washed the dishes and thought of a friend of hers with an autistic son: his tantrums and inability, remote connections, and no one understanding how relentlessly hard it was to raise him. Normality makes us human and disease makes us animals. Her friend said she sometimes felt like the loneliest person in the world, even when—especially when—she was holding her squirming son.

Judy saw Looee's growing abilities, but was ever aware of his limits. The way he fumbled at small things with his half-intelligent stare; how he used the backs of his fingers more readily than the tips. It was hard not to see him as slow sometimes, and ever since the landscapers laughed at him it was also hard not to see him as most others would see him: a figure of fun; a satire of wisdom. A hairy ape in a shirt looked like a mockery of evolution, or progress retarded.

Judy was lonely like her friend. No society, no chance of normality, no school or achievements or growing relaxation. She couldn't grow towards adult communion with him or share ideas as others did with normal children.

But she was not as lonely as she would have been if she had never met him.

Judy had seen things through meeting Looee she would never have otherwise seen. She ended up volunteering again at the hospice—no longer because she was yearning for a purpose, as she had a decade earlier.

She told people stories about Looee. She found that the dying have no need for perfection. They liked to hear her stories.

Now, long after the incident with the landscapers, Judy had said it's best to keep strangers at a distance. She feared he might expect all strangers to make fun of him and that he would have no trust left. She was also afraid of his violence. Since the onset of adolescence she had noticed a defensive posture about him. It had mostly metamorphosed into a swagger now, but she knew it didn't take much to set him off.

He threw a long tantrum one day when Susan visited and Judy didn't let him out of his house. He jumped on his bed and screamed when Susan left, and she and Judy looked at him from outside as if he was a lunatic. Judy said someone looks upset, and left him alone that day.

Walt didn't want him to get lonely, though. I'm going to go to his place more. I haven't been doing that enough.

He bought another TV and one of the new VHS players for Looee's house.

Looee had learned to restrain his habit of grooming because it had grown too painful for his groomees. He made his noises of respect and affection while he ate his popcorn and he liked Walt's company. He watched movies for hours and got up often and brought toys to the couch.

Larry got his hands on a bootleg tape of the new Blue Lagoon with Brooke Shields and the three of them watched it at Looee's place. Walt and Larry grew embarrassed and talked business but Looee was transfixed. He made long affectionate oooos at the blond-haired girlboy who dove in the ocean and foraged for his friend. His eyes went soft when the screen went gold with skin.

Whenever Walt went over to Looee's place The Blue Lagoon was playing. Walt had spent a long time teaching him how to push the rewind button, and Looee didn't understand how long he had to wait, so unless Walt rewound the tape for him he was usually watching the closing credits or the last few scenes.

Walt still thought there was a bit of a unicorn in Looee, something mythical or impossible. No matter how much work or how many complications were involved with keeping him in the family, Walt always felt lucky for having this connection. Judy said how old will he live to. How long do we have him for. They felt the fear of winter.

They were lucky, especially, in how gentle Looee was. A male chimpanzee, deep into adolescence, growing by the week, could easily have torn the house down, and Walt limb from limb. He would soon be as strong as seven men, and by the end of the following year would weigh 170 pounds. He had all the emotions, passions and jealousies of a child; the short attention span; the need for recognition; the need to prove himself while being largely helpless. And he carried those emotions in a body that could lift a thousand pounds and had a bite as strong as a panther's.

The very thing that made him so big was also responsible for his gentleness. Judy fed him constantly. He had masses of food in his own fridge. Like Walt and Walt's cohort throughout the human world, Looee had no experience of starvation, and none of them knew what creatures they would be if they had to find their own food. Looee felt hunger meal to meal but his meals were two hours apart. He got irritable and desperate on occasion and trouble always ensued, but if there was food in his belly he was calm. He could luxuriate in fictions like all who choose their clothes.

And he would find no satisfaction in hurting others not only because no others hurt him but because he was a nice guy.

You're a good man Walt said.

It was obvious. Something you knew from the moment you met him. He's just a nice guy.

He didn't have to do anything. He didn't have to offer you popcorn or do any favours. It wasn't even that he seemed to want to please everyone: he didn't—he hated and was afraid of all kinds of different people, on TV and otherwise. He just had a look about him, a way.

Mr. Wiley said it regularly. There's a joke in his eyes. A smart joke, a slow-builder.

Mrs. Wiley made Vesuvius-mounds of spaghetti with meat-sauce and Mr. Wiley brought it regularly to Looee.

He wanted Mr. Wiley to watch The Blue Lagoon with him.

In The Blue Lagoon the blond beauty takes food to his dark-browed friend. Fish and pearls like mummy's pearl necklace, he would love to hunt like Walt.

Looee and Mr. Wiley acknowledged it with each other, each in his own way, whenever they met: it's great to see you, you're a good guy.

Looee bobbed his head and smiled and went to find something to offer, a gift is the same as some words. Mr. Wiley would hold a greasy fork that Looee had just given him and would say again it's good to see you sir, okay, great great, and Looee would bob his head some more until the fork became a different kind of exchange: Looee would take it back and offer it again and make a gigantic noise that startled Mr. Wiley, who would say okay what's this, it's a fork, it's serious now, and Looee would cast about and display as if he was saying fuck I like this guy, let's go do something important.

When he was calm he wore a look in his eyes like a kind man staring at dawn.

Coyotes yipping at night disturbed his dreams and he woke up and turned on his TV. He used the remote to press play and his dark house bloomed like an electric garden. He slept till mid-afternoon, penis and belly wet with pearls from the lagoon, and he ate from an aluminum tray heaped high with cold spaghetti.

The Senate offered a broad exposure to the world. Mike was able to meet a delegation from Quebec, some of whom actually spoke no English. They dressed well and seemed fine people, but there they were, from a hundred miles away, with nothing to speak but French. He met the Canadian ambassador, the Mexican ambassador. A delegation from Norway came over to look at the Vermont Yankee Nuclear Power Plant. Mike befriended one of them, Thor Pettersen, and has enjoyed a decades-long correspondence with him and has even visited him in Arendal, his hometown in Norway, which reminded Mike of Burlington. Thor is a good man, and their friendship shows that once the whole earth was of one language and of one speech. Thor loved the lakes and trees of Vermont, which for him recalled Åmli and the Sagfjellstigen.

Middlebury College was part of Mike's constituency, and despite its legion of liberals it was a source of new relationships and interesting ideas for Mike. The dean of science was a fellow Rotarian—a good man with whom Mike had had many spirited and gentlemanly debates, and whose ideas were mostly misguided. They had found common ground when the dean discussed scientific explanations of the inferiority of women, and most of their lunches were enlivened by these truths.

The dean called Mike to talk about the establishment of a research wing at the college. There had been discussions of affiliation with an institute in Florida which specialized in research on primates. The dean explained that it was getting difficult to acquire apes and monkeys for research, but Middlebury could benefit from a purchase of animals from this institute. There was much to learn, and it could be a wonderful opportunity for Vermont to get on the map in terms of primate research.

Mike made sure that his smile was powerful enough to be heard over the phone. Let me find out more about this institute and we'll talk some more.

The last thing he could conscionably support was the introduction of more of these creatures to Vermont.

Mike's secretary took the name of the institute in Florida and called on behalf of the senator for a later conversation. The sound of her wool skirt and stockings stayed in his head like unwanted music. It accompanied him as he took a breath outside the State House.

Senator.

Senator.

Senator.

Smitty. How's that mother of yours.

Montpelier is the smallest capital in the United States, sometimes so small that one doesn't know what one yearns for. Flashing lights. A truly feminine woman.

There was a dryness in Mike's throat and a half-seen vision of tethers and confinement, monkeys in cages, a shed in the woods and no meat. There was a thirst in his loins which he did not trust, and a glimpse of Senator Turnbull's immodest Cadillac made him think of floating through imagined blue cities, tasting sweet nights, rolling smooth on American tires over guilt and the perils of having.

He suddenly wanted to free that animal.

When he eventually travelled, in his early sixties, to Thor's hometown in Norway, they journeyed together to ski above the Arctic Circle. They ate reindeer jerky, which Thor had made. Thor had long echoed Mike in saying there is no need to search for food beyond a hundred miles from home.

They were both hardy men with extremely good posture, even under their heavy packs.

Thor said you and I have wanted similar things in our own countries. Maybe we are friends because we are not living together. But I trust you, Mike. I feel like I never got what I really wanted.

They had seen a wolf floating on a detached sheet of ice. Thor said that wolf will starve.

For decades Mike had made coalitions, formed triumvirates, was always a tall and recognized presence in the House, but he often felt alone. Rented mouths and the smell of death at home. Alone, with Cindy and then without.

They watched the wolf drift and Mike said we can't save him.

twenty-two

There were times when Podo, Mr. Ghoul and Jonathan would sit together and play. The men would touch knuckles and roll, and three inscrutable, divided nations would join in a sniggering globe. The ground would shake and the women would be happy and mornings would not be a threat.

A fragrant bundle of sticks would land from the roof of the Hard and there would be no fighting, no teeth. Magda, Fifi, Jonathan and the young ones would sit and savour the leaves. Mr. Ghoul would come and shoulder his way in, and there would be no conflict or worry about who got what.

Everyone was calm, because Podo, like that piece of the sky up there, did the same to all beneath him.

When two bodies want the same thing, a third is needed to govern them. Mr. Ghoul and Jonathan bowed to Podo.

There was oa.

The World needs a leader for stability, and the World will never stay still.

*

Burke charges at Mr. Ghoul and the women, and everyone scatters and screams. Magda hugs Mama and Fifi, and goes to Podo to see if he saw.

Burke settles with his back to everyone and chews on a twig, nervous about what will unfold behind him. He broadens his back and shows that all he cares about is this twig. He has seen Podo do this.

Podo is thinking about Fanta.

Magda takes Podo by the shoulder to turn him so he can see Burke. She bows and looks up but Podo will neither turn nor look her in the eyes. He is tired, and doesn't like her.

Magda pleeps and looks at impudent Burke. Someone needs to show him that his world is not the World. Mr. Ghoul has sought some shade.

Jonathan puts his snut in Magda's rosé and smells tuna and potatoes.

Magda wants Jonathan's help. Jonathan follows her towards the other women and they sit and eat and think. Magda believes that Burke will not dare to run at them now that Jonathan is among them.

Burke will not turn around. The wind behind him has fingers and the leaves are whispering judgment.

Podo is asleep.

Burke stands up and walks to the side, not looking at the group but seeing them nonetheless. He waits until more than one of them lies down.

He clears a space in the dirt, flicks twigs away and starts to sway, standing tall, perfecting his terrible warning.

They all take notice before he runs at them and Magda screams as loud as she can. She grabs Jonathan's arm and begs him to stop the onrushing Burke.

Burke did not expect Jonathan to be involved. He was running at the women. He did not expect the arm of Jonathan to be as hard as the branch of a tree.

Burke is screaming now, side-stepping quickly away from the others. Magda, Jonathan and Mama chase him to the greybald tree which he climbs and swings around until the hools subside, but he does not want them to subside. He screams and hangs from a branch and refuses to be calm.

Bodies scatter and Burke surveys his work.

Podo is awake and feels as clear as the afternoon moon, wise Podo. He senses recent commotion. He walks to the group and sits and Mama gives him an open-mouthed kiss that carries comfort and pictures.

Jonathan and Magda do not come to Podo. They ignore him. He doesn't like this.

Magda and Jonathan groom each other. Magda turns and lets Jonathan groom her swollen fistpips. She is facing Podo and deliberately does not look at him. She looks at tossed-away husks of melon while Jonathan's snut and fingers tickle her pink menace. Jonathan deserves her more than Podo.

She looks at Podo directly now.

Burke is watching to see what power Jonathan has. His face still hurts from being hit by Jonathan's big arm.

Magda walks away.

Podo stares at Jonathan.

Jonathan scratches his chest, looks for a moment at Podo then away to the unknown. He does not get up and greet Podo. He is content to stay where he is.

Podo feels sick. There's a shift inside somewhere. He forgets where he is. He remembers he doesn't like something.

twenty-three

Mike spoke with Dr. Emil Heinz at the Girdish Institute in Florida. It was a large primate research facility that had started in the 1920s. They bred their own animals and acquired them from wherever they could.

Mike said you might be interested to learn that there's a chimpanzee living right here in Vermont.

Dr. Heinz was not entirely surprised. He had acquired chimpanzees from private homes in upstate New York, Georgia, Pennsylvania. He himself had gone to these homes and persuaded the owners to give their pets to Girdish. On one occasion, while trying to anaesthetize a young chimpanzee, he accidentally injected the arm of the woman holding her.

We have a historic relationship with primates and a facility that occupies a hundred acres. The climate is similar to their natural habitat.

Mike shared a lengthy conversation with him, and the man made reference to biomedical experiments, research done for the benefit of all species. Neither trusted the other one whit. But Mike got some sense of the Girdish Institute and Girdish gained the address and phone number of Walter Ribke.

The Fish and Game Department got several anonymous calls about Looee over the years. They had long been aware of his presence, but Walt had got Looee before there was legislation about chimps as endangered species and there was nothing they could do unless he posed a threat.

Walt knew many of the wardens and they never fined him, but they let him know that their eyes were open. They also told him whenever there was a complaint.

Mike was in regular contact with Fish and Game.

This isn't coming from me he said. But I hear about strange goings-on with that chimpanzee over at Walt Ribke's place. I drove past and it was louder than a witches' sabbath.

Mike met the chief warden at church and said Colonel if there's ever a problem with that animal, call me right away. My understanding is that they are valuable and rare, and I know a better place for it than in a human home.

It would be a shame to put it down.

Walt was pulled over as he and Looee were driving to one of Walt's ponds to go fishing.

The game warden looked at the tackle in the back of the pickup and said two rods, two licences.

Looee here is just going to watch.

I'm afraid I'll need two licences, Mr. Ribke.

Okay. I'll take another licence.

The licence has to be for a separate individual said the warden.

Well. You can call him Looee Ribke on the licence.

A separate person. I can't give out a permit to an animal.

Looee was wearing his fishing cap and wanted to put his hand in the man's mouth or trade hats with him.

I'll write out his name for you said Walt.

It's not a thing of writing, sir, it's that animals don't need a permit to hunt or fish.

Well there's your answer said Walt. He doesn't need one.

Walt began to remember that it was dangerous to argue with the wardens. He saw the man's mind turning over the issue.

The warden looked over at Looee, who sensed the delicate mood. Looee looked away through the windscreen, just like scores of other delinquents whom the warden had warned and fined.

I'll tell you what said Walt. I take your point. We won't go fishing today. And next time it'll be just the one rod.

You understand my role, sir.

I do.

If I'd've found fish I'd have to fine you.

Looee was getting restless and making Walt worry.

The way I look at it is said the warden. If we left it up to the animals there'd be no need for regulation. A bear takes what he needs to eat. But human people, we take more than we need. Unless there's some control.

I understand your role said Walt. He looked respectful and sincere.

Looee couldn't wait to catch fish. He thought it was hilarious and scary when they flopped and danced and died and he said oooo and drummed the dashboard.

There was a bill proposed to the Senate regarding cruelty to animals.

A person commits the crime of cruelty to animals if the person: overworks, tortures, torments, abandons, beats or mutilates an animal, ties or restrains an animal in a manner that is inhumane or is detrimental to its welfare, transports an animal in a vehicle that jeopardizes the safety of the animal ...

Cindy told Mike every morning to dare to be wealthy. She held him by the wrists. She took steroids as part of her treatment and her face and shoulders swelled. She turned her back to him at night and he did as he must, and they prayed and pitied each other.

The world is for the taking she said. Do not leave this house till you have straightened as a rod of iron.

He never expected to be in the Senate for twenty years. In those early days he thought that Washington might be the answer. Cindy had reminded him that every great man had a humble beginning. The men in Washington are only men she said.

Would there be this thirst in Washington, this dryness of the throat.

Sometimes his power was obvious to him—when his actions had direct outcomes. He made sure that Middlebury never made a deal with Girdish, that apes and monkeys could never multiply in his state.

But what was real power, that greater power that made men more than men. Not the power of the Lord, but the power that fills a room. What gave people like Walter Ribke that easy confidence, that wordless ability to attract strangers and strengthen friendships. Why did Mike feel nervous—not nervous, but strangely deferential—in the company of men like Walt. Still, after so many years, so many accomplishments and a real ability to have his way, Mike still felt insecure around some people.

The governor didn't have that power. He was a backroom guy, a manipulator. Reagan had it. Some of the men in Congress.

What was it about some men that made Mike think if I could only be like him I would find my ease, my peace. Ugly men. Walt was a petty owner of property, an impresario of a private circus.

What was it like to wake up next to beauty.

The Cruelty to Animals Act would allow a humane officer to seize an animal—to enter a premises with a search warrant and find an appropriate home for the victim. The owner must forfeit any rights to the animal.

Mike had neither been with the bill from the beginning nor acted as its primary sponsor. It was those bleeding hearts, Smith and Warnanke, who knew no more about the rigours of husbandry or farming than a prostitute knows of innocence.

Mike knew that the bill, if passed, would have consequences on the operating procedures at his own plants, at the barns and even the abattoirs of his constituents. Sometimes cattle need to be persuaded by force.

But there was something compelling in the bill. He ruminated unexpectedly over its import. There was a custodial element to it, a satisfying acknowledgment that we are humane, that humans respect their servants.

He was an ardent supporter of hunters' rights. He wanted to leave hunters alone, and only endorsed legislation that kept things orderly—ensuring that everything that happened in the woods was clean and that the woods and animals could, within reason, replenish themselves. Being a supporter of hunters' rights did not preclude him from treating animals humanely.

He never believed that any person had the right to enter the houses or hearts of men. But the idea of a humane officer entering a premises to rescue a tortured soul—that seemed noble. That seemed like the eradication of cancer, removing the bitter crab from the blood of his betrothed. Removing the howling ape from the state for the good of the ape, and for a greater good.

He wasn't sure. He simply wasn't sure.

He let Smith and Warnanke take him to lunches and make

promises. He let them woo him, and there was satisfaction in that. He ate Vermont beef and said no when they offered him wine. Power, like temptation, comes in many forms, and if he could not win the hearts of others he could nonetheless be necessary. The bill would go nowhere without him. These two Democrats could owe him many favours.

Judy watched a TV program about a man who killed his brother. Their parents were interviewed and were asked if they were ashamed of the son who murdered. They said no, he was a good boy. The camera said how can a good boy commit murder.

He was a good boy they said. We're just sad.

Judy understood. He was a good boy. He was a son. The crime is ever the parents'; this world is so before a child comes into it.

All this sadness. Looee used to kiss her tears.

He's such a good boy.

How can we stretch the feeling of kin so that every stranger is a son and every parent takes the blame.

There is so much sadness. Better to be sad than angry.

Judy poured a gin and tonic and got two beers for Walt and Looee.

They were playing Atari, and Looee wasn't very good at it. Beer made him relax.

Judy said I really love Sundays with you guys.

The phone rang and Walt said this is Walt.

Walter Ribke.

This is Walt speaking.

Hello, Mr. Ribke, my name is Dr. Emil Heinz. I'm calling from the Girdish Institute in Florida.

Okay.

How are you.

Walt began to wonder if he had cancer and they had somehow found out about it in Florida.

I'm fine. A few aches and pains.

I know the feeling. It's my understanding that you have a pet chimpanzee. Is that right.

He's not a pet.

I'm sorry—that's just a word. We get very attached. We were in negotiations with Middlebury College about expansion of their work with primates and somehow your name came up as someone who lives with a chimp. I thought I'd try to get in touch to learn more about it. Do you have time for a chat.

I can have a quick talk.

Great. You said he. It's a boy then, is he.

His name's Looee.

And how old is he.

He's. We've had him for about thirteen years. He's maybe a year or so older than that. We're not really sure. He loves cake. We've given him about thirty birthday parties.

So he's quite large then.

He weighs about a hundred and eighty pounds.

My god. And no incidents. No trouble.

Oh, he's been trouble every day. He's grown out of a lot of it.

He lives in a cage.

No, no. He has his own house. We built something for him.

Isn't that amazing. And you have regular contact with him.

He's like a son to us. Who. Could you give me a better idea of who you are.

Of course. I'm a clinician at the Girdish Institute, where we've been studying primates since 1925—so, over fifty years. We have over a hundred acres of land, and a staff of about two hundred and fifty people. At the moment we're working with about a hundred and fifty great apes—mostly chimpanzees. Some pygmy chimps, and otherwise a few orangutans and gorillas. Lots of macaques and monkeys. And what we do is a great variety of research. Are you a birdwatcher, Mr. Ribke?

Not particularly.

You probably know your birds. Let's say you take a red-eyed vireo and put it next to a white-eyed vireo—two vireos with different coloured eyes. Those two birds have less in common with each other genetically than we do with chimpanzees.

I'm not surprised.

So what we do at Girdish is honour that fact, and we learn whatever we can from chimpanzees. We learn about their behaviour in groups, their ability to solve problems, how they communicate—with each other and with us. Do they have a sense of the future and the past.

Looee remembers.

I'll bet he does.

So this is like a university.

We have affiliations with a number of universities. They commission us to do studies and so on.

What I mean is for the chimps. It's like a school for them.

That's a nice way of looking at it. There's lots of evidence of them learning from us, as much as us learning from them. We study their biology in great detail.

Well it's a pleasure to hear from you.

I'd sure love to hear more from you but I know there mustn't be time. Most of the people I talk to in situations like yours, they haven't been able to keep their chimps for so long. Usually two or three years. The oldest human-raised chimp I've met was eleven and she was a female. I'm sure there's more you could tell me than I could tell you. But we've had many incidents. Contact between chimpanzees and humans has to be carefully managed. I'm sure you know. In any case, if you ever want to learn more, I'm going to take the liberty of sending you a package which will tell you about us. And I'll include my phone number.

Sure, sure. But Looee wouldn't want. Maybe if it's like a summer camp or something for him. We could all drive down.

Is he healthy.

Yes. He gets colds sometimes.

Great.

twenty-four

From a tower, someone looks down and takes notes. She uses a voice recorder every five minutes to note who is sitting with whom. She notes that Podo sleeps for an unusually long time, and when he awakes he is off-balance and retches.

Jonathan is bluffing regularly and charges at Podo most days. Burke is Jonathan's helpmate.

Podo is frowning, looking hard at a desiccated flower. When Podo looks elsewhere it is always away from Jonathan, but he sometimes throws secret glances.

Days pass and Podo stands his ground.

But he feels a need for others.

He feels sick and slow and longs for the touch of women.

Mama sits with Podo whenever she can. So do Fifi and Mr. Ghoul. They like sitting with him, showing him that they are his friends. They like feeling united as friends and fear not being united.

But Burke has the women preoccupied. He shakes trees and screams and makes everyone feel nervous.

Jonathan no longer greets Podo. Jonathan sits with his hair on end, his back turned to Podo, and he trumpets a tale of bursting black flowers and birds emerging from dirt. Magda bows to Jonathan and grooms him.

Whenever Jonathan bluffs and screams, Burke attacks the women and keeps them from intervening. Once a fight begins there is little the women can do.

Jonathan runs at Mr. Ghoul sometimes and Mr. Ghoul flees.

Mr. Ghoul has an old habit of looking for Dave, and is blinded by hot light from the windows of the Hard.

These days are noon and midnight and nothing in between.

When Burke sees Jonathan bluffing and about to charge at Podo, he runs at whoever is sitting at Podo's side. Burke chases Mama to the top of the greybald tree and will not let her return until Jonathan has his satisfaction with Podo.

Mama is growing afraid of Burke.

So far there has been no serious biting. In their moments of contact, Podo and Jonathan use only fists and feet. They scream their terrible arsenal of teeth, but no one has been cut.

The new one plays, oblivious to change, but everyone else feels nervous every day.

Jonathan pins Magda close to Podo, and Podo merely turns and moves away. Thereafter if Jonathan wants support he turns to Magda.

Burke cannot stand the sight of anyone having sex. The women all seem like his mother, but none have his respect. He loathes their lekky fistpips. He wants to attack anyone who tries to pin a woman. He blones and drags branches and wants to bite the ground.

There is a reckoning every day at bedtime. As darkness comes they make their way to the tunnels. Some are afraid to turn their backs.

Podo and Mr. Ghoul groom each other longer than ever before.

My friend.

My past.

Where are we.

Video captures every blow. They play it in slow motion and analyze each movement.

Only 0.6 percent of all confrontation between the males in the colony will lead to an actual fight. It is the threat of a fight that matters.

One of the researchers is writing a paper on warfare. She draws conclusions about the relative paucity of actual conflict through human history versus the constant presence of threat. She wants to print Paolo Uccello's painting of the Battle of San Romano. Weapons scattered on a perfect grid. Warfare as ritual and posture.

They pause the slow-motion video. When contact is made between Jonathan and Podo, sweat bursts and hangs in the sunlight like a chandelier of needles.

Jonathan runs at Podo, and Podo holds him by a foot as he passes. He bites Jonathan's leg. Jonathan screams injury and vengeance and he spins. His fist hits Podo's ear and deafens it.

They roll in black percussion and the women are running back and forth screaming.

They face each other with hungry teeth and roar the inevitable future. Podo hears nothing but a low bright whistle.

Boulders are the muscles of the dead.

They are poised on their haunches and neither will run, but Burke makes noises nearby, behind Podo's back. Burke rolls and jumps, throws his hands up and screams. He is cheering Jonathan's fight.

Podo feels Burke's presence and is fooled into running, and Jonathan runs after. They write an arabic chase across the grass and Jonathan bites at Podo.

Podo feels a hot fist inside his chest.

He runs for the greybald tree. He climbs the bottom and spins, fooling Jonathan into climbing, and drops underneath him. He holds Jonathan's foot again, bites off a toe and swallows it.

Jonathan scrambles up the tree in a righteous and bewildered panic. He screams down to Burke and holds a hand out towards him and Magda. She is keening in fear, and useless.

Burke is cornered by Fifi, Mama and Mr. Ghoul. There is a silent acknowledgment amidst all the screams that Podo and Jonathan must fight on their own.

Jonathan is upside down along the body of the greybald tree. His face is a breath away from Podo's and their screams are chilling the wind.

Podo is trying to shake the tree. There's a darkness in the middle of what he sees.

He was the only one who ever climbed and stayed in the electric tree, hair pointed out towards everything he ruled.

He is the fastest.

He can lift this entire old tree.

He is suddenly terrified of Burke and feels a hand across his jaw. He tries to reach but he can't feel his arm.

Nobody is near that tree except Jonathan and Podo.

He feels nails inside his chest, and teeth around his arm, and a bite that bursts, orange and hot. Fanta in his chest, Fanta in his eyes.

Glory glory.

The video from the roof shows the alpha holding the tree and then falling backwards, apparently untouched.

*

Podo is on his back. He looks like he is laughing or afraid, but he doesn't move.

Podo is filling with silver.

The screaming doesn't stop, but it changes.

Jonathan leaps down and shouts at Podo's face, and his fists come down on his chest.

There is no response from Podo.

Jonathan runs with a limp to Magda and hugs her. He runs back to Podo and pounds him, and runs again to Magda.

Mr. Ghoul and Mama are restless and looking at each other in fear.

Podo hasn't moved.

There is screaming and crying and Jonathan charges again.

The body is left outdoors to study their reactions.

Mama and Fifi lift Podo's arms. They touch his fingers.

Mr. Ghoul sits near.

Jonathan charges again and pounds the body.

Mama screams at Jonathan, who limps to Magda.

Mr. Ghoul comes nearer and leans close to Podo's face, three times. He hears nothing. He gently touches Podo's lips. Mama lifts an arm again and lets it fall.

Fifi, Mama and Mr. Ghoul don't look at each other.

Mr. Ghoul picks some grass and puts it to Podo's mouth, hoping he will take it.

Jonathan remains in a frenzy, and his foot hurts.

Everyone wants to go somewhere, but nobody knows where.

Mama comes around to the other side of Podo's body. She rests a hand on his belly. His eyes are hard and flat like buttons on a Visitor's coat.

The new one climbs up Mama and Bootie stares and touches the body, and Burke does not come near.

Mama keeps a hand on Podo's belly.

Jonathan charges once more.

The body is removed at night with a forklift.

The annual electrocardiogram and serial blood pressure had shown moderate amounts of interstitial myocardial fibrosis. It is registered as sudden cardiac arrest. That day's video is reviewed and a short paper is prepared, with a focus on IMF among captive chimpanzees.

In the morning they go to the greybald tree and smell the ground.

Jonathan will not go near it. He had nightmares in his bedroom.

They do not greet each other.

Mama plays with the new one.

Fifi eats.

Magda wants something.

Mr. Ghoul has a feeling in his throat.

He sits at the foot of the greybald tree.

He spends most of his days there.

He looks at nothing and everything and the everything amounts to nothing but a tree is a tree is a tree. He thinks and sees pictures.

He does this for twenty-nine days.

When Mr. Ghoul was smaller, Dave took him for drives to the forest in a van.

Dave had put a string around his neck as if he needed to be held back and they stepped into the woods, Mr. Ghoul's first time feeling dirt and branches underfoot.

He was terrified and excited and wanted to be carried by Dave but Dave said

You're too heavy.

Dave brought the keyboard and Mr. Ghoul tapped on pictures and he squirted white on his leg.

That tree.

That tree.

A stick was a baby tree, a leaf a baby tree, a coloured leaf a flower.

Mr. Ghoul felt shy with everything at first because it was different from the slides and movies and different from the pictures of pictures he tapped on.

A heron flew over and Mr. Ghoul chased it then ran to the pictures that said

That airplane.

He wanted to climb things but felt especially shy near trees.

Mr. Ghoul was at that point twelve years old.

He knew candles and numbers and could remember a random pattern of numbers on a screen and tap them, 5,8,1,9,4,3,11,14, faster than a thirty-five-year-old International Master of chess. And the International Master of chess was sitting on the forest floor asking Ghoul to put it all in a sentence, how many leaves was he holding in his hand.

Dave looked hard at Ghoul and Dave was thinking about time.

This was part of the paper he submitted to Science:

Chimpanzee Mama (MA) was eating cereal and Chimpanzee Ghoul (GL) approached wearing a backpack. GL showed signs of intense interest in MA's bowl of cereal.

Observers Margaret Jones and Timothy Spence recorded the following interaction:

GL motions towards cereal, making food grunts and panting.

Dr. David Kennedy (DK) (speaking): Don't eat Mama's cereal Ghoul. Don't touch it. She'll get mad.

GL observed tapping on lexigram for cereal, repeatedly.

DK (speaking): That's Mama's cereal. Here. How about we make a deal. You show Mama your backpack. If you let Mama wear your backpack, I'll … Mama and I will let you have some of her cereal.

GL is observed removing his backpack. MA leaves her bowl of cereal on the floor. GL eats cereal. MA wears the backpack.

GL is later observed sitting with the keyboard by himself, tapping on lexigrams:

Cereal.

Ghoul eat cereal.

Nut.

We submit that the interaction not only shows proficiency in the use of a visual-graphic-aided language system (lexigrams), but also in comprehension of spoken English and of complex, conditional sentences: *"If you let Mama wear your backpack, I'll … Mama and I will let you have some of her cereal."*

The use of lexigrams among chimpanzees at the Girdish Institute has been well documented for over fifteen years (see Appendix E).

Appendix C shows the results of separate experiments involving 580 novel sentences spoken in a controlled environment. As discussed earlier, the complexity of the sentences was increased by asking the subjects to perform unusual or nonsensical tasks (*"Put the blue hat in the microwave"*), showing a level of abstract comprehension beyond utility and separate from reward.

Proficiency in spoken versus lexigraphical comprehension is roughly equal (+/– 2 percent), at 74 percent correct per 135 trials.

In the woods Dave and Mr. Ghoul shared peanut butter sandwiches. Dave said there's peanut butter on your face. Mr. Ghoul wiped it off with a leaf.

Dave said you can climb a tree like you can climb the monkey bars in the playroom. Trees are like monkey bars.

Dave spoke and used sign language while he spoke, and he tapped on the lexigrams for tree and up and Ghoul.

Mr. Ghoul stared at Dave and various trees and thought about peanut butter.

Dave stared at Mr. Ghoul and Mr. Ghoul moved and sat and sighed.

David rested his forehead on his hand and fingered his hair, pushed it back and thought about how little hair his fingers felt, and reordered it into his ponytail.

It was the ninety-fifth paper to emerge from his department at Girdish. Over eight years of his work.

Unassailable rigour and control of experiments.

Independent witnesses.

David had set out to defy Noam Chomsky's assertion that humans were unique for being born with language, born with a sense of grammar. Linguists believed that grammar and syntax were innate and were the preserve of humans like flight is that of angels.

He had video evidence, eyewitness proof of intentionality, rule learning, imitation, fast associative mapping, sequencing, cognition and meta-cognition. When Ghoul comments on what he is eating, what he is watching, there is no clearer sign of self-awareness, of language as a tool for expressing self.

How many times had he wished that he could tie down Chomsky, seat a roomful of Chomskyans, behaviourists, petty-minded linguists, behind that glass in the observation area and demonstrate that it is not a uniquely human ability to do something so utterly pointless as putting a blue hat inside a microwave because you have kindly been asked to.

The editors at Science called his conclusion an "over-interpretation of stimulus and response" and refused to publish the paper. It was doomed for some other journal in the gutters of the Citation Index.

Language emerged with our early ancestors as a way of coordinating action. That is what David and others believed. The more complex our social life became, the more there was a need to make needs known and to act in unison. This was the real syntax, the real putting together. And as complexity grew, so too did syntax. Ghoul and Mama were demonstrating its rudiments.

But by mentioning syntax and grammar he drew criticism from linguists. For linguists, language is words, not communication. They ignore what words were made for.

*

After the first visit to the woods on their own, David had trouble persuading Mr. Ghoul to return to the van.

David took hold of the leash and pulled and it may as well have been tied to a tree.

He knew better than to try force.

I wonder what Mama is doing he said.

Mr. Ghoul wouldn't look at him.

I bet Mama and Podo are playing Pac-Man he said.

Mr. Ghoul walked with him to the van.

They won't do anything they don't want to do. That has always been part of the problem with ape language research.

So even if he sat Chomsky or Terrace down in the observation room, it would no doubt be a day when Ghoul was tired or sick or ornery like he has been more and more.

And people only see what they want to see.

The next time they went to the woods Mr. Ghoul said

Ghoul put hat on tree.

Dave said what.

Ghoul tapped on the lexigrams again.

Ghoul put hat on tree.

David took off the Greek fisherman's cap that Julie had bought him before she moved to Manchester.

Mr. Ghoul took the hat and walked with it to an ageing pecan tree that was standing apart from others. He ground the cap into the dirt as he walked, and stopped at the foot of the tree.

Mr. Ghoul was climbing a tree.

Mr. Ghoul had been born at Girdish to a mother who produced five chimpanzees for research. He was taken from her immediately and raised in the nursery, and came to David at the age of three and a half years, socialized to both chimpanzees and humans.

At a height of about twenty feet he began to shake and cry out for Dave.

David was thinking about the hat which Julie gave him and how their love had faded.

There were birds in the tree which Mr. Ghoul had never seen. One flew near his face.

Mr. Ghoul lost his grip and threw the hat which tumbled to the outer leaves of the tree and rested. He regained his grip and had no idea how to regain the hat.

He hugged the tree and slid down a few feet, scraping his belly and thighs.

Dave was looking at the hat caught in the leaves beyond his reach. The branch was too high for Dave to shake. He told Mr. Ghoul to shake the branch.

Mr. Ghoul wanted to get down.

He jumped and landed on all fours and wanted to do it again but didn't.

They drove home in the van and David was unexpectedly melancholy, feeling an ache to meet someone new and angry with Ghoul for ageing.

Ever since they compared ape language to Clever Hans, the talking horse, language research had lost credibility. Apes are just mimics they said.

Funding was drying up. He had to broaden his experiments.

When they went back to the woods the third and final time, Mr. Ghoul went back to the pecan tree. He stared at it and didn't climb.

He walked back to Dave and pointed at the keyboard.

? Where hat.

He continued with cognitive tests and realized that all they were doing was testing by human standards. David said if you hang bananas and see if they're smart enough to use tools to reach them, you're only testing if they are smart in our terms. What if they're not in the mood. What if they wonder why you aren't giving them the bananas directly.

Their politics, the subtle emotional variables that are as important to cognition as logic. Those are the things to look at.

David had risen through his profession as a young man, as much through being good with colleagues as through conducting original research. We don't like to see it this way, but a life is shaped less by talent than by handshakes and the right words. He was getting what he wanted by being liked around the table at funding committees.

That was the real essence of language. He was fed up with trying to prove that chimpanzees can communicate. Of course they can. Communication is a process of getting what you want, finding your way in a group. Politics is each individual's struggle to get what he or she wants, in the face of what others want. Language is political.

We are not born with words and symbols, and words and symbols mean nothing without a social context. What linguists and so many of his colleagues don't see is that they protect their fields of interest because they are territorial. David did it himself. It is an inescapable characteristic of apes.

Dave offered Ghoul his cigarette. Ghoul took the Zippo and lit the cigarette, even though it was already lit.

You can't study a chimp the way you can drosophila or even something potentially charming like dolphins. There is more than charm; there is kinship, no matter how objective you remain. There were moments in David's work when that kinship was amplified towards love, towards pure wonder. He knew there was no human/animal divide, there was a continuum. He could never look at Ghoul without wondering what he was thinking, and the lexigrams offered the bliss of revelation. When Ghoul said Dave swing Ghoul, the physical bond of swinging was redoubled by the knowledge of mind.

He felt a need for change, a hunger for some sort of opening. He could look back later in life and say it's what a man starts doing at the age of thirty-five.

He had set things in motion to change the structure of the field station. It was time to move away from language, and away from trials which set out to show how like us they might be.

He thought of Julie again. I don't feel whole without you she said.

Perhaps his work boiled down to an attempt to redress the unspeakable loneliness of humans. Perhaps it was just a recognition that sometimes one ape needs another to show him who he is.

It was time to go, and David thought about the old game.

Ghoul what colour Dave's eyes.

He looked at Ghoul and saw an old-looking, wise-looking, restless but composed hairy teenager, a perpetual but time-worn child, so much bigger than the child in the lab, so familiar but different from the pup he began as.

David pointed at the lexigram for friend.

Mr. Ghoul thought Dave had pointed at the picture for milk, and waited.

twenty-five

Looee bit the tip of Walt's finger off once when Walt reached for a piece of chocolate that Looee thought was his own.

He punched Larry in the eye one evening for no good reason and would only calm down when Larry gave him another beer and showed him his blood on a hanky.

He lunged at a black woman in Kmart when he was little, having never seen a black person before. On TV he had something to say to anyone who wasn't obviously white.

He scratched and kicked and pissed and bit.

He learned to share but usually didn't.

When older, his blackened face and greying frown, his increasingly beastly and hunched-over figure, made him look like a despicable bully.

When he sat on a chair, a chimpanzee on a chair, and looked jerkily around a room, he was everything we have collectively turned from, every gene and culture we have shed across millennia. He looked foreign, hairy, retarded. He couldn't concentrate, couldn't remember enough, couldn't plan far ahead, couldn't control his temper or his jealousy.

This home video of him hammering a nail while wearing a Hawaiian shirt shows a figure to be pitied.

He was a wild animal, is how he was summed up in the Burlington Free Press.

More than thirteen winters had passed since Looee arrived in Vermont and with all the necessity of being indoors he was more sedentary than he would have been elsewhere. He climbed when he had bursts of energy but he was just as happy to climb in his house as he was outside. When there's no need to forage and no enemy to flee from, we might as well stay still until we're bored.

Walt took note of Looee's pleasure in staying on the ground and built a fence around the back half-acre—trusting that he would not climb over. In the summer they had barbecues and parties out there. He was still gentle with children, and Dr. Worsley liked bringing his grandkids over to see Looee. Dr. Worsley could no longer treat Looee at his clinic so he paid visits when needed. Looee didn't trust the doctor, his soft hands and tools, but he loved the grandkids and played tickle-chase with them.

Judy invited Susan over, who had coloured and cut her hair in the manner of Princess Diana. Looee caught a glimpse of her from across the garden and hooted from the basso profundo of his great black balls to the glistening brass of his lips. He ran towards her and she asked Judy, as calmly as she could, if they could go inside to the kitchen.

Looee picked up his pace when he saw her moving away. He was shirtless. He stopped short of the back porch and stood upright and threw a tantrum like he hadn't for several years. Larry and Mr. Wiley were individually unsettled by his shamelessness. He was rolling and pounding on the ground with high-pitched screams and teeth exposed.

Walt waited awhile and said let's go toss the ball and get a hot dog, and Looee calmed down. All of his tantrums and flare-ups passed quickly. But the mood often took a long time to change. As he played catch, Susan was in his mind like a wasp in a tiny room.

He watched her in the kitchen through the window. Instead of catching the football as Walt had taught him, he attacked it. He took it in both hands and brought it down on a flat rock and it popped like a dull balloon.

Christ said Larry, realizing how strong Looee was.

Walt scolded Looee and Looee sulked like an athlete who says fuck this and leaves the team. He ran towards his house and plotted holocausts and flayings, and walked back with his hand held out and Walt said that's okay, sweet boy.

They sat on the lawn and the fullness of the day brought thunder. Instead of rushing in they stayed beneath the warm downpour and laughed at the strength of it. Looee did a ritual dance and pounded the ground as though the rain could be beaten into submission. They were soaked when the rain had passed, and happy, and they were spontaneously silent for a moment. The only sound was the dripping.

Parties faded and Looee watched the trees change. December arrived. Snow was curling into people's collars and the onset of Christmas was reddening the blanch. Everyone was looking for a friend.

Larry carried a bottle of rye from his car to Walt's front door and rang the bell, shaking the snow from his jacket. Judy greeted him and took the whiskey with a hug.

Walt's not here yet, he might be caught in the weather.

Larry felt immediately warm and said you've sure made it cozy in here, did you make all those.

The living room was beribboned and wreathed.

It's my favourite time of year said Judy.

She poured them drinks and they talked themselves out of any awkwardness, Larry and Judy alone. He watched her light candles in the dining room and Larry said they're talking about a season like no other on the mountains.

They heard a hoot from Looee's house, who'd seen Larry's headlights coming along the drive.

I bet he'll want to see you she said.

They opened the door in the dining room which led to Looee's corridor. Judy had even hung wreaths in the passage and there was cedar in the air.

Larry smiled to himself as he always did, hearing Looee's impassioned calls. By now, like Walt and Judy, he had relinquished all pretense in himself of being much more than a talking animal. He was open to error and confusion and had called his elderly brother and said I forgive you, having spoken of it with no one for more than thirty years.

When Judy said we're coming and pushed the bolted door, Looee jumped back and hopped a small hop, two hundred pounds and barefoot on concrete. Larry and Looee clasped hands and men's thick thumbs, and Looee smelled the fresh whiskey on their breath.

Judy said it stinks in here and she wedged the door wide open.

We're having some people over for a Christmas party Looee, remember I told you yesterday. You've got to stay in your house and we'll have our real Christmas in a week.

Looee looked over their shoulders and saw the unusual light in the dining room.

I lit candles said Judy. It's nothing to be afraid of.

There was the warmth of alcohol on their breaths, the warmth of the distant light—and Looee felt immediately removed from both. Concrete at his feet and at his back. Larry and Judy had gathered affection as they had walked to Looee's door, and Looee mistakenly sensed it as affection for each other rather than for him. Judy didn't notice when he made his quizzical noise.

I shouldn't leave the candles burning she said. She touched Larry's arm and said will you come and help me for a second.

Looee watched them leave and pull the steel door behind them. He didn't trust their movements tonight and didn't understand why Larry wasn't staying longer. He stared at the door and listened. He couldn't hear them walking away or talking and thought they were just outside his door. Hiding and whispering secrets. He banged on the door but they wouldn't open it. He banged again and got angry.

Larry helped Judy open a jar of pickled onions in the kitchen. I think I'm getting arthritis she said.

Larry poured himself a drink and Judy said Walt should be here soon. I'll keep an eye on things here. You go bring a beer to Looee if you want and I'll send Walt out. Everyone's coming at seven.

As Larry approached Looee's door he heard screams and felt Looee hit the door.

I'm coming in buddy. It's me. I'm coming in.

Looee was still screaming and Larry tentatively opened the door. He looked in and Looee was in full display. His hair was all on end. He looked gigantic. From side to side he swayed and he pushed his TV on its casters around the room and into the wall beside Larry.

Calm down buddy. Did I scare you. I brought you a beer. Look. Everything's all right.

Looee screamed and walked away and sat with his back to the wall without looking at him.

Larry figured he had probably felt neglected. I was just helping her open a jar he said. Here.

He wedged the door wide open as he had seen Judy do.

Looee saw the hallway and dining room again. His anger seemed to be subsiding and Larry gave him his beer. They sat with their backs to the wall and looked down the hall at the candlelight and gold and silver stars, a spangled and flickering drama beyond his reach or ken.

It's a time of peace said Larry. No sense screaming and breaking your TV.

Larry explained that guests were coming over and they were going to have drinks and dinner. Looee heard Susan's name among them.

He found everything strange tonight.

They drank. Looee wasn't looking at Larry, and Larry wasn't comfortable sitting close to him. There was a prickliness to Looee, and it felt like they were staring forward like rivals at a bar.

Looee was trying to understand why the door was still open. He thought Susan might come in.

They heard kitchen cupboards closing and they both listened for cars.

Looee finished his beer and made a noise. He crushed the can and got up and looked down the hallway and back over his shoulder at Larry to see if he was watching. Looee sat and would only glance at him.

You're not in a great mood tonight are you.

Larry seemed equally confrontational to Looee. He looked at the open door and was all the more confused.

Larry felt he had spent enough time visiting the kid's room. He got up to leave and Looee got up with him. He wanted to wait for Susan in the living room.

All right buddy, I guess I'll say goodnight.

Larry tried to leave but Looee jumped at him and pulled him by the arm.

Walt saw Larry's car when he pulled up.

He knocked the snow off his boots and missed the greeting of Murphy who had died in his sleep in the summer.

The house was quiet and he called for Larry and Judy. Candles were blowing in a draft in the dining room and he could see that the door to Looee's house was open.

He walked down the corridor and called for the three of them. Larry was face down in the middle of Looee's house. His right arm was resting impossibly across the back of his head. One of his buttocks was missing and was lying nearby under a scalp of bloodied trouser.

Walt found Judy behind the couch in the living room. She was missing a hand and her face was split open from temple to jaw. She was moaning sounds so lonely.

Walt heard those moans for weeks. They came from the spans of iron bridges and contractions of the city. The hospital in Burlington was built on a bruise and if you put your ear to the cracks in the pavement or the fold of any curb, you could hear those hopeless sounds.

They say that some of it will heal.

In Burlington the streets were salted and plowed and Walt bought doughnuts, the only food he could eat for a month. He bought them from the same place and always looked across the street at a jewellery store before he got into his car.

Looee had been sitting in a corner of the living room, his eyes slow-blinking and brown. As the ambulance raced towards them through a horizontal snowstorm, Walt chased Looee the two of them screaming into a corner of Looee's house where Looee cowered and hugged himself. Walt had his rifle and aimed it at Looee while the paramedics took Larry out of the room. Larry remembered nothing. Walt couldn't imagine the creature that was taken away. Tranquilizers and game wardens. Was he screaming or muttering his own weird story, that animal they found.

Walt looked at the jewellery store and back through the window of the doughnut shop and saw people eating.

These are the hard questions.

Why can't a man turn his back on his son, and what does it mean to be animated meat on these streets of boutiques and spilled oil.

twenty-six

Mike got a call from the chief warden at Fish and Game. There had been an attack, two people were maimed, and the chimpanzee was in a cage.

He's pretty wild and we'll probably put him down.

Mike called Dr. Heinz at the Girdish Institute, who was more forthcoming than the first time they spoke. Ninety-seven percent of our apes are involved in biomedical procedures. Senator, if you allow us to come and get him you will be helping our research immensely. People will benefit.

For those who walk this earth, Mike thought, liberation and punishment are inseparable.

You will not be setting him free. I will be honest with you. A chimpanzee like that has no place now—not in the wild. But I can assure you that our work has led to countless medical breakthroughs.

Mike thought of Judy being disfigured. The frigid swollen back of Cindy and crouching over the face of beauty. Will illness ever be cured.

He made arrangements with Fish and Game.

Girdish sent a horse trailer which returned to Florida in four days.

Looee felt sharp and regular fists of tranquilizers and PCP.

A long road burned beneath him.

There was a smell of vomit when they opened the trailer.

twenty-seven

Looee's right hand is heavy but weightless. The big black boat could float among the bubbles. He can't lift his hand but it rises like a balloon.

Mummy sang a song.

Looee doesn't trust his hand. He wakes up and it is pulling off the nails of his other hand and won't let him scream.

There's a paint we invented, the colour of sperm: we put it on concrete walls and it's lit by its own smeared fluorescence. There's mould from the Florida heat and the sophisticated nose thinks of Roquefort or something dustier—black ash on chèvre— and a storyteller could conjure from that smell a world of corrupt gentility, a tale of the South of hot gothic moons and florid mildew that puffs up from sheets beneath the bodies of doomed lovers.

CH 488, known as Dusty, is on all fours spraying the wall behind his cage with diarrhea.

Looee is ignoring his hand. He wants to move away from it.

Dusty feels dizzy and collapses.

Looee's hand helps him make a circle. Four sticks of monkey

chow. He thinks about eating the circle. He forgets again whose hand that is.

The CID Wing is otherwise clean.

Looee's name is Lonee now.

Some of Lonee's fingernails are growing back. He needs his right hand to scratch himself. He wants it to scratch his chest and it does.

The scratch feels good. He remembers the swollen itch of summer evenings and someone scratching his mosquito bites. He listens to the sound of scratching and looks down at his chest to see the skin flaking off beneath his fingers. Blood is sticky and he thinks of maple syrup.

Lonee stares at his hand.

Some of the old anger is returning.

He looks away from his hand to make it think he isn't there. He will attack it before it attacks him. He bangs his knuckles against the bars and they swell.

You stick a fork into sausages before you put them on the barbecue, Looee.

Lonee feels pain now in his hand and is confused. He is sitting in a back corner of his cage.

There is a tire suspended horizontally by ropes above his forehead.

Rosie, in the cage next to Lonee's, is sleeping in her tire as though it were a hammock.

Rosie likes the look of Lonee and can't touch him, and while she sleeps her teeth are eating themselves.

Yesterday, Rosie, a thirty-year-old chimpanzee, was knocked down and wheeled to the anteroom where 1 mL of HIV virus stock was applied directly to her vaginal mucosa with a cotton-tipped swab.

Lonee has begun to keen and is craving spaghetti with meatsauce.

The Florida heat enlivens all the other smells of the wing and the smells become tastes and the tastes swell to sounds, the sharp brassband of monkey chow licked, neglected or egested by ten bewildered chimpanzees, blow Dixie, there's the underarm tang of terror to taste before you blast your trumpet in the face of those who innocently crave salvation: there is such a thing as angels, there is.

Caregiver Martha says the smell is like hazelnuts that went sour or something, but boom does it ever hit you in the face some days.

Lonee is keening and staring at his right hand, which is resting on the floor of his cage. He begins to sway as his anger grows. He is sitting and his body is rocking and the hoots are building in his chest but they stop. He won't attack his hand.

The vet gave him clomipramine.

Steady, big Lonee.

The CID Wing is fifty feet long and bright as a gas station's bathroom.

It has emerged that bodies are the products of four Roman letters, G-A-T-C, and the alphabet and numbers also dictate death. ARV-2. LAV-1. SF2. HIV.

Lonee's body is currently leased by a pharmaceutical company in France named Pastora, determined to find a vaccine to prevent AIDS.

The lights go off on a timer.

Lonee floats like his hand.

He will steal a key and break out.

The ten chimpanzees all have their own cage, five by five by seven feet tall, fixed to a wall and suspended two feet above the ground. Five are on one side and five on the other and their cages are two feet apart. Lonee's feet haven't touched the ground in five years.

A new caregiver named Martin arrived at Girdish last week and today he was asked to do a simple walkthrough and tag. He stands at the anteroom door and looks through the window. When CH 563 (Spud) sees Martin's face he raises the alarm and the wing fills with the hoots that say a stranger is coming. Spud doesn't remember Martin's face.

Martin pulls the hood of his Tyvek suit over his head and the mask over his mouth. He puts the face shield on and a third layer of latex gloves and remembers the look on Lisa's face when he told her the chimps might have AIDS. Seven months is the longest he's had a girlfriend.

Martin waits for the labtech, Frank, to dress out, and they open the door and walk. Frank told Martin not to let them know you're afraid.

Martin walks tall behind Frank.

Spud spits on Martin's head and so do Pepper and Nathan. The closest sounds to Martin are of liquid slapping Tyvek but the sound that puts his hair on end is of the ten in unified hostility, reminding the concrete that it wasn't always there and may not always stand.

Accurate Mac fills his hand and flings a mouth-sized piece of shit directly at Martin's face shield. Martin gags and sees that Frank is getting hit by none of it.

Saliva seeps under his hood and he starts to panic and puts his hand on Frank's lower back to hurry him along. Another piece of shit hits the side of his hood near his ear and he thinks he can feel it on his face.

When they are back in the anteroom Martin removes his face shield and a string of saliva hangs from it like egg white and swings towards his nose.

Frank notes in the log that Dusty is looking promisingly ill and that the superinfection is working, and Martin quits that evening.

Lonee and the others take a while to settle down like a crowd watching a detested fighter leave the ring. They want more blood but never want to see him again and don't know what to do with themselves.

Pepper is spinning in circles and screaming and Nathan, in the cage next door, is screaming to calm her down.

Lonee has his hands on the bars at the front of his cage and is looking up and down the room. His cage is the third on his side. He can see the five across the room. He has never had a good look at Spud or Jeannie on his side of the wing, except when they are wheeled in front of him unconscious on the table.

To his right is a droop-lipped old lady named Rosie who has been in a cage for thirteen years. Lonee misses the long bald grace of the women in magazines and their eyes like living candy. Some of the caregivers pull their Tyvek suits back over their arms and let him touch their skin through the bars.

In the midst of his fear and revulsion, Martin forgot to tag the cage of Mac. This means Mac is fed his meal of chow and he will inhale his vomit when under anaesthetic.

Lonee would still prefer to eat with a knife and fork.

There is a storm of brown and white and black when Mac is darted and Lonee and Pepper keen through it. Everyone screams when Mac is wheeled past, and when the procedure fails and Mac is resuscitated he is wheeled back through and placed on his side so vomit can hang safely from his mouth. Dr. Meijer keeps an eye on him and when he is there most of them stay calm. Some of them suck their lips with the expectation of treats.

The vet watches Mac sit up, fall over, and move himself on shaking arms till he falls face forward and sleeps. Saliva pours from his mouth and he rolls on his back. Mac's big lips are relaxed across his ridiculous mouth and his body is spread-eagle, gigantic, submissive, come sun, come women, come bring me your best and worst. The ketamine makes Mac hallucinate and Dr. Meijer wants the bite of vodka to clean the work of blood and breath and will go to his drawer as soon as Mac seems safe.

Lonee is asleep and awakens in the dark. He stares at the handle of the anteroom door, reflecting a light in the room that Lonee can't find. He thinks of Judy's bracelet.

Time is no more contained in a clock than a body is in a cage.

Seven years earlier Lonee was Looee and he woke up with a shaved and tattooed chest, CH 447. He jumped and banged his head on the roof of a cage and was shuttled in transfer boxes from one cage to another with his history preceding him as the one who attacked the people in Vermont.

A labtech who loved drugs gave him diazepam when he arrived and he was lifted an inch above life. For a week he was given enough diazepam to maintain a joyless suburb, his memories and awareness suspended.

Judy had put a thin bracelet on him the year before and it was overlooked when he was admitted and tattooed. He stared at its silver and memories almost came to his eyes but his eyes were too relaxed and all they took in was the silver.

He was anaesthetized repeatedly, kept in a metcage that squeezed him forward till he was trapped and easily injected. His first long-term cage was made from the same grating used on sidewalks to vent the New York subway—its gaps were narrow and the metal was deep so his view from within was limited to whatever was directly in front of him.

He had never seen chimpanzees before. He was put in the darkest wing in Girdish which was nicknamed Congo. It was a long, yellow-lit corridor with fifteen chimpanzees and, at the end, a group of small stacked cages for macaques.

The apes and monkeys in Congo were transitionally used. Many of the chimpanzees were juveniles who had been born and raised in the nursery at Girdish. They were destined to be part of longer-term studies but were kept in Congo until their futures were determined.

Looee spent more than a year in Congo and was used intermittently for rhinovirus studies, mostly for drugs that were meant to cure the common cold. He was now owned by Girdish but was leased that year by divisions of Monroe Pharmaceuticals.

The protocols for these studies required clean chimpanzees, so the vet of Congo made sure they were drug-free. When the diazepam stopped, Looee became more aware of his surroundings and expected Walt and Judy to get him soon. Each time a labtech approached his cage he was friendly and held out a hand or hugged himself to say sorry.

Congo was not a jungle.

It was not a simple prison.

It was not a death or an illness sprung from nowhere, or your family turning their backs. Nor was it a change of culture, an unwanted move, a kidnap and a blindfold lifted in a room of malignant strangers.

Looee was bigger and older than many of the chimps in Congo but was more confused than most because they had grown up in cages. He could see pale young faces like he used to have, staring through the grids, but he wasn't able to associate them with himself or consider himself one of them. They were desperate creatures from some dark dream, the products of dogs and strangers. They made familiar sounds but used them in different ways and were deafeningly loud in unison.

He was naked and never given clothes. He was never let out to go to the bathroom, no matter how loudly he screamed, so he made dirty in his cage and thought he would help Judy clean it up when she came.

All permanent cages in Girdish were fixed to a wall and suspended above the ground. The director advocated what he called the Dry Method. He didn't want cages to be cleaned with hoses because he believed a wet environment would encourage respiratory infections. A long clear plastic sheet was laid on the ground beneath the cages and changed once a day by caregivers or labtechs, who preferred the shift of laying it down to the one of picking it up.

Looee sat in the dark and started shaking. There was a window at the end of Congo but Looee couldn't see it. He needed to say sorry. The light in that long room was like permanent dusk, and darker in the cages because of the thick grates. Looee sat at the back of his cage and waited for Walt and Judy.

People came near to fill the water or the feeder, and Looee waited to be let out.

The cages in Congo were attached to each other and had sliding doors between them. A chimpanzee named Dusty was in the cage adjoining Looee's. Dusty was young and small and wanted to get to know his new neighbour but was simultaneously afraid. Looee wouldn't look at him.

Looee was tired of the snacks. The only food they brought him was monkey chow, a biscuit-like concoction. He wanted chicken. He didn't know how to drink the water. He saw the dogpeople across from him drink it and he didn't want to be like them.

He watched labtechs in white coats and surgical masks wheel transfer boxes to the cages across from his own. He called at them so they wouldn't forget to take him home.

He stared at Judy's bracelet.

A scream made his hair stand on end.

His sleep was a dream of not being able to sleep.

Labtechs finally came with a transfer box and pressed it up against the gate of his cage. Looee shook with excitement. He went in with the relief of a man who has reached the first-class carriage, having jostled through a train full of paupers.

He couldn't see out of the transfer box but was aware of being wheeled, and heard the noises of Congo diminish. The transfer box was pushed up to a metcage which he quickly moved into, and found himself being squeezed once he was in it. He shouted so they knew he had no space and felt a sharp pain in his leg.

The PCP took effect and they took the animal out of the metcage. They put it on a table and drew blood for a virus-serum neutralization test. They took throat cultures by rubbing the back of its throat with a dry sterile swab.

Looee awoke back in Congo but was dreaming.

Another transfer box came to take him to see Judy and he again heard the chimps and macaques of Congo fade away.

The chimpanzee was anaesthetized and strapped to a table. A suspended solution of rhinovirus strain 30 was placed in a number 40 DeVilbiss glass nebulizer which was put in the animal's mouth. Its nose was pinched shut, a plastic surgical mask was placed over the nebulizer, and the virus was sprayed as an aerosol into its mouth. More of the virus was then introduced into each nostril.

Looee awoke back in Congo.

He was very sorry and reached out a hand to a woman in a white coat.

He lay on his side and slept with open eyes.

He awoke with a sore throat. He was hungry and found a piece of monkey chow which he had earlier rejected. He sniffed at it but couldn't smell it. He ate it and his throat hurt.

Rhinovirus 30 was similar to the cold Looee had caught when he and Walt fixed the pickup and they were both laid out for a week. Looee had partial immunity and a minimal response. He was anaesthetized on day 2 of the study for a throat swab and a bleed, and infected with more of the virus.

He slept.

His cage was hot and cold.

A labtech noted diarrhea dripping from the animal's anus.

His neighbours Dusty, Lucas and Tom were treated with the drug bis-bentadazole. Looee was untreated as one of three controls.

The animals were anaesthetized and bled on days 2, 4, 6, 9, 21 and 35 and serum neutralization titres were measured. They were also anaesthetized and swabbed every day for the first nine days.

Table 7 shows results of the study. Note that control chimpanzee 447 had no detectable titre at 21 days and no detectable virus in throat swabs. Note also the universal rise in titres at 35 days among the treated animals, 7 days after cessation of the drug. A cross-infection seems to have taken place.

While bis-bentadazole seems to inhibit virus reproduction, it offers no immunological conversion.

Dusty developed diarrhea from receiving a higher dose of the drug.

The primary investigator and vet could not determine the cause of Looee's diarrhea.

When Looee wasn't sleeping he saw the dogpeople across the room being moved in transfer boxes. He screamed at the labtechs and dreamt that Larry and Judy were being attacked and eaten by Murphy. They were brought back asleep and the other beasts screamed when this happened. His neighbour was taken away and Looee felt he had more room. He screamed at the labtechs and hit the cage and his knuckles were too sore to put his weight on.

During his first procedure at Congo his bracelet was noticed and removed. A caregiver named Consuela took it back to her doily-filled home and put it in a box among poems and detritus from the lab which she labelled The Tears of Tiny Children.

Looee looked for something on his wrist but couldn't remember what. Then he saw light and Judy's face and remembered the bracelet for ten more years like an embittered woman remembers a ring decades after divorce. One of his tics is to rub his hairless wrist.

On the CID Wing it sometimes seems likely that all are having the same dream and they are dreaming what all of us dream, children in adult bodies. The labtechs and caregivers watch them sleep and dream their own dreams at home. Things never done and everything done wrong. There's a skinny woman who used to sell perfume at Macy's who wishes cancer upon all girlfriends, and a man who dreams of ejaculating in a rusty tin can which a moment ago was his wife. They all dream of killers behind their back, of damning those who damn them awake, of joy and revenge not quite attained from the end of floppy guns. They eat what their bodies don't want, dream of the taste of shit, awake to the light with the eyes of a migraineur. The chimps float and fly and are not who they are, and the one thing they do not dream, as Martha thinks when she hears them cough and snore, is of a peaceful jungle that simply never existed, neither in the jungle nor here. This plastic Africa is all there ever was and all there ever will be.

Each study had a primary investigator, or PI, sometimes a clinician employed by a pharmaceutical company, usually a researcher funded by grants. The PI devised and orchestrated tests appropriate to whatever drug or disease was being examined. The PI then worked in concert with a veterinarian and sometimes lab technicians at Girdish to choose appropriate animals and find the right protocol for study.

A product called Narase was being developed by Monroe Pharmaceuticals, and a PI based in Detroit established a correspondence with the vet at Congo to begin tests of Narase on clean research subjects.

Narase was a blocking agent. It was essentially a collection of proteins applied to the nasal cavity, ideally as a spray, with the purpose of preventing the rhinovirus from taking root and causing a cold. It was being tested in various forms, the first in a consistency like petroleum jelly for maximum coverage.

The protocol requested by the PI had various components, most involving direct intranasal challenges. CH 447 was involved in these, but also in one which tested indirect infection.

CH 556 and CH 447 were anaesthetized, bled and swabbed, and found to be both susceptible to rhinovirus 5.

Dusty was infected, and Looee, while under anaesthetic, was treated with Narase by having it liberally smeared within his nose. Although under anaesthetic, the chimps still made gagging noises, groans and farts, and the labtech Bill was saddened by the sounds Looee made when he pushed the applicator to the back of the chimpanzee's airway.

Looee's sense of smell was gone when he awoke. The labtechs had raised the partition between his and Dusty's cage so the two could roam freely between their cages. The purpose was to see whether the Narase would protect Looee from catching Dusty's cold.

Looee hadn't touched any dogpeople yet. He was hiding in the corner of his cage and banging the back of his head against it. He was growing less aware of what was real and had chronic diarrhea which the vet and researchers had come to take as an underlying condition unrelated to their tests.

Dusty had had no body contact since he was brought here from the nursery a year earlier. He was a young adolescent and keen on impressing an older chimpanzee. He was aching to groom Looee.

The vet and labtechs knew that it could be dangerous to house two males together, but transmission of the virus was probable whether they fought each other or groomed.

Looee awoke to the smell of nothing and a dogperson sitting in a close dark corner of his cage. He sprang and screamed and banged his hands and feet on the cage to scare the creature away. Dusty shat and ran through the door to his own cage, and his screams of fear started a wave through Congo till all of them were screaming. Those who were housed in twos and threes could hug while they screamed and those on their own shook their cages.

Dusty made circles in his cage and looked over his shoulder at Looee, and felt like everyone was watching and judging his next move. He found himself going back to Looee's cage without thinking, and he was walking with his hand upturned. The filthy supplicant terrified Looee and he screamed and ran at Dusty. He pounded his eye and mouth and bit his calf as Dusty ran away.

The others were still screaming and Dusty was whimpering in a corner of his cage. Looee was running hard against the cage, ignoring the pain, telling the dogpeople to be quiet.

Dusty was taken away in a transfer box and a missing tooth was noted while he was bled and swabbed and the progress of the virus was assessed. It was at its most contagious and they wanted to ensure maximum contact between animals.

Looee was wheeled away and awoke in his cage with the dogperson cowering in arm's reach. The trapdoor had been closed between the cages and the two were now housed as one.

Both were shivering like orphans in an alley. They wouldn't look each other in the eye.

Looee hit the cage with the back of his arms and Dusty had

nowhere to go. He wouldn't look at Looee but was grinning in fear. Looee saw the grin, saw it as fear instead of a caricature of an ugly man's smile. He understood Dusty for a moment, and then reverted to understanding nothing.

Looee bit into Dusty's head and opened his scalp. The labtechs were alerted in time and tried to hold Looee back with prods while the trapdoor was lifted for Dusty.

Exhaustion overcame Looee and he slept facing the trapdoor so there could be no more surprises. The bottom grid of the cage was dripping with Dusty's spit and diarrhea. Looee's nose rested there but the Narase prevented a cold.

The PI in Detroit was encouraged and wished to test an aerosolized version of the solution. They repeated the protocol with different animals and the thinner solution, but results were inconclusive and never published.

Looee developed a reputation as violent. Each chimpanzee had a chart detailing not only their medical history but also character if anything was noteworthy. One of the labtechs noted "aggressive" on his chart.

Bill would talk about Looee with his colleagues saying he's the one to watch out for. They all had the recurring fear that a cage would be left open, and Bill was afraid it would be Looee's. He heard a story about a lab in Atlanta where one of the chimps got out and it took nine men and a shotgun to restrain him. He knew a hundred stories about chimps biting off labworkers' fingers, and the story where the finger couldn't be repaired because the tendon came off with it and was draped on the cage like a piece of bleeding spaghetti.

Lonee is the king of pus. Lonee is the thrashing heart of an aluminum giant.

Bill loved his granddad's memory and could bench-press 315. And if one sick kid could get better from this research then all this misery was worth it, these days of screams and filth. He respected these animals and gave them extra food and knew it was the little things that could make a day better. From eight to three this place could get to you, could do to joy what a junkyard does to cars, but if one sick kid got better.

Peace, big Looee, peace.

Looee banged his back against the cage at noon and was doing it still when Bill returned at 2:45.

Dusty was now completely in awe of Looee.

Lonee is the king.

On the CID Wing Dusty is across from Lonee and is dying of what some are calling AIDS. Dusty will be mentioned in Time magazine.

In Congo, years ago, Dusty collected things to pass through his cage to Looee.

There was no enrichment coordinator in Congo, as there would be on the CID Wing. No one was instructed to provide the chimps with toys. But Bill gave them whatever he could because it calmed them. He gave Looee a piece of dark blue cardboard from the lid of a box of bottles.

Looee stared at it as it sat on the floor of the cage and it looked like a hole, like the elusive centre of midnight. Looee saw it, then couldn't see it, and realized it was a hole. He looked around to see if anyone was watching and felt the erotic nausea that everyone feels on the brink of a great departure. The woman starting the car after twenty-five years of abuse. He reached for the hole and it moved.

Dusty watched Looee rest his chin on the dark blue cardboard. He watched him pick it up and bite it and sway back and forth on his feet. Looee screamed and wanted to throw the cardboard out of the cage and he smashed it for ten minutes against the grid but he couldn't get the cardboard out of his space.

Dusty was afraid and impressed and he later wanted to push a small piece of old chow through the cagewall to Looee but he ate it.

Bill gave Dusty a drinking straw. Dusty played with it for many hours and wanted to give it to Looee. He pushed it partway through the grid.

Looee sat in the far corner of his cage and saw the white straw moving. He ignored it. He looked at nothing and scratched his chest and was the embodiment of arrogance.

More of the straw poked through until it fell on the floor of his cage. He reached for the straw and sucked on it and remembered the taste of Coke and looking up to Walt.

He sat back in the corner of his cage and stared at the dogperson who had given him the straw. He stared for longer than he ever had and fell asleep staring.

He awoke and found the straw and almost dropped it through the floor of his cage, not understanding that if it fell it would be lost forever.

Dusty saw Looee holding the straw.

He moved towards their shared wall making noises of deference and greeting. Looee made those noises himself whenever he wanted someone to be his friend and recognized them in the dogperson.

Looee played with the straw on his belly and nibbled on it. He moved closer to the shared gridiron and the dogperson held out his hand. Looee pushed the straw back through the grid and Dusty took it and panted. He put it across his top lip and saw Looee bobbing his head. Looee thought it was hilarious to see an animal doing tricks and his bobbing turned to a manic joy which Dusty was proud to see.

Looee wanted the straw back. He banged the cage with the back of his hand and gestured for it. He hated the way the dogpeople never spoke to him. Dusty sent it back and Looee stared at it. He sent it back to Dusty and touched his lip so he would do that trick again and Dusty made Looee laugh.

Dusty turned his back to Looee and pressed it against the grid. He wanted Looee to groom him and he tapped his shoulder. The grid was too narrow for them to get their fingers through.

They had periods of not being tested or moved or knocked down.

PCP was no longer used to anaesthetize them because people were getting high on it and its use in laboratories was abolished. The chimpanzees were now universally anaesthetized with ketamine.

Bill gave Dusty a rubber eraser which he gnawed on and smelled and when he felt the rubber he masturbated.

Looee couldn't find the straw in his cage and couldn't see it in the dogperson's. It had fallen through the floor of his cage and was lying on the plastic dropsheet two feet below. Looee pressed his face against the metal floor and tried to figure out how he could reach down to the straw. He called to the dogperson and called to the straw.

He no longer willingly entered the transfer boxes. The cages in Congo were squeezecages—a rear grid was pushed forward until Looee was forced into the box that met the gate in front.

He nonetheless went through times when he sought to befriend the labworkers just as Dusty did with him. They were the ones he had most in common with. They wore clothes, could talk, had power over the dogpeople. He held up pieces of monkey chow when they passed as a gesture of friendship.

And now he flies at them and can't be liquid enough. He will eat their bloated stomachs.

He goes from one extreme to the other, is how the enrichment coordinator on CID puts it. Makes friends sometimes, and sometimes lashes out.

Bill had a sense that Looee liked people more than chimps and heard he had been raised in a family home. Bill left a Sears catalogue in his cage while Looee was involved in a procedure and when Looee returned he ejaculated on it.

Living rooms.

Hedge trimmers.

Bras.

The catalogue was removed at next cleaning.

Two hundred feet away on the Reproductive Wing they were reminiscing about what everyone called the first wild birth. In the field station, a chimp named Mama had given birth, without help, to a girl.

twenty-eight

This place. This cup of sound.

Mr. Ghoul used to sit with Podo and watch the World's leaves and muscles enliven. Birds and insects and electric piccolos heeming in summer heat.

Fifi complaining to Magda about Bootie's constant noise.

Jonathan whimpering and manoeuvring for Fifi's generous squeeze.

Thunder, and they all worked together after a storm to make a ladder of fallen branches. They rested the ladder against the electric tree and they could reach those leaves they never reached before, and they celebrated all as one.

When Rosie disappeared, Mr. Ghoul sat with Podo, quiet, and the vitreous layer of sadness in Podo's eyes went soft again over time.

Sit with him.

Most of the good sounds have gone.

Dave is in that building, but he doesn't come close anymore.

Mr. Ghoul used to crack nuts for Podo and felt Dave saying good job.

Dave and Podo are watching.

They should sit with him.

When the children pester and the women don't notice me.

Sit here.

I'll look into your mouth for you.

I want to show you something.

Podo was the World.

He was a rich population of virtue and mistakes, and neighbours kind and cruel.

There is open space where there used to be thousands of him.

A weak blue sky and yellow dust.

They watch Mr. Ghoul sit through days. He lies by the greybald tree and tries to feel Podo from the ground.

My friend.

Jonathan gets hard and spits triumph and confusion into Magda's anaesthesis. He flicks grass at her when he's finished.

What do you do when you get what you want.

Jonathan steps testily out each day and tries to make the others aware of his enormity, and what looks like power feels like fear. He looks over his shoulder and thinks Podo might be waiting in the grove. He circumscribes his movements and pulls back others who wander.

Burke tastes lapsy-dulchy pictures of Podo's demise, black fermented berries in the mouth.

He backhands Bootie.

Mr. Ghoul walks straight from his bedroom to the greybald tree, limping. He picks away grass like he is plucking the ground of its youth and his own black hair falls out over days. He moves in slow circles before he sits and he sleeps and drools on the piebald ground, and ticks make a home of him.

There is no unity. No one touches except Mama and the new one.

Mr. Ghoul lies on his back and sleeps. He dreams of plastic trees and windows. Podo wears a ponytail and tells Mr. Ghoul to put it in a sentence.

Jonathan sees Fifi moving towards the shady grove and he goes to her and pushes her away from it. She does not understand.

Burke sees that Jonathan is afraid of the shady grove. He walks towards it and Jonathan gets restless, and Burke sits still and thinks. They sit near each other, and with hair half-raised Jonathan invites him closer. Burke grooms Jonathan.

He moves around in front of Jonathan, who is looking away and trying to be majestic. He begins to trust Burke.

Jonathan doesn't like the way Mr. Ghoul limps in circles. It reminds him of Podo. Jonathan moves away and turns his back. Burke stands up and moves to Mama and the new one, and scares them.

When he turns he sees that Jonathan too is bloning and gigantic and Burke makes himself large again and they square off. Both are standing on two legs and Jonathan, the taller, rushes at Burke, brings his arm above Burke's goon and bluffs over him.

Burke is chastened. He makes noises of apology and wounded pride, touches Jonathan's mouth, and they groom.

They groom for an unusually long time. Jonathan is proud and anxious and tries to see pictures of what might happen. He wants Burke's respect. Each is busy with the other's schemes.

Mama, Fifi and the new one sit at a distance from the men. They wonder what scenes are being woven by those hands. Fifi goes to Magda feeling that if anyone can join the men for comfort it is Magda. They greet and Magda understands Fifi's curiosity. They slowly approach Burke and Jonathan.

Burke does not want women around. As if by prearrangement he and Jonathan swell and bark simultaneously. They fling their arms and chase the women away and renew their strengthening contract.

Stay here lest I hate you.

There is more space without Podo, and more space can feel like more confinement.

Jonathan and Burke see Mr. Ghoul in the company of Mama and the young girl.

Fifi and Bootie join the others and play with the new one. As they move they feel they must look towards Jonathan and Burke.

The men see the group gathering as they groom.

Burke begins to display. Jonathan stands and the two of them grow and Burke begins to blacken a path away from Jonathan but connected to him. Burke picks up a fallen branch and pounds the ground with it. Jonathan sways and runs to a tree and drums its trunk with his feet.

This is the new order. They are not displaying to intimidate each other.

Fifi hugs Mama.

Jonathan is older and knows what to look for when someone tries to take whatever is his. He watches Mama and Fifi, everyone trying to settle after the noise. He does not trust Mr. Ghoul. He wants him away from Mama and away from the greybald tree and memories of Podo. He looks over his shoulder where he thinks Podo might still be. He feels the fingers of Burke and gains confidence.

He stands again, twice his normal size, and he makes a run at Mr. Ghoul. He runs over him.

Mr. Ghoul did not expect to be hit and he rolls on the ground feeling weak.

He sits alone by a different tree and his mouth tastes like a penny.

Melons and bundles are thrown from the roof and they land among fists and teeth. All of them grab and scratch and look over their shoulders and there is guilt and confusion in taking.

Normally they would gather around the heavy bundles and savour their leaves in groups. Burke drags a bundle and drowns it near the blue wall. Mama and Fifi scream and so does Jonathan. They go to the pokol-fear and stare at the soaking sticks and Jonathan runs at Burke.

He cowers at Jonathan's approach and remembers later that Fifi and Mama screamed at him. He grooms Jonathan and he attacks the women when Jonathan isn't looking.

Jonathan pins Fifi and the afternoon widens like an artificial smile.

Mr. Ghoul shakes in his legs and shoulders when he walks and doesn't know where to sit. Jonathan hates the way the women go to him, and the way he is walking like Podo. He runs at him and Mr. Ghoul is scared.

The new one goes to Mr. Ghoul and sits with him. She grooms him with a taste for play and her sweet bright face brings colour to his sight. He tickles her sides and she laughs. She wriggles on her back and he prevails above her, avuncular, a storied old tree in an otherwise empty field.

On the periphery Burke is bluffing and clearing a path towards them, sweeping stones and twigs away with a long swinging arm as he puts his weight on the other. Mr. Ghoul tries to keep a playful face and not be intimidated, but when he sees Burke's approach he shows his teeth in fear and the new one sees Burke fly above her, an airplane into a tower.

Burke bites Mr. Ghoul's neck and holds him to the ground face down. He jumps up and down on Mr. Ghoul's back and Fifi and Mama hug and cry as they see their old friend screaming.

Jonathan and Burke focus on Mr. Ghoul to avoid fighting with each other. They don't let him rest or think. They corner him and beat him, they set him up as a common enemy and are stronger and closer for it.

Mr. Ghoul is better than this. His memories are bigger than these days.

Burke waits near the hole, and when Mr. Ghoul comes out of the tunnels in the morning Burke runs at him from the side. Every morning, before he steps out to the World, he has to think of Burke.

Bootie and the new one play like Burke. The new one goes into the hole to the tunnels and jumps back out, and Bootie runs at her. He bluffs and stomps and tries to be scary and the new one wants to try but Bootie doesn't let her. Bootie is Burke.

They rumble. It's funny. Bootie hurts her.

Fifi and Mama watch them with concern and Magda is nowhere to be found.

Burke sees Fifi, Mama and the young ones gathered and he runs at them.

Mama tries to bite him, and he grabs her by the wrist.

He wants to pull off Mama's arm and beat her with it.

He swings her by the wrist and throws her.

No one can find a scream that makes a difference.

From above they note that Ghoul walks with a limp as if his right foot has been injured.

He remembers Podo and walks like Podo in the view of Jonathan, and Jonathan cannot stand it. Mr. Ghoul limps to Fifi and Jonathan runs at him.

Mr. Ghoul crouches and tries to protect himself and hopes the hitting will stop.

Later, when Burke is asleep, Mr. Ghoul walks low to Jonathan and offers a salaam. If Jonathan would meet his gaze he would see pictures of the past.

These trees were smaller once.

Was Mr. Ghoul not one of the first to see all this.

He will not bow to impudent Burke.

He doesn't leave his bedroom for three mornings. There is no longer food inside.

Burke runs him down when he emerges. He stands over Mr. Ghoul and chases him and the older man stumbles and the ground insults his face.

He is hungry but can't eat and he sucks on his cheek and drinks the red salt.

He sits on his own. Jonathan will not let him sit with the women.

A sociogram is prepared after six months. It is clear from the graphic that Mr. Ghoul is completely isolated—the only association with others of more than ten percent is with the juveniles.

Two researchers study the sociogram and conversation drifts to family and how much it can mean sometimes just to get a phone call.

The new one ranges far from Mama now. She is broader and thinks more and more about what is beyond the wall. She goes away with Bootie to the shady grove. She wants to sit with Mr. Ghoul but Burke chases her away.

After all those years of nursing, Mama is pink again.

Jonathan watches her closely.

The World is surprised by her Apriling body, how a pale honeyed light can warm this air so sad. She quickly yearns for touch and a space beyond her daughter and no one knows what race or desolation exists on the other side of the blue.

They have all had glimpses of others in the Hard, and heard sounds from distant corridors at night. From trees they have looked over the wall and seen different fields and people.

Mama feels no choice but to turn to Jonathan. Who else can offer safety.

New flowers bloom among dry husks and the seasons mock each other.

Burke swings a heavy stick in front of Jonathan's face and Jonathan moves backwards. He grooms Burke and it seems that Burke is in the ascendant but Jonathan later runs and bluffs over him. They sit together and groom.

Mama and Fifi watch and wonder which of these pretenders will offer oa.

Where is stability.

When can we all play again.

Jonathan pins Magda, and Burke is disgusted. Bedoulerek fistpips and vulnerable noises.

Jonathan sees Mr. Ghoul trying to move towards Mama and Fifi. Burke doesn't notice. Jonathan grunts at Burke and nods towards the angling Mr. Ghoul. Burke seals the coalition with Jonathan again. He mounts him, and then walks to Mr. Ghoul. He carries a stone behind his back.

Mr. Ghoul turns in time and feels the stone come down in front of his face. His lips feel numb as he runs and now that the World no longer has mirrors he is the only one who doesn't know that his face has changed forever.

He runs to anyone, Bootie, for comfort, and Burke now chases Bootie. Mama and Fifi scream and run at Burke for bullying the younger one, and Burke is frightened for a moment. But instead of running, instead of going to Jonathan, he turns and attacks the women.

He is not as big as Jonathan but he is younger and quicker and fists will seldom catch him. Mama and Fifi scatter.

They tremble later as they bow to Burke and the past is silenced and supplanted by the present. They feel closer to Jonathan, but are frightened into paying equal respect to Burke.

As the new one walks, something stirs in Jonathan. He looks at the other women and rises above the World.

Jonathan gathers Fifi by the hips and finds oblivion. Magda is also pink and he goes to her soon after. Magda eats lettuce while Jonathan troubles her rear end.

There is sugar on the wind. Jonathan can't get enough. He pins rare Mama and his vision is sweetly blurred.

He no longer thinks of Podo. He sleeps and wakes and pins someone else and subsides into the ground like it's a cake. When he walks he is weak.

He keeps an eye out for trouble, for movements and suspicious connections, and when he sees them he sends out Burke. He is able to notice manoeuvres more keenly and quickly than Burke, and Burke is the better to stop them. They rule together.

They gather much of the food to themselves and the others grow beholden.

Mr. Ghoul eats leaves through the day. No one can touch his breakfast in his bedroom, but he doesn't feel like eating it.

Mr. Ghoul whispers salaams to Jonathan's back as Jonathan regularly walks away.

Mama and Fifi have wanted to sit with Mr. Ghoul but they are always prevented. They can no longer bear the trouble. Fifi grooms Burke. Mama and Magda bow to him in fear.

Mr. Ghoul tries to find company with the children. Mama worries that the new one will be hurt by Burke. She is happier seeing her daughter running away with Bootie than playing near lonely Mr. Ghoul.

Burke can't stand this village of weak mothers. He turns his back whenever Jonathan pins a woman. When Fifi walks away from Jonathan, Burke chases her sometimes. He hits Magda on the back. Jonathan beats Burke for doing so.

Burke sits coiled and ready to pounce. Loathsome scarlet drops drip lightly down the legs of moody women. Jonathan sleeps and drools and sits unabashedly erect. There is nowhere for Burke to turn but to the pleasures of pounding the vulnerable and weak.

Jonathan keeps trouble in view, and the trouble is coming increasingly from Burke.

They are all sore for different reasons and the World rests trapped beneath that sky.

A season passes and Jonathan awakes in the itchy bed of an estrus garden.

Everyone is turning inwards. The women sit with Jonathan but each is lost in her own pictures. They are torpid in the afternoon heat. They lazily allow themselves to be taken by Jonathan whose klopsiks seem to heave a relentless flood. The more he has the more he wants. He looks in and looks out and sees nothing but pink and he rises and swoons above the slopes of delectation.

As if by edict they have followed his example and think only of themselves. They are united but only in solitude. They sit and dream together but their private pictures tell them they are not in the right place.

The only thing that breaks the torpor, and reminds them all that there is no oa, is the temper of Burke. His shadow is over their shoulders. He has run at the women so often that when Jonathan calls on them to support him in fights with Burke, they are too afraid to do so.

Jonathan is no longer strong enough to fight Burke on his own. He needs the help of the women or Mr. Ghoul. Or he must somehow keep Burke close.

There is an outbreak of chlamydia in the colony. It is a recurring phenomenon. It may have originated from the females in the breeding program.

Four of the apes are treated with tetracycline.

A widespread respiratory infection also requires antibiotics.

One researcher says to another that it started with a bad summer cold. My husband has it.

Another says it's not really summer. It's more like late spring.

For a while a heaviness lifts. Strange tastes in the mouth disappear and everyone breathes better. Jonathan's cock no longer oozes and there are no more sneezes and sniffles.

Jonathan and Burke have naps on warm dirt and relax together when they wake.

Mama and Fifi sit quietly with the new one and Magda eats a peach.

The new one wanders.

Mr. Ghoul sits with the children. Bootie is half his size but his hugs feel good nonetheless.

twenty-nine

Not long before Looee was moved from Congo, two adolescents escaped. They were housed together in one of the cages across from Looee. A labtech came to put one of them in a transfer box and the other kicked it away on its wheels and they both sprang out.

A high-powered hose was used to contain them in the corner and one of the labtechs fired tranquilizers at them. The entire wing was flooded by the hose and the day's waste was soaked and sprayed all over the room. The wing had to be aired and cleaned, and for the first time in over a year a door at the end was opened. Congo was on the third floor of Girdish and the door was to a fire escape. A new light blew in with the breeze and smells of tarmac and oranges. Many of them pressed their faces to the front of their cages and a hoot arose in Looee which several of them echoed.

The water sprayed the nameplate on his cage and the chalk now read:

CH 447

Lonee.

Other names were washed away and there was administrative

confusion for a while. A new vet redrew Lonee's chart and for the sake of economy he omitted most of Looee's personal history.

They prepared him for transfer to the Chimpanzee Infectious Diseases Wing. CH 447. LONEE. He carried no known diseases.

The CID Wing is separate from the Girdish main building and sits on higher land. It's a Biosafety Level 2 isolation facility, equipped with an air filtration system to control airborne viruses. Lonee was squeezed into a transfer box and anaesthetized. He was left for hours near the door while staff were distracted by the death of a chimp named Fred. Lonee was taken out of Congo, conscious, and wheeled to an elevator. Two labtechs talked about the Toyotas they both owned and the lift went silent when another man entered. Looee had a view through vertical bars if he twisted his head and looked to the side.

The labtechs wheeled his box down a corridor and Looee realized he was finally going home. He moaned once like a woman surprised by how good something feels.

They went outside, the first time Looee had been out for seventeen months. The wheels struck pebbles and made the box unsteady. At first the labtechs thought it was this alone that made the animal thump against the metal, but Looee was banging his head to ensure the fresh air was real. They felt the heavier banging and looked at each other.

They wheeled him through a parking lot and up the driveway that leads to CID. Looee was banging steadily now and screaming like chimps do in the wild when they have caught a colobus monkey and are about to taste its meat.

One of them rang the buzzer and said over the intercom that they had the transfer but they needed a rifle and drugs.

The process had been delayed because of the death of Fred and it was now approaching four o'clock and most of the staff had gone home. One of the labtechs was sent back to retrieve a rifle and ketamine from the main building and Looee continued to scream.

The other stayed behind atop the hill, outside CID, and lit a cigarette. The transfer box was moving every time Lonee shifted. The labtech thought about money and friends and how his life lacked everything, and he smoked, and his thoughts were as full of feckless elbows as the chimp in the steel box. One bash from Lonee made the box roll away two feet, but the labtech reached and held the handle with his fingers.

The other ambled up the hill with a pistol and rifle. He fired the pistol through the gap in the cage and waited for someone to come out of CID.

Looee felt the familiar dislocation once the ketamine took effect. He was limp and his screams dissipated to a wheeze. He couldn't feel the eight hands on his limbs and the sky was green and sweet.

The four men held his wrists and ankles and carried him face upwards, a comrade, a carpet, a grinning deplorable truth that each of them had to ignore.

Looee smelled Judy's perfume and looked forward to his bed. He looked at the chin of the stranger who held his right wrist and reached to squeeze that pimple and his hand extended to the top of a tree and he hung there and sucked a strawberry.

The four men put Lonee on a scale and confirmed his weight at 171 pounds, thirty pounds lighter than when he arrived at Congo. They lifted him onto a table and the vet shone a light in his eyes and checked his teeth.

They dressed out in Tyvek and face masks and couldn't think of small talk.

Looee saw the top of the anteroom doors push open and heard the panic of other chimpanzees. He knew wolves had found the carcass of a fawn. Judy was in his bedroom when the four men lifted him into it. She was wearing her apron and said come on sweet boy put your feet up.

She sat on the floor and filed his toenails and he sang and she said tell me everything.

Looee sang a dirge and chuckled and spat through every confusion and showed her how his hands had swelled from banging daily on the grid that had kept them apart. She forgave him for hurting her hand and face, and she opened a sluice, and a cageful of poison poured over the floor and dawn descended from the top of the room, it was brighter here, and she held his head and neither could believe it. His body submitted to peace.

Judy held his head and they drove through a carwash and she told him to stop screaming, it was nothing to be afraid of. He was calm but all he could hear now was screaming.

Eight other chimpanzees had been pounding and hooting since the stranger was slung into his cage.

The vet of CID was usually a calming influence, but the other three men, now gone, had raised the alarm and it was hard to change the mood of that room some days.

The vet, Dr. Meijer, wrote Lonee's name and number on the blank metal nameplate with a felt-tip pen. He kept an eye on him as the ketamine peaked and subsided. Lonee was lying on his side and twitching, a visionary mute and inglorious, and his bottom lip hung low and made him look like a picture of stupidity. Dr. Meijer's depression was young but gaining strength.

Looee was looking for the key to get out of his bedroom and Judy was laughing like a dogperson.

Dr. Meijer made a round of the room, touching the backs of the fingers of those who wanted to be touched and wondering which of them he should worry about through the night.

Dr. Meijer lives in a new apartment building and has never talked to the people across the hall. Spud didn't like the look of Lonee. Rosie groomed Dr. Meijer's Tyvek suit. She was scared of what was in store and had barely noticed her new neighbour. Dr. Meijer drinks in bed every night till he is numb behind the eyes, and wonders if nature is our handmaiden.

The chimpanzees on the CID Wing were involved in several studies at once, studies involving several institutions and companies. All of the research was HIV related and most had to do with finding a vaccine to prevent the spread of the virus in humans. One of the greatest and recognized challenges was the fact that HIV had so many different strains, making a single vaccine elusive. Other challenges emerged over time.

Lonee's body was leased by Pastora, based in Paris. They also leased Dusty's, Rosie's, Nathan's and Spud's. Mac was leased by Pfintzer, and Pepper intermittently by Pfintzer, Marck and Quest. All of the chimps had various lessors over the years, all pharmaceutical companies or laboratories associated with them.

Dr. Meijer was responsible for looking after the animals' general health and administering the protocols dictated by the various institutions involved. Aside from whatever a study demanded, he would ensure that each chimpanzee was weighed every week, its teeth and nails checked, that it was fed and watered when appropriate. His team of labtechs and caregivers did much of this, but he was the one who was ultimately turned to by everyone on CID.

There were politics involved in his relationship with the researchers. Only occasionally did his name appear in the papers they published, usually in the first footnote in association with the Girdish Institute. But none of the studies would have proceeded without him—the authors knew that, and usually had to defer to him. He and the animals were the reality check to the ambitions of the researchers, many of whom never met the chimpanzees.

He was involved in every surgical procedure. He was at hand for all emergencies. He knew their idiosyncrasies, their flesh, what it was like to push the needle in.

The remoteness of the researchers allowed them to think of the chimpanzees as a crop of data, numbered bodies to be harvested for information. Dr. Meijer had to know them by name as well as number.

Girdish was a perverse abattoir where the animals were efficiently denied their death. Altogether Dr. Meijer worked there for sixteen years. When enough conversations with researchers accumulated, when he got to know each chimpanzee by character, he began to feel like a failed colonist—sent to a dark continent to exploit and find information, he fell in love with the natives and became a man without a country. In his tenth year at Girdish he stared at his hands, which were busy in the body of Rosie. She died of heart failure. He was removing tissue from her liver, brain, lymph nodes and spleen, which he would mince and send for analysis. Something about seeing his hands at their task that day made him lose all sense of whose hands they were.

Apes have hands that betray them. Last night Looee's hand tried to float away from him.

The cages on CID didn't squeeze their occupants forward to be anaesthetized. They were bigger, with bars far enough apart that you could extend your hand between them or fire a gun from outside.

When Looee awoke in the morning after being moved from Congo he hung from the bars of his cage and screamed. He screamed at all these new dogpeople, at their noises and smells and hunched despicability. He screamed at Judy and the hunger he felt, and

screamed at the screams he made, and his screams became a relentless fugue of insanity, of muscle, teeth and diarrhea responding:
and surely this was madness, this was what we are all afraid of, the
rest of us, cowering on the sidewalk while the schizophrenic with
his bags of garbage screams murder and makes all commerce and
congress quiet; he was the man on the bus who stabs at passengers'
heads with a pocketknife.

Everyone was terrified and shivering or screaming and a man in
a Tyvek suit and face shield walked in and fired a pistol at Lonee.

He was lifted onto the wheeled transfer table which was used
for most operations and was given Fluothane and atropine in the
anteroom.

Dr. Meijer had never seen teeth as good as Lonee's. And even
though his muscles had atrophied over the previous eighteen
months, he was in better physical condition than any chimpanzee
the vet had ever known. He rested a latex hand on Lonee's chest.
He's a healthy boy he said to the labtech at his side.

Dr. Meijer filed Lonee's nails, remarked on the swelling of his
hands. He took blood and told the labtech to fetch a stool sample
from the sheet beneath Looee's cage. Dr. Meijer gave him mebend-
azole for worms. He admired the texture of Lonee's hair and shaved
it off his chest to reveal his tattooed number.

The labtech marked the time in the log when Lonee came to
in his cage.

Over the coming days Looee witnessed the procedure of knockdowns. Men in Tyvek suits, sometimes one, sometimes two or
three, would come into the room and the populace would scream.
The men would walk to a cage and fire at least one pistol. The
dogperson would fall down and the men would lift it onto the table
and wheel it away while everyone screamed.

Looee felt a bit of a thrill when he saw it happen the first few times, seeing a dogperson get shot—similar to the thrill he felt when Walt shot a deer, the wonder of what will happen next. Then he felt sad and scared when the body was wheeled by him.

And once he felt it happen to himself a few times he never felt that thrill again. He moved to the back of his cage when the men walked towards him and screamed for them to go away. It was just one man at first, but Looee learned how to dodge the dart sometimes.

He had built up a tolerance for ketamine and required more than one dose to be anaesthetized. By the end of his second week two men approached his cage and there was nowhere to hide. One dart hit his lip and chipped a tooth, the other did its job.

He was weighed and got his nails cut and Dr. Meijer drew some blood.

Dusty arrived at CID soon after Looee. His body was wheeled in and lifted into the cage directly across. When Dusty awoke he was happy to see Looee, the friend he was in awe of. Looee recognized him and when Dusty reached out his hand from his cage Looee reached out his own twelve feet away.

Besides Dr. Meijer, the people who were a daily part of life on CID were the labtechs and caregivers. The caregivers were lowest on the hierarchy, divorced from the research except that they sometimes did the rounds with administering trial drugs and medicine. Their role was to keep the premises clean, to provide food and water as directed, to tag the cages before knockdowns, and to provide some sort of care to the animals in terms of enrichment or warmth or diversion. There was an enrichment coordinator, a former office manager named Pam, who determined what sort of toys were allowed, what sort of contact and for how long.

The range of personalities who worked at Girdish was as broad and varied as in any other collection of great apes. Some of the caregivers and labtechs were studying to be primatologists or clinicians. Some were there because, as they said, they loved animals. Some were simply locals, like Jerome who had grown up half a mile away from the white main building and had worked there for twenty-one years. Jerome had held a variety of jobs and had watched the institution grow, and at the peak of his abilities he reached the role of lab technician and disliked most aspects of his life except his fishing trips to the Everglades.

Some of the workers despised the animals, some thought of their jobs as nothing more than jobs, and some had their hearts broken daily.

A few of the often changing employees were young and came from all over the world, specifically to work with chimpanzees and the other apes and monkeys. They had read of some of the fascinating social research that was going on in other parts of Girdish and hoped to play a part somehow in the discovery of what it means to be an ape. Few of them ended up doing what they wanted. Most went away with ideas of only the most negative aspects of what it means to be an ape.

The caregivers and labtechs also worked in other biomedical units of Girdish, including the nursery—only a few were permanently dedicated to duties on CID. The reality of their days was often of long shifts and tedious work, of gossip and politics like most other jobs. The caregivers resented doing the dirty work and were sensitive to the arrogance of those who were there for science. The labtechs resented the occasional imperiousness of Dr. Meijer, who resented the same in the PIs. Martha, the caregiver, knew that the reason Pepper screamed at Jerome, just now as he passed by Pepper's cage, was that Pepper was about to get her period and it was really nothing personal. Jerome, who often fantasized about fucking Martha's big ass, was tired of the way she treated these animals as human. Another labtech, Simon, was sick of Jerome's negativity, and Dr. Meijer was sick of Simon's incompetence when assisting him during surgery.

The greater reality was that the work was dangerous and always ugly; a walk along CID or any other wing usually meant being spat upon, shat upon and screamed at. At best it was like working in a hospital where the patients never got better. It was a place that offered no praise.

And while there were some who truly saw it as nothing more than a job and some who never questioned the nature of apes and life, almost everyone felt a need at some point to justify this work and almost everyone had the same justification. It was for the benefit of humankind.

When it comes to disease and death, hunger and survival, there is no right or wrong. Rachel, who came from San Francisco to work at Girdish for a year while studying primatology, was aware that a bright and talented generation of men was being decimated by AIDS. Her brother was among them. She knew of the spread of the plague. She left Girdish because she couldn't stand what she saw, but signed their confidentiality agreement and told herself it was for the greater good. Those corridors and rooms of ugly industry might offer hope.

Hepatitis C. Parkinson's. Cancer. Alzheimer's.

Girdish is funded by a species trying to survive, and a country that can't get used to sadness.

The long shifts and turnover in staff meant that those few care-givers who were there for several years had little time or energy to spend more than half an hour each day trying to entertain or comfort the chimpanzees.

Jennifer was a caregiver who worked in the nursery. She had raised Dusty from birth, until he had been moved to Congo at age five; she had bottle-fed him and played with him and had grown particularly attached to him. She was sad when he moved to Congo because caregivers played a small role there. She was even more sad to hear he'd been moved to CID because she knew he would be infected with HIV.

She made an effort to come over to CID in the evenings. She had kids and a husband and a job volunteering at the hospital on the weekends, but she tried to spend half an hour with Dusty when she could. She dressed out in all the gear they had to wear on CID but took off her face shield and mask once she was inside.

Dusty liked anything rubber and was especially fond of shoes with rubber soles. After getting over their mutual excitement at seeing each other, Jennifer held her shoes up to the cage whenever she visited and Dusty smelled, groomed and chewed them.

Looee always watched from the other side. There was a nice smell when Jennifer was near. He didn't know why she always went to the dogperson and he sometimes shouted at her. He wanted her to come over but he didn't trust her either. He sat at the back of his cage and turned sideways to her, looking at her only when she had her back turned.

The chimps always hooted when someone familiar came in, and once that noise died down it was replaced by individual pleas, complaints or Bronx cheers. Looee had been taught not to spit, but it was an effective way of getting someone's attention when bars prevented movement. Jennifer expected to be spat upon or somehow harassed by the others whenever she went, and in the half-hour she could spare she tried to give everyone a little attention. But when she came to Looee's cage he sat back and ignored her.

They all figured out that when a cage was tagged it meant its occupant would soon be knocked down. Dusty's cage was tagged, as was Lonee's.

They spent a night of anxiety, and in the morning Looee watched Dusty get shot and saw his body on the table. Dusty was taken to the anteroom where Dr. Meijer used a two-pronged needle to scarify his upper back and inject him with an HIV-1 isolate as directed by the PI.

Looee watched Dusty's body getting lifted back into his cage and shouted for him to wake up. Soon he saw two pistols pointed at him through the bars of his cage. His bowels went liquid and he heard a scream and he stared at the fluorescent ceiling and thought of icing and a white couch he sat on, who loves cream, cream Christmas. He felt loving hands, warm light on his face, wanted a hand on his ass but where is it. He was turned on his side and felt a pain behind his hips that made him scream, and ketamine screams aren't heard. Dr. Meijer removed a four-inch needle from the back of Lonee's hip bone and had a clean sample of bone marrow for baseline analysis.

Lonee was a control in that study. His antibodies were measured at the same intervals as Dusty's and Nathan's, who was now HIV-positive like Dusty. Their counts were regularly measured through lymph node and bone marrow biopsy. After four months they showed positive signs of infection. Dusty and Nathan were fighting the disease.

Lonee screamed at everyone. He was unconscious regularly and felt the same disbelief each time he woke up.

Pam, the entertainment coordinator, had arranged for Lonee to be given a bucket as a toy. She had meant a plastic bucket, but he was given a metal one.

When Looee wore it on his head, the fluorescent lights turned off. He liked the sound of his breath.

Jerome and another labtech came in to knock down Dusty, and Dusty, while cowering, turned and blasted diarrhea through the front of his cage. Jerome backed up in case Dusty had more to offer and, unthinkingly, held on to a bar on Lonee's cage.

Lonee took his bucket and smashed Jerome's knuckles, rendering his fingers unusable for two weeks. When Jerome realized the pain he screamed and wheeled. He tried to use his gun with his left hand but he missed.

Lonee rang the bucket off the bars. His hair was on end and he wailed and thrashed the bucket and Jerome ducked and made a noise. Lonee awakened a fear that Jerome had always had of these animals and their fangs, and he felt humiliated for ducking.

When studies were in full swing they were all knocked down at least once a week.

Lonee now leapt at anyone who came near his cage.

Dusty and Nathan were showing few obvious outward signs of disease. They had lymph and bone marrow biopsies every two weeks at first, and every eight weeks by the end of the year.

A vaccine for that strain of HIV had been developed through earlier studies—a combination of HIV antigens and canarypox. Lonee and Spud were given the vaccine over a period of eighteen months and challenged with the same strain of HIV.

Jerome was asked by Dr. Meijer to gather a stool sample from under Lonee's cage. Lonee pissed on or screamed at Jerome whenever he could, and even though Jerome found more straight-forward revenge in various ways he cleverly gathered some of Dusty's oily stool and presented it as Lonee's.

Dr. Meijer grew worried about Lonee's health as a consequence. He gave Lonee doxycycline for an apparent bacterial infection. Lonee broke out in a rash from the unnecessary antibiotics, and there was now concern that the rash and diarrhea were signs of an unknown disease.

So for a time they insisted on stricter protocols and more

cautious behaviour on CID. This meant that when Jennifer visited she no longer took off her mask. This bewildered Dusty. He was feeling ill.

Researchers waited for results.

Mothers waited for babies.

Cities waited for better times.

Dr. Meijer made them wait for grape juice, one cage at a time. Jennifer did the same. Martha brought other treats.

When the women did their rounds, Spud climbed all over the front of the bars, stabbing his hard pink penis towards their faces like their husbands did on their birthdays. Spud was proud and playful and aching, and screamed for just one touch.

Each of them did his or her own thing, depending on who was visiting the front of the cage. Mac would always do a slow and deliberate display for Dr. Meijer, one which showed his belief that he and Dr. Meijer were both leaders, Dr. Meijer out there, Mac in here, and uneasy lies the head that wears a crown.

Rosie loved to groom and would get down as low as possible, though two feet off the ground. Dr. Meijer leaned forward and rested his white Tyvek arm for Rosie's busy fingers to clean it. Her grooming noises were frantic and she picked and rubbed at the Tyvek with a business and passion that made Dr. Meijer smile at first. He marvelled at how she could imagine all those faults and nits and concerns on that flawless piece of Tyvek. They really have imaginations. And after a while he realized that it was nothing but worry and fear. She would do him endless favours, anything he wanted, if he would only stop turning the lights on.

Right now Lonee's hand is floating, an endless salute to Dusty.

When people came to the front of Lonee's cage he either lunged at them or sat in the back corner, looking either through them or away.

Martha didn't bother lingering in front of Lonee's cage. Here's your chow you old bully.

But Jennifer always tried.

She thought of a guy in her local family restaurant. He was there most Sundays, sitting on his own. He had a way of seeing everything that was going on in the room without making eye contact with anyone. It looked like arrogance, but Jennifer figured it was insecurity and loneliness. He didn't want to be seen, but wanted to be noticed by one perfect person.

Looee watched Jennifer remove her face mask. She took off her hood and hairnet and put her arm against the cage saying I see you handsome boy, I see you. She was pretty and Looee sighed. He moved a little closer.

Jennifer pulled back the arm of her Tyvek and showed her skin to Lonee.

Pretty.

He put the back of his fingers outside his cage and she rested her skin against them. Nobody believed her when she said he was the sweetest.

He has memories. You can see them.

Sometimes when Dr. Meijer left the room, his mind stopped at the anteroom door. The wing was quiet behind him for a moment of contemplation—he was a father putting his children to bed. He thought how none of them knew when they slept that he was the one who opened their bodies and shared the diseases we were ashamed of.

Lonee was infected with a different strain of HIV. He was knocked down and it was administered intravenously at a hundred times the infectious dose.

He liked it when Jennifer visited. When she didn't come regularly he blamed her. He was harder to cajole from the corner of his cage and she had to show more skin or stay longer.

He began to display for her to impress instead of frighten, like the others did, jumping from one wall of bars to another in a rhythmic pattern, up and around like a hairy rollercoaster, and Jennifer was impressed.

He swung on the tire in the middle of his cage, thinking it might make her laugh because he was so big.

She always spent a little more time with Dusty. Looee and Dusty developed the further bond of rivals. Dusty had always admired Looee, but now Looee admired more deeply some of the things the dogperson did because Jennifer was impressed.

Dusty was good at making Jennifer feel guilty. If an irregular amount of time passed between her visits he would sulk in the corner of his cage and not look at her. She would have to stay longer and bring him sweeter treats. He got her to take off her shoes once and leave them in his cage, and he slept with them.

Lonee gestured for her to take off her mask and hood and he saw her pretty hair.

They had good dreams some nights.

Their health went up and down. Dusty was so listless sometimes that he didn't bother moving when the pistols were pointed at his cage. Looee screamed for him to get up but he only flinched when the darts hit, and slumped when the ketamine took effect.

Lonee was too angry to be listless.

Needles went blunt on his bones.

Frank and Simon watched through the window of the anteroom door sometimes. Lonee spinning, Lonee holding the bars and shaking his cage getting all the rest of them agitated.

Simon had been raised by an uncle who drank too much and backhanded him, and Simon had gone to school some days with ears swollen and lips inflamed. Lonee made Simon nervous.

And when Lonee wasn't angry he was sad and bored because

when there were no knockdowns, no visits, no deaths, there was absolutely nothing to do but sit and think and remember.

Dreams of a house and Larry. A horrible night. He was closest to death when memories were strongest. They flashed and changed. What was Larry's name. These days of torture are the same as mummy's screams. He remembered Jennifer, and saw her, and didn't know whether he was remembering her or not, and there were things he didn't want to remember. He screamed and spun not only to get out of his cage but to get the memories out as well. His habits became an unconscious discipline, a way to find oblivion.

Sometimes Jennifer put her hand in his cage, which she was not supposed to do. Once a chimp has a hold of you, he won't let go until he doesn't want a hold of you, till he's hurt you or used you for whatever it was he wanted.

Don't wear shoelaces. Tie your hair in a bun and keep it under the hood. No necklaces. Wear nothing they can get a hold of.

The cardinal rule at any institution containing chimpanzees is to lock the doors.

Posted at every exit in Girdish was HAVE YOU CHECKED THE LOCKS. Padlocks were ubiquitous—on cage doors, transfer boxes, fridges, cabinets—and the protocol was to make sure each was secure and hanging straight downwards. A glance back over a room you left would be satisfied if every padlock was hanging straight downwards.

And every time the lights came on in the morning on CID, a glance would find every lock askew. In fact, every worker at Girdish in every corner of the buildings over its long history would tell you that last night the chimps had tested the locks.

They tested them throughout the day, whenever a back was turned, and every night when the lights went out. Those dark eyes in cages saw everything. Over the years there had been many escapes, but rarely on the smaller wings like CID.

Cages were cleaned every thirty days, each of the ten cages on a fixed schedule. The outside doors at the opposite end of the wing were opened and some mouthfuls of fresh air came in along with the fumes of a forklift. The occupant of the cage to be cleaned was knocked down and manoeuvred into a transfer box. The forklift removed the cage from its mooring on the wall and took it outside, and the chimp in the transfer box was wheeled out with it. The cage was hosed on the driveway and a caregiver would wash the back wall where the cage had hung, mopping away the artless finger-painting that each of them did with their shit. Each chimp had a monthly moment outside and they were usually anaesthetized lightly because the process rarely took more than twenty minutes.

The outside doors opened and the forklift appeared. Jerome came out of the anteroom and shot Lonee. Jerome recorded the time and he, Simon, Frank and Martha lifted Lonee out of the cage, struggled to get him in the transfer box which they righted on its wheels. Simon pushed the box outside and the forklift came in and removed the cage. Martha mopped the wall.

Ten minutes later Lonee was loose and the general alarm sounded, and every door and window across the hundred acres of the Girdish Institute was locked.

Simon had closed the padlock on the box, but the lock was rusty and what felt like a catch was the shifting of grit. The ketamine did little more than make Looee think of bubble gum when he was wheeled outside. Cherries in the air and metal pink and chewy. He looked through the gap and watched his cage getting hosed like Murphy after the skunk.

His fingers reached around through the gap and felt the lock. They pulled and the lock came loose.

He stood upright on the driveway and fell over. He wanted to get to a telephone or at least as far as the Wileys' house.

Simon was looking at the forklift driver and finding him kind of sexy. He thought of Richard, his ex, and how good he was at fixing the car and the coffee-maker—anything mechanical.

Looee smelled the tarmac. He got up on all fours and ran, and dreamt that he was running, and nothing looked familiar but he felt like he was home.

Simon was hosing the cage. He looked idly towards the transfer box and saw its door ajar. He cried for help and held the spraying hose like a bayonet.

Girdish had had a long and fragile understanding with the municipality and county that they would keep the strictest control of their premises, and that they would call the police if any of the animals escaped. Not only were the animals dangerous on their own but many of them carried infectious and fatal diseases.

Once Simon radioed in to CID, the central call went out to all corridors of Girdish. Labworkers locked their doors. At the field station they looked outside and counted, and all of them were there.

Internal policy was to call the police only after thirty minutes of not finding an animal. The police had killed a gorilla several years earlier and the institution got too much of the wrong attention in the press. Animals were to be darted, or ideally coaxed back into a cage by someone familiar to them like a caregiver.

Few of those who escaped ever went far beyond the walls because most of them knew this as home. They sought out cafeterias or comfortable hideaways within the grounds or buildings. When a baby crawls away she always looks back for her mother.

Looee was at the bottom of the hill, looking for a telephone. He moved in spurts and collapsed, and sprang up again like a push puppet. The footage later showed that he was stumbling in circles on the driveway before he made his final run.

Simon had been certain that Lonee was hiding and that he would leap at someone like he did in his cage. He went inside. Jerome was out with a rifle. Jennifer had been called as someone who might encourage Lonee back inside.

Forty minutes passed and the police were cautiously notified. The minimum physical value of a chimpanzee to Girdish was fifty thousand dollars—that was what they could sell them for if other labs were interested; but the information a study animal like Lonee contained was invaluable. Girdish wanted its trained employees to capture him, but the institute was obligated to inform the police of all likely dangers associated with the animals.

Once word was out that the escaped chimpanzee was HIV-positive, the police had orders to shoot to kill.

Florida Animal Control was notified as a matter of course. Their preferred trapper in that county was Wade Henderson, who knew how to catch everything from alligators to bobcats.

Jennifer looked around from outside CID with her hand shading her eyes.

Looee walked into the diner and climbed onto the counter. He took a glass and ran cold water into it and wanted to meet the other customers. He liked the waitress and wanted to lie back while she rubbed her ass on his balls. He smelled bacon and burning onions and he drooled.

Simon watched from the side windows of the anteroom as the security staff moved down the driveway. They were met by others coming up.

Staff had fanned out in all directions. The guard at the gatehouse had seen nothing pass, but the perimeter fence was no obstacle for a chimpanzee.

Wade Henderson assembled his collars and guns and drove towards Girdish with no idea of how to capture an ape.

Police patrol cars were scoping a one-mile radius and focusing on the businesses along Jackson Avenue, which was busy with a lunchtime crowd. The chimpanzee would likely not travel far and would probably search for food sources.

Looee tugged on the trouser leg of one of the customers at the diner. He wanted help. The man stood stiff as a tree. Looee stood upright and came to the man's shoulders. Everyone in the diner was still. Looee looked around and saw nobody familiar. He had never been here before. He felt frightened, and when he called and showed his teeth everyone flinched and the man said okay, sweet boy, it's okay.

Looee looked around for a telephone and went back to the sink for more water. He was dying for a strawberry milkshake and made loud calls which upset the customers all the more. Dust blew into his eyes.

The public relations staff at Girdish were beginning to be concerned and the director was briefed. For the most part, people drove by the gates of Girdish with no idea of what went on inside. There were occasional flare-ups with animal rights activists but most of those people did not live locally. Girdish had managed to exist quietly, a business like any other, rarely troubling the local community—the escaped gorilla had been quickly absorbed into the lore of alligators in swimming pools and other Floridian oddities. But Lonee's escape could easily shut them down. They urged the police to be as discreet as possible.

The police walked into restaurants carrying rifles and asked proprietors if they had seen a big monkey.

Jennifer could do little more than pace. Jerome was wandering the grounds. He knew how much ketamine he had given Looee.

And Looee's mouth was dry. The light through the windows was so bright. Genuine, painful sunlight that he hadn't felt in years. He couldn't see anyone for a moment and wanted to find a corner to be sick in. The countertop felt like heated dirt and he smelled women and licked metal and wanted milkshakes, strawberries, that's a spoon. He hadn't moved like this in years.

He slept while Wade Henderson spoke to the sheriff. Wade had a prosthetic arm.

The sheriff's radio was full of chatter. An officer had shot a black bag of garbage in the alley behind Annie's diner.

Looee remembered about menus. He found one on the floor that felt like dry leaves and pointed at a tiny picture of something that looked like a milkshake. He looked over his shoulder to the waitress. She was pretty in white but scary. He looked at the menu but it had blown away and he looked again over his shoulder at the waitress who looked exactly like Jerome.

While the search first concentrated on the driveway and then spread out, Jerome had a hunch that Looee wouldn't be far. He helped with checking the kitchens and cafeteria, then wandered to the south of CID. There was a grove of poplar trees on the grounds near the storehouse that seemed a likely place to look. He watched Lonee falling over and babbling, using the trees to pull himself up.

Jerome had waited awhile, had watched Lonee sleep, and he thought about options. He stood not far behind Lonee and aimed the rifle, and the dart pierced a testicle with no satisfying pop.

Lonee was slung into the back of a short-bed pickup and driven to CID.

Jennifer transferred from the nursery to CID. She wanted to be close to Dusty. She arrived at seven most mornings and manually turned on the light.

She looked at the protocol book to see who should eat and what procedures were planned for the day, and she went from cage to cage to note how much each had eaten through the night.

She fetched the food bucket—a yellow plastic garbage can on wheels—and for those who weren't scheduled for knockdowns she opened each feeder and poured out two scoops of chow. The room was filled with food grunts and hoots, even from the sickly. At lunch she came around with fruit and water and noticed their barks, uniquely reserved for the prospect of fruit.

The next and last meal was at 3 PM, and most of the staff went home. Dr. Meijer arrived and left late.

Jennifer was allowed to visit during the evening. The lights went off automatically at eight. If she was late she sometimes turned on the anteroom light, which suffused through the main wing like the light around bedtime stories.

Lonee wasn't sleeping and his hand had started to float. Jennifer thought they were connecting some nights, those intelligent eyes of his reaching out, but he would suddenly look away or attack his hand. He was pulling off his nails.

When he seemed lucid he sometimes came to her at the front of the cage and lay on his back. He pulled his feet back and looked at her through his legs while he felt his diminished scrotum. It had been more than a year since his testicle was removed.

They were all now chronically infected with HIV. The progress of the virus in chimpanzees was not yet fully understood. Biopsies showed that they were clearly infected, and clearly fighting infection, but the outcome of the infection was a mystery.

It had been decided that Dusty would be superinfected with several strains at once.

Jennifer got a special dispensation from the entertainment coordinator to bring a television and VCR into the wing. She wheeled both on a trolley to the far end, and at moments when there were no scheduled procedures they all craned their necks and watched.

Lonee wanted to show everyone that he knew how to use the remote control. Jennifer couldn't understand why he was jumping and displaying so loudly and said you really are a moody boy. They watched Three Men and a Baby.

Dr. Meijer felt like he no longer could tell anyone about his work. He could barely talk to colleagues.

Rosie was eating her own shit, to savour and savour again the food that was each day's only diversion. She was growing obese and Dr. Meijer knew neither how nor why to stop it. Staff were instructed to keep a careful eye on her whenever she returned from a knockdown. They stood near her cage with broomsticks to prod her in case she slumped and choked.

At night when Jennifer visited, Lonee played a song for her, rattling the door of his cage rhythmically, repeatedly, a metal song of train tracks shivering under maniac commuters. Jennifer took her hair out of her hood and danced like an idiot.

She told Dr. Meijer she couldn't do it anymore. I'm either going to quit or I'm rescuing every one of them.

Protests outside the main site became fervent, and some of the labs were broken into. Macaques were freed to the Florida suburbs and a labworker beaten by activists till he trusted no one ever again.

When Dr. Meijer performed the autopsy on Rosie, he determined heart failure to be the cause of death, but her liver was in pieces and dispersed around her body. He stared at a print of a seashell in his office and couldn't remember where or why he got it or why anyone would make it and his lungs felt full of snow.

Research had slowed and the wing was like a hospice for eighteen months.

But Dusty's death prompted a renewed interest in HIV studies. As the years had passed there were very few publishable results. Some vaccines seemed to work on some of the chimpanzees, but none could cover every strain. And some that were safe for chimpanzees ended up being pernicious in human trials. There was accumulating doubt about whether the experience of the disease was the same for chimps and humans.

As a consequence, funding for many studies dried up and there was talk of closing CID. But Dusty's superinfection eventually developed into symptoms like those of full-blown AIDS.

After five years of infection, his diarrhea became fulminant and relentless. He was treated with five different antibiotics and showed little response. Cryptosporidium was rampant in his intestines, and it was this which the researchers called "AIDS-defining" in their paper. He wasn't treated with any antiretroviral drugs, as some of the others were, because the researchers wanted to see how the virus progressed.

Jennifer watched his weight go up and down. After a year she no longer wished he would rally. She spent a night on the floor by his cage thinking it would be his last, but he made it through hundreds more. In their night sweats and fevers Lonee and Dusty called mournfully to each other like neuters across a chapel.

Dr. Meijer began insisting to the PI that they euthanize Dusty. The PI, after consulting with his peers, told Dr. Meijer to wait and perform a blood transfusion. They had found that the virus they had isolated from Dusty's blood was different from what he had been inoculated with—it had undergone a genetic mutation. A new quasipecies of HIV had developed in Dusty's body and they wanted to see now how other chimpanzees reacted to it.

Lonee was knocked down and 40 mL of Dusty's blood were transfused into him intravenously.

Dusty was killed when his weight dropped to thirty-five pounds. He weighed less than Jennifer's six-year-old son, who was ten years Dusty's junior.

Altogether, Lonee spent fourteen years in those cages.

Jennifer resigned.

Lonee saw and smelled her in the dark sometimes with the tall men Walt and Larry, with rainstorms and meatsmells and friendship and lipstick: all of them bugs in the woodwork, distractions from the sleeping that had to be done.

thirty

Mr. Ghoul is led into a room with a plekter wall and the room is dark in the corners. On the other side, a yek appears. He walks oddly.

Mr. Ghoul sits. He doesn't challenge the yek. He watches.

The yek is sitting in a corner. He looks around the room.

Mr. Ghoul moves closer to the plekter. He looks for something in the room to play with. He sees something on the floor, moves to it and holds it up, as much for the yek's analysis as his own.

It's a tooth.

They both stare at it.

Mr. Ghoul shows his teeth briefly to the yek to remark on the fact that it's a tooth. The yek does not move.

At midnight through a high window, a star shines so dimly. Sometimes it doesn't seem like it is there, but Mr. Ghoul knows it is.

The yek doesn't move or make a sound. He is black in the corner. Mr. Ghoul keeps holding the tooth. Something about it pricks the darkness of the yek.

There is no fear in that room.

Mr. Ghoul stares at him.

Quiet star. Silver coin in a dirty pond.

All of them meet the yek. Some are brought in separately, some in groups. Fifi, Mama and the new one are brought in together. The yek watches from the corner. The women and the girl are eager to meet him.

Fifi turns in a submissive posture, but the yek doesn't move from the corner.

They clap, as Podo used to clap, to initiate a skrupulus. They groom, and the new one gestures towards the yek, inviting him to come closer to the plekter.

He stays.

Lonee sleeps.

Dusty's malignant blood fizzed and mixed with his own.

He sleeps for two years while his muscles melt, and once the pain has climaxed he enjoys the deliquescence. He will flood the floor and suffer no longer.

Bill the labtech is transferred from Congo to CID and recognizes Lonee as Looee, though he can't believe that it's the same animal. He corrects the name on Looee's chart and asks: remember me, old soldier.

No papers are published. Nothing can be gathered from his body's data except that a massive infection has come and gone.

There is no final submission. For months he feels more than ever as if he is floating. Two feet above the ground for fourteen years, this aluminum air has become the new earth.

He rallies and sits and can adjust his posture now when the

bars dig into his ribs. The knockdowns have stopped. He misses the ketamine.

There is something about having shared this space with the others—all the dogpeople screaming, succumbing and surviving. Dusty and Rosie are now long gone, their cages never filled, but the others have hung on. Looee survives by watching the others surviving. They have always called in support and screamed at the men with guns. Each of them is isolated, but looking around for all these years they feel that no one is alone. Looee screamed with the rest of them, felt jealousy and sympathetic joy when the others had their cages cleaned. He has yearned for touch, and died like everyone else.

New caregivers tie colourful streamers to the corners of the wing and bring balloons. They give everyone a piece of cake. Looee eats his and Mac makes noises of delight so excessive and pure that the caregivers remember that moment for years.

HIV research on chimpanzees has grown too costly and inconclusive. The CID Wing is to be closed. The chimps will be sent to other laboratories.

Dr. Meijer does what he can. The placements are dictated by the arbitrary needs of strangers, but most of the chimps will escape these cages. Pepper, Spud and Nathan are sent to sanctuaries in Quebec and Louisiana, others are sent to Spain and Uganda. Mac endures ten more years of biomedical testing in New Mexico. Looee remains at Girdish.

He is knocked down and transported in a van for half a mile to the field station.

He is kept in a concrete room with bars on one side and is brought vegetables and fruit.

David Kennedy says let's get you healthy.

He puts a television in front of the bars and Looee watches footage of a group of dogpeople in an outdoor enclosure. Looee wonders where their cages are.

Another man comes to the bars and offers Looee grape juice. As Looee sucks on the straw, the man masturbates him with a long-handled device. Despite his missing testicle his sperm is adequate and motile.

He is given blankets and toys and he sleeps.

He dreams of a garden with a tall blue wall.

He dreams of bananas, watermelon and strawberries.

He doesn't trust this space but he is dreaming.

No one knows if he is aware of what a dream is.

A woman points to the TV screen and says that's Magda ... that's Jonathan ... that's Bootie.

Looee wants her to talk to him all day.

He attacks his hand sometimes.

He is led into the room they have always used for introductions. It is divided in two by a wall of iron mesh so the chimps being introduced are unable to hurt each other.

He sits in the corner so his back is protected and he can see anyone coming with a gun. A low door opens from the outside and two dogpeople come into the room on the other side of the mesh.

Bootie sees Looee and barks in alarm. His hair stands on end and he goes to Magda for support.

Bootie reminds him of Dusty.

Magda comes up to the mesh. She looks deep into the corner while Bootie makes a racket behind her.

Magda looks hard at Looee and barks. She's what Larry would have called an asshole.

Stencilled memories of a past long gone take colour for a

moment and Looee is overcome with fear and sadness. He pushes hard into the corner wall.

They feed him parsnips, lettuce and red peppers. They fill a rubber hose with peanut butter and he occupies himself with sucking it out.

David Kennedy sits on a chair. He watches Looee eat. He senses vulnerability and defiance, some otherworldly wisdom. He feels irrationally drawn to this injured chimp like students are to certain teachers. Charisma is one of those forces that unite us with other apes. Alphas, male or female, are those who attract others to them, sometimes regardless of what is said or done.

He thinks about sending Looee out into the colony, an emissary of sorts. David hasn't had any physical interaction with them for over fifteen years.

Looee will be killed if he joins the colony now. Some of the males will have to be sequestered. There will have to be introductions.

David feels a strength in his hands as he watches Looee, an unconscious force that he reflects on later. A shared determination.

He wants Looee to be strong. He wants to see if others feel his charm.

Looee gains weight and gathers strength. His hips and legs are permanently damaged from being in the cage for so long.

Burke comes into the introduction room looking massive and invincible. He paces his half of the room, several times with purpose around the perimeter. He pounds on the low iron door with room-shaking strength. It slides up and he walks outside.

Jonathan is in the room when Looee is next brought in. He fills the room with sounds that make Looee shudder, but they continue for so long that Looee eventually relaxes.

Looee sits in the corner and watches the rangy dogperson leap around the room. Jonathan hangs from the mesh and pisses and his penis surges and flags.

He holds a low pipe that protrudes from the wall, too low for him to swing around it. He moves to and fro and tries to break the pipe and he jumps again onto the mesh and screams.

Where Burke walked, Jonathan runs, pounding randomly on the walls, and there seems to be no end to his mania.

He runs unseeing into the pipe mouth-first and knocks himself backwards and flat.

Looee meets Mr. Ghoul the same day, who finds Jonathan's tooth on the floor.

He watches Mr. Ghoul walk out to a sunny garden. Looee has been naked for years but not outside.

When food is brought to him later he tries to tell the man that he wants clothes.

The new one waits outside the door some days. She wants to see the yek again.

Jonathan watches her with suspicion. She has grown and is beginning to ripen. Jonathan sits with Burke and they groom each other.

Mr. Ghoul is trying to rest. Burke had hit him so hard yesterday that he cannot see properly and he has trouble standing.

Jonathan and Burke allow him to pay them obeisance but there is no benefit to him.

After all this time Jonathan occasionally thinks that Podo will emerge from the shady grove and he tries to keep them all from going in. The new one looks in and tries to understand. Bootie goes to Burke when the others go into the grove. He wants Burke to like him so he acts as an informant.

When Jonathan and Burke are having naps, the others feel more free. Fifi and Mr. Ghoul have snuck into the grove together. There is a single cure for most fear and worry, one answer to most questions. Their sounds blow birds into the sky.

Jonathan awakes, and when he sees them coming out of the grove and knows they have been together he screams as if a thick stick is being forced up his ass. He pounds the ground and cries like a child.

Jonathan has been throwing these tantrums more and more. He knows he can't hit Fifi because she and Mama will turn on him, and if he attacks Mr. Ghoul right now it will be the same as beating Fifi.

Burke will not console him through his tantrum. The new one goes to Jonathan and hugs him from behind. Closer to childhood, she understands his behaviour better than the others. The spectacle of Jonathan being hugged from behind by the girl makes Burke feel powerful.

Burke later beats Mr. Ghoul and runs at Fifi as she tries to sit with Mama. He and Jonathan sit apart, the older man looking over his shoulder and trying to look big.

The same cast of animals enters the room over the coming weeks and Looee watches them on TV. There are long periods of stillness interrupted by noisy fights, and he doesn't understand what happens.

He gets stronger but David remarks his many tics. Looee's stare grows absent and he has pulled off some of his fingernails.

David thinks it's a good idea to let him out into the enclosure on his own so he gets a real sense of it. If the others are around he will be attacked.

They keep the night cages locked in the morning so the others can't go outside. Looee is brought to the outdoor side of the introduction room. The low iron door is raised and the sun shines in horizontally.

Looee walks tentatively to the doorway. He sits down beside it, looking back into the room, and he won't go outside. He stares at the rectangle of sun on the floor and feels the room warm up.

He wants to go back to his cell.

He hears local birds and cicadas making sounds he has never heard. He peers out and sees the beautiful garden he has seen on TV. He can't see any of the dogpeople.

He stands on the concrete ledge and leans forward, touching the dirt with his knuckles. He doesn't understand whether this is television or not.

Fresh air blows softly into his face and something awakens. He sits back and breathes and stares out at the sunny garden. He cautiously sighs, a pensive ape in a concrete frame. A camera captures him looking out from the doorway, a postcard from one of evolution's abandoned neighbourhoods.

David has had the courage to touch his hands through the bars. He sensed that Looee is comfortable with people and surmises that he spent time in a human environment. His records have long been lost.

We trust each other. I tell him that. I trust you Looee.

I bet you could tell me stories.

Looee's eyes follow him, and look away before David turns to leave.

He willingly enters transfer boxes and presents his limbs for injection.

He has been broken.

David believed that there was value in trying to communicate with other apes, but that more could be gained by trying not to fit them into human culture. Seeing how they communicated among themselves seemed a less narcissistic sort of inquiry than trying to make them communicate with us.

He and his staff have thousands of hours of video footage and volumes of meticulously noted interactions, upon which hundreds of papers have been generated—papers on customs, politics, empathy, conflict, child-rearing, personality, topics so far-reaching that he is often invited to speak at conferences that ostensibly have nothing to do with chimpanzees.

Occasionally they test social behaviour in various ways—dropping melons or nutritious foliage into the enclosure, for example, to see whether they share and what sort of conflict arises. For the most part they try to let life unfold without interference.

Outdoors there are five acres of land including several species of trees. The climate is so like their natural habitat that there is seldom need for prolonged indoor housing, but their sleeping quarters are easily modified in the winter.

A concrete wall surrounds part of the enclosure, with two observation posts. Its base is moated because chimpanzees cannot swim and are generally afraid of water. At the end is an electrified fence. One of the old sweetgum trees, which could provide escape over the wall, has also been electrified.

The population has largely been static—most of the babies were delivered in clinic and taken away for other studies in Girdish. This is one of the institute's longest-running projects.

He responds to the name Looee but sometimes wonders whom people are calling. He remembers Looee, who lived in a house.

They no longer introduce the apes by name. The female born in the colony to Mama was never named, though the staff call her Beanie. David points out, obviously, that names don't exist in the wild. I wouldn't be David if my grandmother hadn't been Welsh.

Looee walks tentatively out into the sun.

Jonathan runs and throws a handful of shit at him.

Looee retreats inside and they make the iron door slide down.

He goes to the corner and tries to sleep.

A system of tunnels is controlled from within.

During power struggles and times of uncertainty, fights can escalate to the point of fatality. Individuals and groups are carefully monitored. As much as the staff try to keep their hands off, they don't want them to die.

Looee is anaesthetized and moved to the sleeping quarters. He wakes up in a very large cage with a concrete floor. It is nine feet tall with an elevated platform. There is room to nest on the floor or on the platform.

The iron grids are broadly spaced and there are large high windows and skylights in the room. A catwalk traverses the cages and leads to the various tunnels. The cages are opened or closed with electric locks. The chimps amble at will along the catwalk and find their own cages.

When Looee wakes up he finds new blankets and a GI Joe doll.

His cage is where Podo last slept.

He is excited by the prospect of sunshine but is nervous about being naked outside. He knows that even on warm days the mountains share their chill with the valleys and campfires are needed in the woods.

He finds his way nervously through a tunnel, touches the dirt and feels grass and sun. Hot sun and summer smells.

Jonathan and Magda see the yek emerge and they raise the alarm. Magda screams and throws her hands in the air and runs to the women and Bootie.

Looee sees a dogperson running at him and it looks like he won't stop. It's the crazy one who lost the tooth. He gets hit and is scared despite feeling that he shouldn't be afraid of these animals. He cowers while he is hit, and then runs.

Jonathan runs after him but not to catch him. Jonathan makes sure that others are backing him. He watches the yek stop running at the bank of the pokol-fear.

Looee looks at all of them screaming and bustling. He is weak and sweating. He scoops water from the moat into his hands and drinks. He quickly plunges his head underwater like Walt taught him when they went fishing.

They watch him emerge from doing what no one has done and they scream and Magda hugs Jonathan. He jumps and screams and runs to others for a touch of hands.

Looee looks at a nearby eucalypt, the likes of which he has never seen. He pulls his broken body up the branches.

Jonathan hools and drums the base of the greybald tree and knows he can climb but doesn't. He runs through the rest of them and hits Mr. Ghoul and shows the World who truly sits atop it. His violent run stirs many and Mama is in ¡harag!

She hates the men's constant abuse of Mr. Ghoul, and the presence of the yek is a brief new perspective, a momentary catalyst for correcting the state of the World. Soon there is a fight involving six of them.

Above the noise, no violence worse than that of his adult life, Looee sways on a naked branch, a fruit reclaimed by the sun. As the fight plays out and some uneasiness flares about this strange new space below, he feels the heat on his face and smells fresh air.

He sees fields and buildings and cars and people. No one can see his face.

He sways at the top and the tree nods and dips like an absurd and sage old dancer. The long melancholy sound like wind through wide pipes is Looee's nervous song of joy, too soft for anyone to hear.

Mr. Ghoul's bedroom is next to the yek's. He wants to show him that you can fold back the upper platform and have more space.

Everyone has underestimated Burke. He has grown faster, cannier and stronger by the year. They redraw the hierarchy and sociograms and wonder how the introduction of Looee will affect the colony.

Burke and Jonathan corner the yek at the wall of the Hard and they beat him, fists like axes to wood.

There is a dedicated infirmary to deal with illness and injury. Both are carefully monitored but selectively treated. The chimps help each other and have learned to indicate when other help is needed. Some of them are able to apply ointment on themselves or others.

The philosophy of the project, though altered over time, is to see how these apes behave when they are well fed, well housed and benefit from medical care, but the latter is only offered when injury or illness is grave.

Video footage shows Ghoul sitting by Looee's inert body as he had with Podo.

Staff were alerted and Looee was taken to the infirmary. Three of his ribs were broken, a lung was punctured, and his face had several lacerations.

The facial injuries are left unstitched because such wounds are common and heal surprisingly quickly.

There is a television in the infirmary where they play Sesame Street and Gorillas in the Mist.

Looee is strapped to a bed at forty-five degrees. There is television and good food and when he is not sedated he spends much of the time in a tethered panic.

For these, his past, and most of the rest of his days, he does not know where he is. A diplomat's son.

He is not Looee. He is not a number. He is not he without others to need and define him.

There is a truth in every corner of Girdish. Every ape has a home and leaves it; every ape is lost without other apes.

He wants to climb again in that warm sun to verify that all the mountains have truly disappeared.

When he is returned to his cage, his neighbour is repeatedly raising and lowering his platform bed, and pointing to a board with symbols on it.

Looee wearily pushes the platform bed against the cagewall and feels there is much more space. He makes a nest on the floor with his blankets.

Mr. Ghoul is lazily, autistically, pointing at the symbols for up and window and vodka, meaning that when the bed is up you can look through the windows at the moon.

Looee relaxes on his blankets despite the noises of others. Fourteen years of nightmares have made this warm and easy.

He nonetheless has nightmares. He wakes in the middle of the night, sweating and screaming and believing that labtechs are aiming at him with guns.

Mr. Ghoul and several others wake up and wish that Looee would be quiet.

*

In front of each of their cages is a trolley with a small supply of food. They reach out and take what they want. In the morning they go outside as they please. A large quantity of food is laid out for them in the vestibule and outside the tunnel doors, so they are usually motivated to leave the sleeping quarters.

Cameras film their behaviour during these communal feeding sessions. Who eats first, who shares with whom, what conflicts result and how are they resolved.

Looee's liver and kidneys are damaged from the years of biomedical challenges and his appetite wavers. He is often nervous and nauseated and eats things selectively. He only eats the skin of apples. The clinical staff know that the skin is rich in quercetin and is good for the liver. They know that Looee doesn't know this, of course, and they ask if all knowledge is truly seated in the brain.

For weeks he tries to avoid everyone. He feels simultaneously superior and nervous.

Several of them make threatening gestures at him whenever they can. He is frightened of Jonathan and Burke and knows they will attack him again. Yet he is also not frightened of them. He feels their fists and feet but they also don't seem real.

They attack him again and he runs away. He has nowhere to turn. He runs up the electrified tree and feels warm while his memory and emotions are cleaned, reordered and toasted. The dogpeople are all screaming below him. He jumps down carrying a charge and he is insensitive to the fact that perceptions of him are changing.

Fifi wants him.

He runs and sits and doesn't know how to fight.

*

The ache for oa is universal. The arrival of the yek has provided some diversion but there is also even more instability.

The women don't support Jonathan because they can no longer bear the pointed reprisals of Burke. His vigilance is greater than Jonathan knows. Jonathan writhes on the ground having far too many tantrums and they are all unwilling or afraid to give him comfort.

They feel that they are always being watched. Every movement can meet with Burke's or Jonathan's disapproval. Nothing can be done without consideration. Fear is in the air, even for Jonathan now as he tries to keep the women in his fold. Burke stands big whenever Jonathan makes overtures to someone. He stands over Magda when she leans forward for Jonathan. He seems twice the size of both of them. She bows low and trembles and Jonathan aches while the union is thwarted.

It is to this increasingly sexless place that Looee has arrived. Some are sympathetic to the fear of others and some are vigilant of misdeeds—eager to report the errors of others to win favour from Jonathan or Burke. There is skulking and looking over shoulders and constant silent scheming. Nothing grows but fear—desire won't take root.

When Looee was on the CID Wing, he spent so long trying to survive that his sexual desire has effectively disappeared. He has breathed an air of fear more concentrated than this.

There could be a release. He could feel an opening here. But the dogpeople are as unattractive to him as the mothers are to Burke. Something stirs when he is allowed a glimpse of the researchers. Nail polish. Bermuda shorts. Like Dusty, he has developed an attraction to rubber and he ejaculates when he thinks of smelling a boot.

Burke squirts white when he sleeps. Fists, teeth, dying screams from the daughters of loose mothers. He pounds on Bootie who himself has grown into this taboo World of a sister and men and frequent masturbation.

Mr. Ghoul has escaped with Fifi to the grove but the appointments grow more costly and less possible. Everyone is watching, wanting to join or wanting to report. Jonathan's constant arousal has to be somehow hidden from Burke and there are times when he must use his hands to cover his urgent and telltale twig.

Looee has arrived in Berlin.

The new one shows an irrepressible interest in him.

He walks like a dog and is naked and he can't believe the weather.

He is always the last to leave in the morning. He likes sleeping in and wants to avoid the communal breakfast, like anyone intelligent who stays at a B&B.

He craves the fresh air, and when he is outside he sits with his back to the wall of the building. The wall gets hotter in the sun as the day progresses, and he moves. He keeps his side or back to things whenever possible.

He has realized that Burke is the one to be afraid of. He knows that others are watching him and he tries not to make eye contact with anyone.

He isn't able to distinguish them all yet. When he sees them alone he sometimes can't remember who is who, but when some are together he can tell the difference.

Fifi is very fat. She seems to be gesturing for him to come over all the time, but she does it furtively and doesn't look directly at him.

Burke is obvious because his hair is always on end and the others seem constantly aware of what he is doing.

Looee moves if any of them come close, and he moves especially quickly if Burke or Jonathan approaches. He makes the effort to climb a tree.

The view is endless and reassuring.

He watches people on the roof of the building and on the observation posts. They come and go and eat sandwiches. Occasionally they throw things down, watermelons and bundles of sticks, and they point a camera at the pandemonium below. Looee watches with an arrogant eye and they point the camera at him. He is tempted by the watermelon.

He looks down and watches the dogperson who sleeps in the cage next to his. Mr. Ghoul finds a piece of watermelon that nobody has noticed. He quickly buries it. When noise dies down he goes to the edge of a thick group of bushes and trees and raises an alarm. He looks into the dark and hollers and the others are all curious. Burke runs in with some others and while everyone is occupied with the fiction in the grove, the dogperson comes back to eat his buried fruit in peace.

Looee thinks this is smart. His neighbour looks up to him in the tree. He holds up a piece as if he is offering it to Looee or is acknowledging that he has been caught.

The only tangible legacy of language research at Girdish, besides published papers neglected by the academy, is the piece of cardboard printed with lexigrams which Mr. Ghoul keeps in his cage.

Mama is the only other who was conversant with those symbols but she has been too busy with motherhood and negotiating the weakness of men, and she was never as good with the language as Mr. Ghoul was.

He offers things to the yek through their shared wall. He points to the pictures for Visitor and friend and he lists various things that he has eaten today.

Looee sleeps as much as he can. He feels safest in his night cage, but can't stop fearing the approach of men with guns.

The grids between the adjoining cages are much larger than those in the distant dark of Congo. Like Dusty, the dogperson next to Looee passes objects to him through the grid. He can also extend his hand into Looee's cage.

Bootie is in the bedroom next to Mr. Ghoul and Mama is next to Bootie. Mama can see through to Mr. Ghoul and the yek but can't reach them. She watches Mr. Ghoul moving around and muttering and tapping on pictures.

Mr. Ghoul's hand is dangling in Looee's cage, hanging and waving.

Come here.

The researchers note that some of the females are carrying their pink swellings around like yesterday's luxury.

For Mama, hope still drifts and struggles like a butterfly in the wind. She looks for change and sees it in her daughter and she wonders about the yek.

When she is pink she feels vulnerable. She wants someone to sit with.

Mr. Ghoul feels a protective urge towards her but he can never get near her.

Mama sees his back in his bedroom and wonders what he is doing with the yek. She finds the yek more interesting the longer Mr. Ghoul has his back turned.

And Looee remembers Larry.

He remembers his friend trying to get in his way and lock him in his house when he wanted to see Susan. Larry so brittle and weak.

Looee barks and Mr. Ghoul wonders why he is barking.

Looee screams and tries not to think of Larry and he jumps and finds all memories confusing. He screams and jumps up at the dogperson. He does so repeatedly to get the memories out.

He wanted to get outside. He wanted to see Susan and was tired of mummy always being in the way.

Mr. Ghoul is frightened.

Mama and Bootie see the yek looking huge and scary and soon all bedrooms are screaming.

Mama wants to touch the yek.

Mr. Ghoul walks in circles and sits in the corner and taps dirty dirty Visitor dirty.

Looee doesn't remember what he was doing.

He looks at Mr. Ghoul with the cardboard symbols and the lights go off.

He remembers doing puzzles with Walt.

He wants to do the dogperson's puzzle with him.

In the morning there is no one else in the cages and the sun shines brightly through the skylights. Looee's better health and less constant fear of pain have made more space in his days for remembering. When he shifts he sees dust rise in the sunlight. He taps his blanket and sends up more. He remembers sitting on the living room couch when sun came through the windows, the same puff and smell of dust.

There is the loneliness that feeds on itself and turns one inwards till there is nothing left, not even breath. And there is the loneliness that sends one out to dispel it.

He wants to bring the dogperson's puzzle to him outside but he doesn't know how to open his cage to get it. He walks along the catwalk, out into the sun.

Mr. Ghoul is sitting alone. He sees the yek walking cautiously towards him. The yek keeps close to the pokol-fear and is oblivious to the movement of others.

Looee walks like some mythical god of boundaries, all rivals ignored as he claims his line. He sits near Mr. Ghoul.

They look at each other and Mr. Ghoul's hand says come here.

They grunt and touch and each looks like a man who calmly sits with a struggling son and says okay let's get this done.

They groom, assess, correct and reassure, two mirrors deeper than any made by hand.

Magda delays the serving of dinner by not coming inside. She wants attention. In the morning several of them beat her.

Looee learns the rules.

In the evening Mr. Ghoul puts his arm around Looee's shoulders and encourages him inside.

Burke seems ever larger. His back is often turned, shoulders forward when he sits, and no one dares to go near him. He seems to be staring at some black domain that darkens the deeper he looks. But he is aware of what everyone does behind him.

In the evening he shoulders his way through the line towards dinner.

Looee feels a flash of heat behind one of his legs and he falls down.

Burke pushes through and the others find their way to their cages.

Looee is unable to put weight on his leg and he limps along the catwalk to the roof of his cage and climbs in.

His hamstring has been cut and partly severed by Burke's teeth. It will be stitched in the morning. He can't see it so he shows it to Mr. Ghoul. He lies on his side, pressed up against the partition, and Mr. Ghoul tries to push the wound together with his fingers. He licks it and eats his dinner and spits his flavoured saliva on the wound.

Looee is afraid and dreams of retribution.

thirty-one

When Dr. Heinz, now retired, tried to encourage people to send their pet chimpanzees to Girdish, he delivered a brochure with photos of the field station. The photo on the cover was taken from within the enclosed garden. It is a typically sunny day. A stylish white building is blurred in the background, behind several chimpanzees who are sitting pensively on the lawn. Mr. Ghoul and Podo sit side by side and the caption reads Much of Their Life Is Spent in Thought.

For those who lost their pets, there was meant to be comfort for lonely moments.

Walt and Judy had kept the brochure.

He's happy now sweetheart. I know he is.

I want him to forgive us.

Judy had nerve damage and a permanent swelling on one side of her face. Larry had to travel on a mobility scooter. Walt still met him a couple of times a month.

Walt took Judy to a speech therapist for two years after the attack, and it always felt like Looee was sitting in the backseat of the car, staring at them, threatening them, silent.

Neither Larry nor Judy could remember much of that night, and Walt selectively focused on having pointed his rifle at him, Looee trying to hide from the gun in the corner with his arms protecting his head. Years after the violence and shock, they felt ashamed.

There were reporters and intrusions for a while and then long silence. Producers of a TV show approached them one day to be part of a feature on animal awareness. Judy thought it would be an opportunity to tell their story. She spoke for hours and showed them photos, and took them into Looee's house, which she had avoided for a very long time. The feature ended up being called Wild Love. It had dramatic, cautionary music, blurred re-enactments, and focused on people who foolishly raised tigers, panthers, violent and endangered animals. Larry was shown toodling around Burlington on his scooter looking sad and fat. Walt looked even fatter. Stills of Looee's house were flashed on the screen in a way that made it look like a dungeon. Hours of Judy's conversation had been edited to a few short sentences. She held a picture of him when he was four, saying he was just so cute … He tore the house down … I miss his hugs. Her face was disfigured. They were three suitably bloated freaks on the fringes of America.

At Viv's the question was asked.

What the fuck were they thinking.

Walt had a dream, more a sensation than a dream, that woke him up regularly. He was against a body. Lips, hair, warm breath on his face. Arms that were strong on his behalf, a father's or a friend's. It was Looee, but it wasn't.

Most of their friends avoided them. Mr. Wiley remained an unexpectedly good neighbour. Soon after he died they moved to

Burlington. Judy said she wanted to leave the woods. Some days they thought there was too much colour and noise in the city. Walt felt oppressed by opinions on the news, but delivered more himself.

They went out to the mall on a sunny Saturday and someone bumped into Walt's shoulder and walked on without apology. Judy said cheer up. I'll buy you some shorts. She wore a lot of makeup and said I'm not covering up. I just like playing the game. Clerks in stores tried not to look at her face.

She stayed positive. She lifted Walt's chin. She felt pleasure in survival; not survival in terms of overcoming injury but survival as the process that few people notice and none can control, the hum of energy that fuels the machine. Survival isn't always an act of will, and when she realized that, when she was carried through the years and felt healed, she began to see beauty in all those things we try to run away from. There was beauty in the loss of beauty, in loneliness, in sorrow, some inarticulate vitality that was greater than the celebrated signs of joy, a different joy not obvious but more constant. To see herself as a body in the mirror, death in the middle of life, was to see a beautiful truth. This is me and it is not how I see myself.

She and Walt hold hands and know what each other is thinking. Walt goes to the freezer and Judy says we know the address. I've thought about driving down there and buying him ice cream.

Their apartment looks over a quiet street. Usually it's the same people who pass below, different clothes through the seasons. Their neighbours have a five-year-old boy who was frightened of Judy. He stared at her face and hugged his mother's legs. Judy crouched down and laughed, and said I *know* you.

They stare at the brochure from Girdish and say would he still be there. Is he still alive.

They used to puzzle through that night with Larry, wondering what had set him off. He was excited and confused and wanted to be at a party. Rooms lit by candles, surprises coming in from somewhere behind the door.

thirty-two

She loves the way he limps.

She really wants friends.

Pink skies grow gold and the upsides of leaves flash white in the sun.

She is scared and small and growing bigger and she wants them all to be her friends.

She is first out in the morning.

She loves Fifi and sits beside her and they hug.

Jonathan sees how the new one is growing.

The researchers note that with each monthly cycle her swelling grows larger and more roseate.

She is last out in the morning.

She calls the yek through a thornbush of plekter.

She hates Bootie.

She loves them all.

Jonathan scares her and Burke is everything she cannot see in the dark.

She walks lightly through the World. Her knuckles tell some that there is more to get from this ground.

She and Mama stare less at the wall and more at the yek.

A researcher goes home and feels there is possibility everywhere. She wants to have children despite a preponderance of misery on TV and she buys her boyfriend a T-shirt that says 98.4% CHIMP.

The generation, diversion and ruin of life stand proudly embodied as Jonathan looms and swaggers near the new one, he will be her beginning and end.

It is common for adult males to threaten young females as they reach adolescence. You may feel the world is yours because I want you, but it is mine it is mine it is mine.

Jonathan rips a weak and leafy branch from a tree and whips the wind and jumps on all fours from tree to tree, and kicks to show that he can bring each down.

He takes a heavier stick and beats the ground near the new one until she adopts a submissive posture.

At this time of year the moon shines in through the skylights above the sleeping quarters.

You who stand on the tower, can you hear their whispered orisons, their heads full of mice. Can you depose these tyrants or do tyrants stand untouchable on towers.

The moon is on a stem.

It illumines white flowers.

David Kennedy thinks of them all as his family. He loves them and wants to let them be. He wants to leave them alone completely, as much as we are left alone in our neighbourhoods and countries. Don't you see that cruelty and forgiveness are everyone's inheritance, that this is a neighbourhood and a country.

Their fights make him sad and fill him with worry, yet everything gets resolved more quickly than with humans.

He reminds his staff repeatedly not to intervene, no matter how attached they become. But he lets them intervene sometimes because our attachment is another shared inheritance. Empathy comes from a fear of being hurt oneself, but it's still a beautiful thing. He saw Mama find an injured crow one day. She gently picked up the bird and climbed a tree, put the bird to her mouth and dropped it so it could fly again, its one good wing taking it just beyond the wall.

He and his staff have always decorated the sleeping quarters and provided enrichment and treats. They planted moonflowers across from the cages and they have grown to ten feet.

The flowers bloom at night and Mama and Looee, in separate spaces, stare at them.

Looee can still feel the pressure of the floating cagefloor at CID. His bones remember it, even though they rest comfortably on blankets now. Every night he waits for his cage to be tagged.

Mama didn't like today and is worried about tomorrow.

Worry lights fires in this ape-ruled earth and runs cold in all the pipes. Worry seeks the death of itself and makes tomorrow better.

Looee's eyes grow bigger as he stares at the bloomed moonflowers. He and Mama, at different times, make the noise of a man who is modestly surprised by something happy he has discovered.

Hmh.

The flowers are very pretty.

The women who wheeled their dinner trolleys to them, their salad, peppers, bananas and beef stew, said goodnight crazy lovelies, and, be good to each other tomorrow.

*

From the tower David watches Mama kiss and hug the other females and gather their support. He sees her act as a peacemaker. She goes to Ghoul and grooms him and Ghoul wears a nervous grin. David can feel Ghoul's excitement from the tower and he feels his own when he watches Mama going back and forth between Jonathan and Ghoul. He can feel how much they wanted to be touched.

Ghoul and Jonathan groom each other. It's the first time he has seen this for more than eighteen months.

He has his stopwatch and timesheet, and it is all being recorded. He will have to describe it in the language of his trade and the data will have to be mapped. With his colleagues he will talk about side interventions, new coalitions, eye contact and posterior grooming. His assistants will help him put a paper together.

For now he feels happy seeing a group of women deciding that they have had enough. While Mama brings about the reconciliation of Jonathan and Ghoul, Fifi prevents Burke from doing any harm. She settles his display and takes a rock from his hand that he had been hiding behind his back.

He struggles to describe them sometimes, to make the larger world feel the way he feels. When he sees a reconciliation like this he feels it in his chest. His papers and data are dust and chips of ice.

He wants to describe Mama at rest. One hundred and thirty pounds of vitality. Fear, humour, jealousy and peace. Every day he sees empathy, shame, the will to heal, but he fights sometimes to discuss these things credibly with those who have no sense of their own bodies.

Lobbyists.

What lobbyist thinks of himself as an ape, one who brings other people's hands together for the sake of something fruitful. Isn't Mama, here, a lobbyist. An ambassador.

Are there ambassadors—in Savile Row suits, heads full of histories of Byzantium and Talleyrand—who think of themselves as apes. Do apes wear suits and dine with Kissinger.

Is Kissinger not a man obsessed with power, who boasts of women, who does indeed digest food, and need to have the respect of certain people.

What do I know of Kissinger, yet I speak of him. What do families arguing around dinner tables know about the president, yet they fight over who he is. We are born with the need for a leader, someone to control the conflict between each individual's need. An alpha in the house, an alpha at work, an alpha in the church and in the White House.

Mama reminds him that the women have equal power. Beaten and despised, but just as strong as the men because the men can do nothing without them. He thinks of that Aristophanes play where the women end the war by withholding sexual favours.

My mother was ninety pounds when she died. She fell asleep drunk and her cigarette lit the chair on fire. Ninety pounds but her coffin weighed so much I thought my brother and I would drop it. Tiny charred woman inside, ragged bird in an iron box.

I went to a conference once where a man delivered a paper claiming that all scientists were looking for their mothers. He named it the Call of the Inquisitor. We all want to know how it started. We want our mother to tell us. We'll get it right if we can only know how we began.

Mama rejoins the women, and, after Jonathan and Ghoul stop grooming, Looee walks to Ghoul and offers what can only be described as a human handshake.

Fifi and Mama rub their asses together.

At work he occasionally thinks of masturbating in the

bathroom. His assistant Sarah taking her glasses off, cute short hair and a flash in her eyes.

The day is done when he says it is done. So many years of hard work.

I have my own family. I have a daughter whom I want to be strong and confident. But this is my family too. I worry and wonder.

He has kept the project going from his own pocket, those times when funding was scarce. They thought about raising Burke as their own, remember, when Rosie didn't want him.

Mother.

He lives in Jackson Heights, a suburb forty-five minutes away. There's time for thinking each way, morning for planning, afternoon for contemplation or not thinking at all. Dad was a salesman and said that sitting still wasn't natural, wasn't the way we're meant to be. He thinks of that often. It's abundance that keeps us still. Abundance of food, abundance of love. Or fear that both are lacking and at least we have this house.

With chimps it's the girls that wander away. The men travel to fight and claim territory and the girls travel to find new men and friends.

We have good friends in the house two doors away. It's her second marriage. She said with her first husband, they moved into a house and he said I love this place so much. I want to live here forever. When she heard him say that, she said she couldn't breathe.

Looee has a favourite spot outside, near the eucalyptus and its smell of menthol. It is where Podo lay, dead after his fight with Jonathan. Mr. Ghoul sits uneasily when Looee rests there. He wants to go to him and he wants to watch, and some inarticulate speculations make him move and sit and move again.

Looee walks to Mr. Ghoul. They sit and look at each other

testily, and groom. Looee sits behind Mr. Ghoul and his fingers make Mr. Ghoul drift off, nod into soft pools of sleep.

Looee looks around. He goes back to the tree and watches the others. Some are thinking. Some are sleeping. Some are watching him watch.

He walks, and the new one thinks that he walks like no other.

David watches from the tower and also thinks that Looee has a strange walk. It's more than the product of injuries. He ducks and stretches, hides and yearns, acts like something he isn't.

The observation posts are considered part of their territory by some of the apes. When new staff members appeared over the years they would sometimes be treated to stones and pieces of wood, missiles being thrown at their heads, usually by Podo.

There is a calm today that everybody senses.

Looee looks up at David and reaches out a hand.

You want to come up.

I've seen lots of human-raised chimps, and few of them get along with their own species. When Washoe, in Oklahoma, first met other chimps, she used sign language to call them black bugs. It's an ape characteristic to look down on other apes.

Looee wants to use the man's binoculars. He wants to climb up the tower to look. He climbs a tree to the height of the tower and he softly trumpets an ache and a fragile feeling of peace.

David likes him.

There is always a third enemy, who keeps the others together. Like Russia or China. When Podo was alive, he and Mr. Ghoul had Jonathan to villainize. Then Jonathan and Burke used Ghoul to keep themselves from fighting. If we don't choose enemies we fear there won't be peace.

Looee climbs down from the tree. He feels sick.

David has a budget meeting to attend. He has three papers to edit. Debate at the University of Florida. This house believes that science is unethical.

There's so much noise, he thinks.

Everybody thinking our small concerns are the height of useful inquiry. Everybody thinking that everything we make, once made, cannot be a fiction.

Looee wants to climb again to look over the wall, but he's tired.

thirty-three

I try to think of this house as shelter, my daughter as my offspring, and my wife as my temporary companion. I try to be reductive and realize I am an animal with animal needs and nothing will ever be perfect. But every corner of my house means something more than shelter. I believe in love and beauty. I've known them and felt them, and even if I reduce them to the hunger for procreation and power I'm unable to cancel the warmth I feel.

Complete consciousness is unattainable. I'm aware of the things in my life that are fictions but I enjoy them nonetheless. I understand my motives, and my wife's and Tilly's. Understanding rarely stops any of us from doing what we do.

Knowing I am an ape doesn't stop me from being an ape.

We've done all kinds of tests to show that chimps are self-aware. Not just that they recognize themselves in a mirror but that they are aware of the consequences of their actions. And they therefore must act despite themselves, sometimes, because the consequences aren't always what they would want.

I'm not sure what I am looking for anymore, except comfort.

I like being the boss.

Sometimes David is afraid of sleep. He worries about his daughter and his wife being hurt, and on very few occasions he thinks of the attrition and cirrhosis of those invisible organs he normally takes for granted.

His wife is doing a residency in Seattle for eight weeks, and it is the longest they have ever been apart.

Each time they talk on the phone she reveals some new pleasure she has found in being alone.

I like not eating so much meat she says.

He gets a little drunk some nights when they are apart.

It's funny, isn't it she says. Seeing things on your own for a change.

She has always said that talking makes everyone feel better. He says talking is the equivalent of grooming. The tongue and fingers are governed by the same parts of the brain. He marvels at how close they can be some nights on the phone and how words really are the equal of touch. Bakelite pressed hard against his ear.

She says it's not just the freedom from him and from their daughter. I feel some sort of opening. I saw things so clearly today.

He thinks about the solitary figure in every religion, the monks, saints and shamans in every tradition who walk out into wilderness on their own and find revelation.

It's what solitude does to a social animal he says.

People talk of recognizing something greater than themselves when they're alone because we finally have to realize how helpless we are as individuals. There's a freedom, a sense of wonder in feeling for a moment that we don't have to please anyone or adjust to the needs of others. And there's a fear in realizing how small we are, how much those distant others normally insulate us from seeing the limits of our mostly incompetent bodies. When we're on our own we seek solutions and speculate and fictionalize because that's what we do when we're confronted with survival. That's revelation.

Maybe she says. I'm just saying I'd like to eat less meat. We could have fish.

He drinks and listens to music and some nights they spend longer on the phone than others. After a month he decides that words are actually not the equal of touch.

I miss you.

He listens for telltale modulations in her voice but nothing is complete without sight and the feel of her body.

Did I ever tell you about the work we did with facial recognition. We showed them pictures of the faces of some of the other chimps in the colony, and some of the staff as well, and we wanted to see whether they could identify them. Match them with names or other photos. There were photos of strangers too, other chimps and people. They were a hundred percent accurate in identifying the familiar faces, even when some were wearing hats or were at strange angles. Actually, we did other tests where they identified rear ends. All the ones they knew, they got right.

The strangers made them curious or anxious or uninterested, but the ones they knew, they knew.

I like thinking about how the world is mapped for them. How they spend so much time grooming and scrutinizing, that they are aware of any change in each other. We do the same thing, so much more than we acknowledge. People's eyes looking all around your face, making infinitesimal judgments and looking for stories while you talk. If I could see your face right now.

I'm fine she says.

I really want to see you.

Some nights the silence over the phone is quite beautiful, and sometimes it makes him anxious.

Are there people there you like. Anyone new.

He finds comfort in the fact that many psychologists are unattractive outside their practice or have off-putting tics.

There are some really interesting people she says.

He wants to go back in time, when they were so hungry for each other.

Maybe I should come and see you on the weekend. I like Seattle.

The whiskey that helps him sleep keeps waking him up.

He was in Seattle for a conference on climate change two years ago and he dreams about the fact that most amphibians are dying. Frogs absorbing toxins through their thirsty skin. He awakes at four in the morning with a dry mouth, and calls her.

I wasn't very popular at that conference.

I remember.

I remember there was a guy from the World Wildlife Fund who said the planet is under assault and we must shift our economy in favour of conservation. Another man from the Sustainable Development Commission said overpopulation was the problem. He said he was tired of people focusing on the economy. And another guy from the Nature Conservancy said I'm not sure the conservation movement has got it wrong, I just think we should stop talking about the environment as a separate problem, it should be a central part of our economy.

I was the quietest person on the panel. I kept looking up and down the table and out to the audience thinking we're apes and we're doomed not to know it.

You know how I undress people. I was picturing everyone naked and wondering how their opinions would change. Would they offer opinions or just touch and fight and choose similar factions.

I was wedged between a scientist from the World Bank with a dark suit and a bushy beard. And this other guy from the WWF who had a neat beige shirt which he probably thought would be great for mountain climbing. All kinds of pockets. I was watching him speak and I was staring at his feathered grey hair and I started laughing at the way his hair jiggled when he moved. I hadn't said anything so far and the first thing I contributed was to giggle at this guy's hair.

I thought: here is a group of men, and one woman, sitting higher than the audience. We make gestures of goodwill to each other and respectfully insist that each of our viewpoints is paramount. We are here for a cause that is greater than all of us so it allows us to come together. What we call saving the planet. Some things will be agreed upon, there will be a couple of villains, there will ultimately be no concrete result, and we will all feel a little bit better for having got together as a group. And we can distance ourselves once again from those who go on with their lives, ignorant of climate change, in the pursuit of consumer goods.

I said there is no greater example of ape behaviour than what is taking place in this room right now. Finding friends and imagining enemies.

Change the words coming out of our mouths and this could be a town council, a parent-teacher meeting or a Beer Hall Putsch. The issue isn't the issue.

We're talking about saving the planet but we're not really looking at ourselves, we're just trying to gain power. Each of us.

I'm grateful that you've invited a primatologist I said.

I'm really thirsty. Wait a second.

He drinks warm water by the bed.

I said I'm glad you've invited a primatologist, and I acknowledge that I have my field of expertise as much as anyone. But when we're sitting here asking what can we do, how can we save the earth, we're not asking who *we* are. There's lip service paid to human beings as a species but we really don't talk about what that species is.

I said this room is what this species is. Us up here debating, you down there judging. All of us wanting to be heard. Everyone seeing things through our own eyes yet believing that what we see is reality or the same as what everyone else in the room is seeing. We're happy when we hear opinions that agree with ours, and unhappy or surprised when it seems that someone is seeing this room differently.

We're born as individuals with an equal need for others. We have hair, skin and teeth. Some of us produce milk. Most of us have no sense of our bodies until something goes wrong.

We're talking about global consciousness and enlightenment and progress and we have no sense of the fact that we are talking apes. You laugh when I say ape. We're not talking about saving the planet, we're talking about the survival of our species. Let's at least start there and forget about our species for a second. We're talking about the survival of things like trees and mild temperatures and exotic animals, anything that nourishes our fantasies about deathless gardens.

You should have heard me.

I told them about Podo.

I said years ago we had an alpha male in the colony who was the champion of supporting another chimp's cause. If that chimp was down or beaten up he would make sure that the other chimps who hurt him or her would feel what we call justice. And if the next day the tables were turned and yesterday's victim was the bully, Podo sided again with the victim. He kept one chimp, Jonathan, as a sort of perennial scapegoat or whipping boy, and the rest he won over by siding with them whenever they were losing. It didn't matter what the issue was or whether he had beaten them up yesterday. The issue wasn't the issue. He stayed alpha for a very long time.

And there are chimps who bully and only support the victors. They too gain power. We can think of these types as Democrats and Republicans.

Honey she says.

And I don't think that any of their machinations are elaborate products of consciousness or are wicked or planned far in advance. They just do them. They want power.

Honey.

And I can't remember how I finished exactly. I said we're bald, bipedal apes. And I shouldn't even say bald because we actually have more hair than chimpanzees it's just less visible.

We will never change our behaviour, we will only change our words.

Please honey she says.

Yeah.

It's one o'clock in the morning. I'm speaking today and if I don't get more sleep.

I'm so sorry baby. I couldn't sleep. I'm afraid of sleep.

He is neither awake nor asleep nor here nor there. He still thinks he is in his early twenties and pities or despises the man he sees in the mirror.

When he looks at the older ones like Ghoul or Mama he can't believe how they've changed. And Burke with his gigantic swagger. He was a baby.

My daughter was a baby.

My mother left my brother and me when we were kids, and while I never once have blamed her I wonder sometimes who I would be if she had been near me. I find more answers as I age, but some of them seem even further away.

I call old friends and feel embarrassed for the fact that the only time I call is when my wife is away.

I call my brother who seldom answers the phone.

I feel proud of him, and close to him, though we have no real idea who we are anymore.

I think about the different directions two bodies can take from the same womb.

I think I would feel less lost if I kept in touch with everyone I ever befriended.

I see the chimps' need to reconcile and I feel some sort of awareness that no matter what my body's needs might be, it will never be complete without friends.

At that conference in Seattle I felt powerful, really satisfied for a second, but nobody talked to me.

After seven weeks of being apart from his wife he drives home after seeing a fight. The girl his staff call Beanie was found injured in the morning. She has lacerations to her face. He hates not having footage of everything.

He watched Mama fight with Magda, so Magda was probably the culprit. Mama turned to Ghoul for support, suggesting there is a real shift in power and Jonathan, at least, is not so much in the picture.

Mama fought with Magda and then Burke joined in to fight Mama. And then Ghoul joined in and Jonathan, and it all went on too long.

He feels raw when there is a fight like that. He wishes he could somehow tell them to stop.

He saw Looee far away from the fight, running in circles and hitting himself.

He wants to talk to someone.

Seven weeks is almost long enough for yearning to expire.

He thinks about flying his daughter in from Austin.

He sighs when he walks through the door and pours himself a drink.

He thinks about the fight he watched.

Sometimes he can't shake the feeling that someone is watching over him and he is certainly not religious. We're born with the feeling that there is something greater than ourselves, first our mothers, then school, god, bosses, a vigilant sky blemished with guilt and remorse. God is the alpha. Taxes.

He turns on the radio, then the TV, and later he listens to music. He drinks wine that a friend in California made and knows that it will give him vivid dreams. He thinks for an eyeblink about fishing out some pornography or even calling Sarah.

There is something greater than ourselves and it keeps us from being ourselves.

He drinks more and thinks he might as well sleep in the chair, and he doesn't know if he is sleeping or not.

Legs on the leather sound like someone shifting in the bath upstairs.

Those nights you took vodka to the bathtub while we played in the basement, sad mother.

We drank Coca-Cola in bottles with dad, who mourned his weakness for women.

A child swims through sea lice and is stung from lips to ankles and your cells are pierced by vodka in the tub.

This suburb is your body.

Dad said that even if she's an old family friend, when a woman sits across from you, pulls aside her panties and shows you her pussy, you guys will understand when you're older.

Mother.

The oceans are your bathwater.

Did you know ten thousand years ago, as blood vessels colonized your face, that a human nose could one day be grown in a jar.

Why don't you come downstairs. Come back.

His breath wakes him up.

He awakes and the house is empty.

I'm so glad you're coming home soon.

Me too.

This place is cleaner than you've ever seen it and I've mowed the lawns he says.

thirty-four

Everyone takes as much food as possible and they carry it outside with their lips and hands. It's a beautiful day again and Looee sits in the shade eating bananas and grapefruit and he fishes through a bag of peanuts.

He is getting better at recognizing his friends. Mama approaches making soft noises and she grooms his shoulders and neck. Her fingers are practical and rough.

Sometimes she turns and presents her pink rear end to him. She rubs it on his arm and he gets up. He doesn't know where to look.

Some of their customs will be forever foreign to him.

On sunny days and rainy days they sit under trees and think. He sees memories in their eyes. He feels tired. It rains prettily and he sits under a tree. He turns to his side and briefly looks at Mama and the girl. They're sitting and Mama is hugging her from behind and the girl is using her like an old chair.

Looee gets up and walks in the rain. He stares at the blue wall. He doesn't think mummy is over there but he thinks of her and sits in the light rain. He can go back inside whenever he wants. The rain is sweet on his lips and the sun comes out again.

Looee hurt mummy and that night is a red flash. It bursts when he blinks. He wants to say sorry. His need to say sorry to Judy has become a calcified reflex. It accompanied whatever memories were left, it sat with him and settled through fourteen years and grew into a bone lying crosswise in his chest.

No one loves this sun as much as the one who has been tortured. The sun and this apple are beautiful. The apple is in his hand, he can feel his hand and the sun. He is here. He eats the skin of the apple.

Mr. Ghoul sits with Jonathan, grooming. The yek seems to be inching closer and Jonathan starts to feel rinjy.

A foreigner takes our jobs and our women. He has greasy hair, kinky hair, blond hair and no hair, smells like armpits and cumin, patchouli and Ralph Lauren, and I swear I can smell his ass. He has a big nose and doesn't know our ways. He's a kike, a goy, a cracker and a paki. He's from the city and won't fit in. We used to know everyone here.

Mr. Ghoul strokes Jonathan's arm to calm him as Looee looks towards them. David, from the tower, sees Ghoul resting the back of his hand, gently and briefly, on Jonathan's testicles. Jonathan's hair relaxes and the grooming is resumed.

Looee walks by and sits with his back to the wall of the building. He gets hungry and finds more peanuts. If he stays away from Jonathan and Burke he can move wherever he wants.

He sits with his bone of guilt and appreciates the day.

This is not the time of life to stoop and cower, my brother.

Mr. Ghoul and Looee sit together and Mr. Ghoul shows Looee how to crack nuts. Looee knows an easier way but there is no nutcracker available.

Mr. Ghoul can't steer a car, make drinks for the ladies or control a VCR.

Burke walks near with hair on end and Looee and Ghoul both cower. They stare at the nuts with greater concentration and bond through the act of sharing their fear, and hating it. Burke passes by.

Mr. Ghoul looks handsome for a dogperson, more man than animal, and is endearingly weak.

The yek has the marks of many battles but would not survive without Mr. Ghoul.

When Burke is safely distant they eat the walnuts and think of other things. Mr. Ghoul taps Looee's shoulder with the back of his hand, let's go, and they sit by the pokol-fear. Mr. Ghoul wants to see him put his goon under again, and gestures to make him understand. The yek is not fast sometimes. Eventually he understands and does it.

Looee's head emerges refreshed from the water and Mr. Ghoul is standing on two legs, arms swaying, uttering low ritual whimpers: high priest to divinity incarnate.

He turns his butt submissively to Looee and Looee is offended. He pushes the dogperson's butt, and Mr. Ghoul is satisfied.

Mr. Ghoul sits near the water and timidly scoops some in his hand and spritzes his face. They look around at the sun-filled bowl of possibility and deliberately ignore the troubles that randomly wander.

Mr. Ghoul grooms Looee, who is getting used to the roughness of their nails—the aggressive way his chin is pushed up while his neck is getting inspected. Judy used to clean him like that when he had been naughty.

Mama watches Mr. Ghoul and the yek spending time together.

David watches Fifi licking her fingers and casually rubbing her clitoris, and he wonders what that's all about.

As dinnertime approaches, Mr. Ghoul goes to the yek and puts his arm around his shoulder. They briefly walk with their arms around each other and file into the tunnel and catwalk.

The high-ceilinged chamber is filled with food grunts and farts while all of them dine privately from the trolleys in front of their cages. Mama takes an armful of fruit and climbs up to her lowered platform. She likes to eat up high where nothing can bother her.

The sounds of chewing mouths would be enough to make children laugh.

Looee can never eat much of what he is given, though some-times the cooked food goes down regardless of how he feels. When Mr. Ghoul sees that Looee is leaving something aside he taps on the divider and holds out his hand. Looee passes a half-full bag of nuts to Mr. Ghoul.

They sit close to their shared wall and eat. Looee used to make Larry laugh by putting something on his bottom lip, pushing it forward and staring at the object cross-eyed. He does this with a plum pit and Mr. Ghoul laughs, a quick and quiet wheeze.

Mr. Ghoul eats and grunts and taps the grid and carefully makes a nest of blankets. He eats nine soporific bananas and taps banana banana banana on the cardboard beside him while he eases into sleep.

In the morning he grooms Jonathan outside beneath a needle tree. The cool smell of the needles soothes them. Jonathan watches Mama grooming the yek. He wants to run at them, but he knows that the yek is a friend of Mr. Ghoul's. He knows that Mama, Fifi and the new one are bowing to Mr. Ghoul and that Mama and Fifi will get in his way. Burke is no longer his ally. He feels calm with Mr. Ghoul.

He tries to pin Magda later but she hits him and screams and runs away. She feels that Burke should be respected.

Burke watches Jonathan and Magda.

Jonathan stares at the new one and his cock arises. Burke sees it.

No one predicted it.

Magda gradually resented the new one. She had seen Jonathan's interest and did not want a new woman to complicate the World. She had attacked the new one through the plekter at night, scratching her face and pulling on her arm. She fought with many the next day and learned how things were changing.

The new one no longer slept near Magda's side of her night cage. She was afraid and wanted friends.

Burke made sucking sounds and lured her in the dark. He pushed his mouth through the bars. He dangled both of his arms into her room and she did not trust him, but she couldn't resist. Her fear made his invitation more compelling.

She turned submissively and he touched her. She sat nearby and he chewed some fruit. He offered her the chewed wad of fruit from his mouth as if he were her mother. She stood to take it with her mouth and his hands trapped her hard against the bars. He opened his mouth and sucked, salt fruit and bone. He held the back of her head and ate her face.

The staff heard alarm calls in the morning. They came down before opening the cages and saw several of them jumping hysterically and pacing. The girl was lying in a pool of blood. Her jaw was hanging by a tendon and what was left of her tongue drooped unsupported to her neck.

One of the staff went into her cage and picked her up. Magda made threatening gestures at him.

He walked through the vestibule carrying the eleven-year-old girl against his chest. David watched him come into the study area covered in blood. She was still alive but sounded like she was drowning.

Looee and Mr. Ghoul, at the far end of the chamber, didn't know what was going on. They were kept in their cages all day, food brought out on trolleys.

Mr. Ghoul could tell that something was wrong with Mama. She was keening and screaming and leaping at the side of her cage.

He paced and made desperate noises and intently touched and groomed the yek. His fingers told stories of need.

Fifi was in the night cage next to Magda's. She was Mama's informant. She touched Mama and screamed pointedly at Burke. Mama learned that Magda had not been involved.

They were kept in their cages and fed for three days. The staff naively hoped that things might settle down. What little Mama ate she choked on.

The locks buzz open. Mama pushes her door and runs along the catwalk and stops above Burke. She screams and tries to break the iron, and diarrhea sprays down over Burke. He will kill her when he comes out.

By the time he does, Mama has touched or been touched by everyone but Magda. Burke runs straight for Mama, and Jonathan is the first to knock him down.

It is the most vicious and prolonged beating they have on record. David feels sick but he is the best at identifying the actors and actions. Even he needs to review the footage closely. When fists stop rising it eventually looks like a group of wild dogs busily feeding on a carcass. There is jostling, and side fights, and some of them come and go. Mama walks away from Burke and throws something into the moat. Fifi is notably on the fringe of the attack.

He finds the gradual lack of emotion on their faces to be the most unsettling, the way they eventually walk away and seem to go about their business. He is trained to read subtleties and knows there is more than meets the eye, but he is acculturated to expect keening, remorse, articulate shock and grief.

When they are locked in at dinner the staff retrieve Burke's testicles from the moat and take his body to the main site. Some organs may still be of use.

David feels a strange need when he goes home to come clean about every lie he has ever told, and to tell his wife that he loves her and knows what is important.

For weeks there is a bruised and chilly calm, an air like the early northern spring, weak promise amidst bad memories. Among all of them is a fragile mood of mutual respect. The staff agonize over the condition of Mama. She wastes in her grief.

Fifi too is grieving. At first they assume she is grieving for the girl, but the extent does not make sense.

Despite her hatred of what Burke did, he was hers.

It is proof to some that adoption was complete, that apes can call anyone a son. Her interaction with the group is uneasy.

The girl's jaw was reattached in the hospital at the main site. She has been fed by tubes. There was extensive plastic surgery and she is kept in clinic for two months. She won't be able to function without human help while she recovers.

So while the staff rejoice on the one hand, they wish they could somehow put Mama at ease.

Looee grooms Mama, as roughly as he can.

*

The new one is released from the introduction room. She wears a helmet and jaw-brace and her sounds, forever altered, combust against her palate.

Mama runs and throws her arms up repeatedly, and vomits from shock and joy. As the news spreads over the acres, all arms go up as if a war has ended.

They gather around the new one, and poke and smell her helmet.

She gets special meals that she drinks through straws, and Magda and Bootie are jealous.

The radio says it is ninety-eight degrees.

Looee steps out onto the grass.

They wear the same skin, no difference in temperature between Looee's chest and the air that rests on the grass. They sit in the body of the World, and the earth, Looee, the leaves and that tower are equal and temporary facts.

One of the researchers wants to show her new baby to Mama. She takes him out to the other tower and waits for Mama to look up. A few of them are curious. Mama comes closer, then looks for her own daughter. The woman hears Mama issue a telltale hoo whimper towards Beanie: come and let me feed you. But the new one is older and wants her own baby to play with.

Looee naps on the grass under a threat-free sky. He hasn't done this since he was a child. He awakes and sleeps again. Jonathan is sleeping nearby and neither minds the other. Two hairy men dreaming on the grass.

Mr. Ghoul sits with Fifi and Mama and it feels like the three of them are sharing a secret smile. Warmth and wet arise in Mr. Ghoul and Fifi. She turns and manoeuvres and grips his curiosity.

He holds her hips while his own roll and jerk. Mama turns her back and presses her backside against Mr. Ghoul's while he is inside Fifi. This is a pact, a trusting sweet agreement. Fifi squeezing tight, Mama on his doojy.

It is most enjoyable.

He eats and thinks of Podo for a moment. He smells Fifi on his fingers and feels a dulchy sleep approaching.

He sees Looee sleeping in the warmth. He sits nearby, flicks away a stick, and lies on his side. Their long arms are extended towards each other, their fingers almost touching.

They sleep and twitch through dreams and Looee's arm tingles under the pressure of his body. He moves and his fingers touch Mr. Ghoul's. He is not fully awake and is frightened by the touch, but he relaxes when he sees Mr. Ghoul's face.

They both grumble and try to sleep but their fingers keep touching. Mr. Ghoul tickles Looee's palm and Looee tries to ignore him. Mr. Ghoul leans over and puts his fingers in Looee's armpits.

Looee laughs and puts his feet in Mr. Ghoul's face. He gets on top of him and they roll, and Mr. Ghoul nibbles Looee's neck and his breath makes him giggle. Looee runs invitingly and when Mr. Ghoul follows he spins and tickles Mr. Ghoul's ribs until he can't bear it. Mr. Ghoul runs up a tree.

Looee feels sick and delighted. He is no longer young.

David wishes he could wear their skin.

Listen to that sound.

At dinnertime this is a cathedral of honesty. So many gigantic and short-lived confessions.

Let me be inside that throat.

That sound is Looee.

He sits under these yellow lights. He sits on a blanket on

concrete, a squat ape with a secret history, my cousin and a stranger.

Listen to that sound he makes, richer than a howl and long. Chin up to the moon.

Looee smells a blue plastic bowl and holds it up, above his head.

He sings that note that wood and brass yearn for, grief embodied and beaten.

He moans and snaps and coughs and eats and speaks a language almost human. Pentecostal kitchen gossip. Brandy swoons and lonely comfort and orgasms baffled by swells of new delight.

He is calling for someone.

Laughing.

He stops and hools that song from where beginnings and endings join.

¡Hooooooooooooooo!

He's eating spaghetti with meatsauce.

¡Whooo!

Friends too far to hear him.

acknowledgments

I am grateful for the generous support of the Canada Council for the Arts and the Conseil des arts et des lettres du Québec.

This novel owes a debt to the research and stories of Frans de Waal, Sue Savage-Rumbaugh, Roger Fouts, Herbert Terrace, Jane Goodall, Rachel Weiss, Maurice Temerlin, Vince Smith, as well as to the stories of many like Pepper and Billy Jo who neither wrote nor spoke.

On the publishing front, my usual gratitude is to Doug Stewart. Thanks to Penguin Canada, especially Nicole Winstanley and Stephen Myers. Thanks also to Jessica Craig, and to Max Porter and everyone at Granta.

I would like to thank Dr. Jarrod Bailey and Dr. Theodora Capaldo at the New England Anti-Vivisection Society.

My great thanks go to Nancy Megna for being generous with time and recollections. And the same to Gloria Grow and assistants at the Fauna Foundation, for showing me medical files and letting me meet your friends. It was a genuine honour to spend time with Sue Ellen, Rachel, Jethro, Regis, Spock, Binky, Chance, Yoko, Maya, Petra, and the noble, storied Tom (RIP). I mourn the loss of Pepper.

And Suzanne, for everything. I'll speak the words.

Keep in touch with
Granta Books:

Visit grantabooks.com to discover more.

GRANTA